THE SOLDIER AT THE DOOR

On 28th May, 1953, twenty-year-old soldier Jack Parrish is killed in Korea just before the Armistice: a meaningless, confusing death. When ord re Jack's mother in the mall villag of C but deter ined for some e t llage recto , a , Mrs Parrisl r the churc ything more about dyin t the simp tense reluc why, touc at the mys em. It is fi to be calle ds within him world with e but voli

THE SOLDIER AT THE DOOR

Edith Pargeter

CHIVERS PRESS
BATH

First published 1954
by
William Heinemann Ltd
This Large Print edition published by
Chivers Press
by arrangement with
Headline Book Publishing Ltd
1997

ISBN 0 7451 8736 6

British Library Cataloguing in Publication Data available

Photoset, printed and bound in Great Britain by
REDWOOD BOOKS, Trowbridge, Wiltshire

CONTENTS

CONTENTS

CHAPTER ONE

THE VICTIMS

The small, wet wind came sighing down between the graves, and stirred the grass against his face, and he came back to consciousness after what seemed to him a very long sleep. It was then that he knew he was dying.

His body had known it ever since the grenade went off. From the breast down he was resigned to dying. Either there was some degree of paralysis, or else from the breast down he was simply not there any more. He could not lift his head to see how much remained of him; it had become so heavy that nothing would ever raise it from the earth again, it was settling slowly, slowly into the new, soft mud of the shattered rice-paddies, digging itself a grave. But his mind was so little resigned that until the coolness of the wind blew his senses back into him he had not realised the inevitability of death. Now he knew. He was done for. He'd had all there was for him. No, not all there was for him, but all that *they* had let him have.

He did not know who *they* were, but he felt how close, how very close, he was growing to the enemy, those slender, child-size men with the unbelievably young faces, who came out at night and crept silently among the hills, blowing their bugles and fingering their tenacious way through the lines like fearless children playing an elaborate and sacred game. No, the enemy were almost friends of his, in spite of the terror he had felt of them many a time in the night, in

1

spite of his blood ebbing away dully now into the odorous mud. If only he could have got to know the enemy, between them something might have been done about *them*, and he and a lot more like him, and that little man who had thrown the grenade, and a lot more like him, might have gone on with their legitimate business of living.

But now it was too late. He was a dead man already. He was never going home.

He struggled feebly for a moment to raise himself, in panic at the thought of extinction, and the mud pulled at him protestingly, so that all he achieved was a flash of returning pain, and an instant of blindness. Then the waste grey acres of the sky came back over him, that May sky which had glistened from horizon to horizon since the month's beginning, to darken in rain at last for three long days and nights before the attack began. The serrated edge of the land bit at the greyness just within his vision, a fantastic line of saw-tooth peaks like a child's drawing of mountains, the characteristic skyline of Korea. Bluer now and more distant in the lingering softness of the rain, they withdrew before his straining eyes into the recesses of memory, and he saw them white again with the glittering veil of snow.

He blinked the winter away, because he had only moments left, and he did not want to remember the cold. If he turned his head an inch or two in the mud, and forced his eyes to the limit of their range, there was still so much that he could see. The slope of the hill above him, pitted with foxholes between the rounded beehive graves, the broad, abandoned valley carved into terraced rice-paddies below the dryer strip fields, the distant high curve of the track, raised six feet out of the clinging mud, and the little hillside opposite, marked with the three ugly purple blotches of naked ash where the napalm had fallen, and the single tattered huddle of walls without roofs where once the village had been. A village like any other Korean village now, dead as he would soon be dead, the people gone from it, some southward in one retreat, some northward in the next, looking for a place where they could still grow rice and keep a family alive. Looking for the chimera. Looking for peace.

All the thatch from the roofs was gone long ago, pulled down and burned before the frosts ended, to keep some poor devils alive through the murderous cold of the night; all the burnable wood torn down after it and used for the same purpose. Wherever there was a flame, the children crawled out, God alone knew from where, and came sidling to share it, wrapped in their silken rags, their bright acid colours of tragedy—magenta, viridian, lime-yellow—setting the teeth on edge with their delicious bitterness. Even out of a landscape as utterly void of human creatures as this one now, a fire could draw forth creatures who at least had once been human.

He stirred his hand painfully along the mud, and found an edge of the crumbling clay dyke which fenced in the terrace on which he lay. They were broken up beyond repair now, all those tiny, laborious evidences of man and growth. The higher manifestations of civilisation, the bomber, the jeep, the flame-thrower, the jellied petrol bomb, had come and smeared the outdated rice-paddies away with their villages and their villagers, and all their innocent worn-out values of life and living.

His hand stopped moving, and he knew it would not move again. He could feel his blood ebbing

3

steadily, like a falling tide, and his life going out with it. He was obsessed with a terrible loneliness, because there was no one there in all that sweep of land to speak to him in any human tongue; only himself, and somewhere along the terrace there, out of the range of his vision, the slender, delicate young body of the Korean who had thrown the grenade. Perhaps the boy was quite near to him, how could he tell? But he felt alone. No faces would come back to him even out of the past, out of the fabulous distance where home was. He could not remember what his mother looked like, or feel anything at all of what he must once have felt for Renie. It was all so long ago. And all over.

He could remember nothing with any distinctness before Korea, and even Korea was shrinking into a few symbolic recollections, the little coloured cards of the stages of his passion. Clearest of all was the whiteness and the cold, the diamond air, the withering, blasting cold of the long winter nights, the killing cold that felt its way through layer after layer of clothing, through the shrinking flesh, through the bone and the marrow of the bone, into the violated spirit, and reduced a man to the feeble, desolate tears of childhood. He had cried with the cold many a time, as he was crying at the memory of it now, and the tears had frozen on his raw cheeks and multiplied his misery. In hell there would be no fire, no fire at all, but a cold like that cold, and *they* would be there in it for ever and ever. Or if there were fires, they would be the sudden, appalling, gold and black fires of napalm, enveloping *them* with a crust of black, roasted flesh for a skin, and leaving *them* alive inside it.

He believed in hell, because he had had a lot of previews of it during the last year. It was heaven in which he no longer believed, heaven and the things of

4

heaven, truth, justice, mercy, forgiveness of sins. Beyond a certain point forgiveness of sins becomes itself ludicrous, a rather shameful sin.

He could not move his lips, or make his tongue articulate, but within his groping mind he was saying over and over and over: 'Damn *them*, damn *them*, damn *them*—!' He said it very steadily and earnestly, because it was a prayer.

Not only for what had happened to him, nor even for all the years he should have had. For all those others too, for the families stumbling south with the bundles on their heads, for the exhausted old men, for the women screaming in that house in the town of which he'd forgotten the name, the respectable young women who didn't want to be raped, even for a good cause like the United Nations, for the two men contorted upright in the mauve residue cold after napalm, the blackened roasts of men without hair or eyes, for the men and women and children stumbling out of the trucks toward the unexplained trench in the ground, prodded forward by South Korean guards with guns, that day when nobody thought or moved in time to prevent what was, after all, only a little bit of all the murder going on within this liberated land. Only a little bit, but ours. A small thing, but our own. 'Damn *them*, damn *them*—!' he prayed in absolute, devoted reverence, calmed by the assurance of damnation.

The clouds had broken a little over the saw-tooth mountains. There was a thin gleam of sun, and the larch branches on the hill above him gleamed bright as emeralds, and cast a luminous green shadow over the rounded graves where the luckier dead men sat, each with his knees drawn up to his chin in the burial chamber. A diffused shining of water came up from the valley fields where the cranes dabbled. He remembered the incredible coming of the spring, the sudden thinning of the blanket of snow, the clouding of the hills with the first delicate green smoke of foliage, the eruption of the whole earth in a sweet pink foam of flowers. And the smell of death, as the frost released its hold on the bodies of man and beast long buried in the snow. And the epidemics which came with the sun, and sprinkled the countryside with warnings to keep away! Keep away! Flee from the wrath to come!

He had never wanted to come there at all. He'd wanted to go on learning his trade at the works, and walking out with Renie until he was earning enough for them to get married. But he'd been called up like the rest, and sent where he was wanted. He'd read all the polite banners of welcome, believed all the smiling and bowing, at first. But who could be in Korea for more than a year, and still believe that he was wanted? Napalm, and high explosive, and trucks driving through the terracing of the paddies, and big-booted unbelievers bedding down in the church—that's what he was to them, he and all his kind. Disruption, destruction, death. From the north or the south, what difference does it make?

Now even the remaining shapes of reality kept floating away from him, and the sun had gone again, and he could not see more than a greyish, dissolving shadow before his eyes. His anger had become a kind of comfort, as if he had created another person of his own will to bear him company, but even this ally had begun to fall away from him. The soft mud had taken him deeply to itself, moulding closely about his shattered body. The evening was folding in from the dimming hills, but for him the light did not change, was no longer subject to change. He wept still, in the desolation of his loneliness, but feebly; and after a while he did not weep or think or feel any more.

He was dead long before the Chinese came looking for their wounded in the dark of the spring night, after the moon was down.

This was the manner of the death of Private Jack Parrish of the 4th Midshires, on the 28th of May, 1953, on the west central front in Korea. He was within three months of completing his National Service, and was just twenty years old. If he had lived two months longer he might have received his life back, only a little soiled, from whoever *they* were who had laid claim to it.

* * *

He had disturbed the others a good deal, earlier in the day, by groaning, and even by talking to himself in his intervals of more complete consciousness. The post was hardly more than a hut of two rooms, a hut on stilts, that swayed lightly when any of its inhabitants moved, and a crazy little wooden watch-tower that lifted their view above the rim of the jungle below, and gave them command of the village and the opening undulations of stony savannah beyond. Regnier and Coustin in the outer room were sick of listening to the groans and the tangled words. They had no room to escape from him here, and he knew, in that clear-sighted way that considerate people have so long as they have life, that his pain was distressing them, in spite of all the worse things they had seen and heard. He was trying very hard to keep silence until the Moï recruit should be able to reach Dak Song, and bring back, if the luck was good, some

7

truck and driver to take him away.

They would know already that the convoy had been ambushed, and driven through with the loss of two lorries and several men; the only news to them would be that the M'nong Gar women had found the last casualty wandering in the jungle with three bullets in him, and brought him here to die. They naturally did not want him to die on their anxious hands. Let the French, his own people, bear the expense and the burden of paying him the rites.

All the same, he did not want them to come too quickly. The hut swayed on its long legs, the bamboo floor swung, but the jolting of a truck along that path, where the wing-clipped jungle was already encroaching again with seedlings and roots and taut little trees, would be far worse than anything that could happen to him here. He lay on his back, staring into the dim arching of bamboo under the thatch, and tightening his hands upon his swathed middle every time the pain jarred him more fiercely. He could not suppress the pain, but sometimes he could keep himself from crying out, so that the other two would not be offended.

He had been in Indo-China more than a year, first in a precarious post in the confused country down towards the Mekong delta, where the Viet-Minh used the tracks by night, and the French controlled them from their arrogant little watch-towers only by daylight. Everybody knew that trade and traffic went back and forth steadily, but nobody could stop it; and the villagers in their swampy creeks and on their neat vegetable-gardens were at the mercy of both sides, if either side had any mercy. They lost everything in some battle, their homes, their crops, their stock, and they took to the jungle in fright for a while; and then, when some new and apparently sturdy French post went up in the district, they would come out of hiding and crowd in thankfully under the walls, like chickens huddling under the wings of the hen, put up their little grass-and-bamboo houses again, lay out their industrious gardens, and resume their business of living. In time the enemy would take advantage of this affectionate proximity to fill the village with his irregulars, and one night there would be an unexpected attack on the post, and a lot of killing, and a swift and shadowy withdrawal into the forest with whatever arms they could capture.

After that, because someone must have known, and no one had spoken, because even someone *might* have known, and to let the occasion pass would be to invite its repetition, there would be horrible reprisals. Since the Viet-Minh had vanished by then, it was the villagers who died. He had seen it and taken part in it. He had done what he had been told to do, and hoped to be justified, but he knew that he was without justification.

He remembered the woman in this moment as vividly and fatally as the day of her death. He had never been able to get her out of his mind. Because of her he was a little mad. Cochin-Chinese, young with all the delicacy and grace of a townswoman, though she had fished for a living in the creeks and the shrunken irrigation ditches, wading to the thighs in the greasy mud. They had found a grenade hidden in her garden after the raid was over. He had done what he had been told to do.

The feel of her long hair was still live and violent about his left hand and wrist. The fountain of blood from her taut throat, instant, scalding, a world of red, had spurted over his right hand and arm. Afterwards,

9

when the scarlet fog had cleared from his eyes, and the long convulsion of nausea had left him half-dead, he had crept away and waded into the river to try and clean himself; but the blood had gone through the skin, and she was in him for life.

She was not the only dead person, not even the only dead woman, who came back to him whenever the light was between day and dark, and the shapes of things began to melt and become other than they normally were. But she was the sum of them all. That was why he could remember everything about her but her face. Like that of a classical statue, her face was without identity, because she had to be everyone. Those broken-down, bewildered scarecrows on the plantations, too, those degraded caricatures of the handsome Moïs, though he had killed none of them. And the tamed villagers, adapting themselves to subservience, resigned to the humiliation of trying to be a little French in order to please, putting upon their beautiful, seemly bodies the unsightly, incongruous inventions of European clothes. It was only after he had become a little mad because of the woman that he had noticed all these offences.

The sergeant had humoured his sickness of the mind at first; it was nothing out of the way, plenty of young soldiers took their breaking-in just as hard, but they got over it in a few months, and took the dirty work in their stride with the decent. Only this one lacked some inner security of soul, and he had never got over it. That was why they had moved him up here, into country less frequently troubled with raids. And that was why, though this they did not know, and now there would never be anyone to tell them—that was also why, when the firing on the convoy had begun, he had swerved his wagon aside

10

from the track into the dusty confusion of the trees, towards the machine-guns.

It hurt, but it was what he wanted. He hugged the bullets to his flesh almost jealously, and out of the darkness within the thatch he recalled suddenly the whole green dimness of the jungle, the corrugated trunks draped and strangled with lianas, the thick bearded tree-ferns climbing, the bright, parasitic orchids, the sombre, splendid butterflies swarming astonishingly upon every corruption, turning every foulness into a radiance. The first excitement came back upon him for a moment, the sweet, ingenuous enthusiasm which had made Lyons seem well lost for so much beauty, though he had cried quietly to himself under cover of the darkness the night he had left home, and there was no recess in the whole waste of homesickness he did not know.

He could hear them talking in the other room, in low tones, so that their words should not reach him; but he knew they were saying that he would not last long. Once or twice one of them put a head in the door, and looked at him. He could no longer distinguish one face from the other, they were blanks like the woman's face. Sounds swayed momentarily into his consciousness out of the dark, and were gone, but vision was almost over.

In the end there was nothing left but the one thing he had not expected; no anger, no relief, only an inexpressible and destroying grief, the groundless, irremediable grief of a child, draining his life away in an inward weeping for which his eyes had lost their aptitude. Everything he had had and lost was borne away from him in the torrent of his sorrow. He had no mother, no fiancée, no home, no family. The stream of tears was the stream of his blood, bathing

11

the hands of the faceless woman, who alone kept him company in his departure.

When Regnier approached the mattress and looked down at him, the stillness of the body needed no explanation.

'He's gone!' he said, not ungratefully. 'Just as well! He'd never have done any good.'

Over the open savannah, over the village with its stilted long-house and its scattered flowering trees, the light still clung. The jungle was already a deep green night, grimy, mysterious, adhesive with the gossamer webs of spiders, tenacious as human fingers. Moths were beginning to beat inward towards the light of the fire in its earthenware bowl, and the watchers by the mattress saw the lines of the dead face relaxing at last from the intensity and accusation of its sorrow.

This was the manner of the death of Jean-Pierre Duclos, on the 28th of May, 1953, in a French outpost north-east of Saigon, just over the border of Annam. He was a conscript from the Rhône, twenty-one years old. He was engaged to be married.

*   *   *

He never passed by the resettlement village without averting his eyes. It was not that the place itself looked so bad, but rather that he could not look at it without seeing the other one, the village from which these silent people had come, the village he had helped to destroy. These new huts and sheds were better, if anything, than those he had burned down, though the over-crowding was more intense here. The high barbed-wire fence looked grim, but without it, so the authorities said, the villagers would still have been subject to the old blood blackmail, would have had to find food and shelter for the terrorists on demand, or pay the penalty. Now they were safe inside the wire, with guards and guns to fend off their enemies. They had every reason to be grateful, hadn't they?

It was a pity, of course, about their little houses up there in the forest, and their fields in the clearings above. The destruction of food and razing of roofs could never be very acceptable to a boy raised in a village, and used to the careful harvesting of the land. It went against the grain with him to see standing crops sprayed with poison, and little dwellings burned to the ground, however excellent the reasons for the abortion. But it was war, wasn't it? They had to do what was necessary to win it. There wasn't much the other fellows stopped at.

But, for all that, there was something about the new village that stuck in his throat. It might have been the height of the wire, it might have been the hard-trodden, over-populated look of the nude space within, scorched clear of grass, or the sight of the gun on the hip of the guard by the gate. Or perhaps it was only the way the people inside the wire sat listlessly about on the ground, their slight dark bodies bowed forward, their faces blank. Or, worst of all, the live, attentive precision of the eyes in those dull faces, as they followed every khaki-clad figure unwaveringly round the wire, and watched him out of sight. The faces might be heavy and lifeless, but the eyes missed nothing. They were submissive, but they were not grateful. He knew hate when he saw it. Every time he passed across a segment of the wire he felt them focusing on him, pouring out their secret longing upon him, waiting for him to drop dead. Even the

13

children, brighter and more intent than their elders, had that still, expectant look.

Why did they take it like that? Was it fair? Was it his fault? Had he wanted the job of turfing them out of their homes and herding them down here into concentration camps? He felt the injustice of it scalding his senses as the steady, covert glances of the eyes he would not meet slid down his cheeks and felt hopefully at his heart. If they'd played the game in the first place, their village would still be standing. The law's the law, isn't it? They'd been feeding the terrorists, so the sergeant said. Or if they hadn't been feeding them, they wouldn't give any information against them. There must have been somebody up there with some to give, if only he'd chosen to speak. It did seem hard to punish the whole community for the silence of one or two, but how could you prove they weren't all in it together? And anyhow, this war was a desperate business, it couldn't be run on sentimental Christian lines. An officer and three men had been ambushed and killed up there; that was something that couldn't be passed over. Not strict curfew, nor cuts in the rice ration, nor preventing them from going out to work on their fields, had produced any co-operation. What conclusion could you draw, except that the whole village was on the other side? They'd gone over to the enemy. They were disloyal. If a few helpless sympathisers suffered with the rest, how could you prevent that?

But now there were no sympathisers. All the eyes had the same look, they felt along his ribs furtively as he walked by, for the place where the knife would slip in easily and let out his life. Some day it would really happen and he would be picked up somewhere off the track, under the tangled creepers and the soiled

14

growth of shrubs below. He told himself that it was morbid to let the affair get on his nerves like that, but there the miserable place was, and almost daily he had to move within sight of it at least once. How could he get it off his mind?

Up-country, on that last little sortie with the Dyaks, he'd first slipped into this bad habit of brooding about things. It wasn't like him, either. The first severed head had turned him up a bit, naturally, especially as it was a woman's; but very few fellows can take that sort of thing in their stride, and he'd soon got over it. He'd behaved sensibly enough, too, hadn't gone off by himself and struck any attitudes, or let his mind dwell on the inevitable nastiness with any offensive assumption of superiority. He knew very well he was in it with the rest. He'd let himself be involved in all the horseplay with the bodies, made one in several of those photographs about which there'd been so much fuss afterwards, complacent groups with the Dyaks grinning in the middle, and the slender, doll-like Malayan dead laid out in a row in front, like the bag after a hunt. He'd tried to shove himself a bit too far, holding a head in either hand by the long black hair, but his whole idea had been to get himself well blooded and broken in, and have it settled once for all where he stood, since there was no getting out of it. But it hadn't worked out quite as he'd hoped. In the night, with the great stars pulsing in the sky's blue-black infinity, everything came back heavily upon his heart, and he knew that he hated it, that it was not what he had been meant for, that all he wanted on earth was to go home.

He had been in Malaya only six months, and he had nine months' service still to do. He thought he could stand it, with the certainty of England then,

15

and a good job waiting for him on the farm, and his life still before him. He rationed out his emotions carefully, to make the time pass without breakages. He was too sensible to let his imagination run away with him, just because he'd had to do a few things he didn't much care about. Let him once get a tractor under him again, and a nice open piece of ploughing before him, and he'd soon get those poisoned crops out of his mind.

And so, perhaps, he would have done, if he had not come back into camp alone past the resettlement village, after dusk on the evening of the 28th of May. It was already shadowy and dim under the trees, and he never saw his assailant. He heard the light snap of a twig under an insignificant weight, behind him and on his left, towards the mesh of the wire. He turned sharply, aware of a soft, hissing breath, light and excited like a child's, very close to him in the darkness. A *parang* struck downward into the hollow between neck and shoulder, shearing his head half from his body, and the last thing he saw was the sullen, twilit brightness of the blade sweeping upon him out of the dark, in a little, delicate hand. Then he was in the grass, his life pouring out of him in a throbbing stream of blood, and slender dark feet stepped over him and ran on into the forest, towards the secret places of the enemy.

They found him next day, the soaked ground round him swarming with ants and gaudy butterflies. A sixteen-year-old boy was missing from the imprisoned village. The wire nearest the trees, two or three strands of it cut and bent aside near the ground, showed where he had crawled through. The hole was so small that only an undersized adolescent could have negotiated it without damage.

16

This was the manner of the death of Private Joseph Greenslade, in a village in Selangor, in Malaya.

* * *

On the same day died also, in a mountain skirmish in east Burma, not far from the borders of Thailand, Ling Sien Yu, an orphan of the Chinese civil war, from Yunnan Province.

He had been taken over the border from China by the retreating Kuomintang troops in 1949, as a boy of twelve, and he had never had any choice about becoming a soldier himself as soon as he was old enough. He believed in the Kuomintang, because he knew nothing at all about any other China, or any other theory of living; but, even so, in his heart he did not want to fight, for that cause or any other. He wanted to go back to his village, so well remembered, so far from this alien land where he was a fugitive and an enemy. He wanted to take a wife, and raise a family in piety upon his own small farm, as his parents and grandparents had done before him. Instead of that, he was a soldier in exile, in a country which hated him and wanted only to be rid of him.

He was returning from a food raid with a dozen others when he was picked off at leisure by a Burmese rifleman from among the dappled rocks of a hill-ridge above him. It was a clean shot. He died without even the realisation of pain.

* * *

In Egypt, about the same hour, in an alley in Ismailia, Private Andrew Burns was knifed in the back, and left to bleed to death in the gutter. A girl who had

17

looked out of an upper window at the slight sound of the scuffle, drew the casement to again very quietly, and went in, and said nothing to anyone. She wanted nothing to do with Private Burns, in life or death. It was not that she had anything against him personally. But he was English. He was the enemy.

Nor had Private Burns ever wished to come to a country which had no feeling for him but hatred. He was very young, and very inexperienced. A part of his nature had died of the hatred, some weeks before he died of the knife.

*　　*　　*

After the Englishman stopped moaning, there was hardly a murmur to disturb the limitless silence. All the planes were gone out of the sky, and the rainy wind had just sufficient strength to stir the larch-branches, without drawing from them so much as a sigh.

He lay on his face in the thin, fresh grass, his arm doubled under his forehead to keep his nose and mouth out of the soft, yielding ground. The hand stretched beyond the edge of the grass, into the cool and glutinous mud, where the tiny clay wall of the rice-paddy was broken away. He had tried to draw himself a few inches backward, to have the support of the grass more firmly, but he had not the strength to move. All the time he could feel the blood flowing, flowing out of the bullet-hole in his breast, a steady, quiet stream. Sometimes also it bubbled up into his mouth, and gushed out of his parted lips irresistibly, hot and angry, spurting over the crimson clay.

They were all gone on, over the ridge, through the hill of graves, down into the next valley and beyond, advancing once more, after so long of tedium and stillness. His heart was no longer with them in their thrust forward. Jealous and careful within him, it pumped slowly, that the blood and the life might stay in him, that he might not die. Let them go, let them have their triumph. What was it but another valley like this valley, burned, abandoned, desolate, without people. How often had he run uphill with them, fierce and eager, towards his death, and felt no fear and no reluctance. And now he had encountered it, and he knew the truth about it. It had all been for nothing, all vain effort in a contest which no one could win.

He had known it at the beginning, and he found his way back to it in the end. Everything between had been a killing fever, for which this, at last, was the only cure.

Against the dimming blueness of the distant hills, sharply serrated against the sky, two cranes rose out of the shallow standing water with a vast spread of white wings, and arched their slow, indolent, beautiful way across the line of his vision, lambent silver in the dusk going homeward. Their beauty was like the thin, emerald leaves of the larches, something left over from a former world. He remembered that world, distantly through his pain, for he also belonged to it.

His father's land was in the north, good rice-land, five acres, and well-kept for generations. A man and his wife, and his children, and his old parents, could live on that land, and be content. He had never wanted anything but that, the good life season by season, the well-walled terraces, the small thatched house, the daylight labour on his own ground, the evening rest in the warm room, bright silks for the wife he would take when the time came, bright silks for the children in the years to come.

But the army had come and taken him, and sent him southward on this endless and profitless mission, a soldier against his will. He had done what was required of him, fighting his way for ever back and forth across the disputed heart of his land, three times up and down over country grown neglected, depeopled, unproductive. To end here, in the May mud, with a bullet through his lungs, himself despoiled like the soil.

'If I can live until tonight,' he thought, 'they will come looking for us, with nurses and doctors. Perhaps I shall not die, if they find me in time.' And he breathed gently and slowly, not to force out the blood more strongly than he need, for he wanted with all his heart and mind not to die. But waves of heat rose in his throat and burst out at his mouth, flooding the clay into a swamp of blood; and then it was as if his very heart came up into his throat after the blood, choking him. He struggled for a moment for breath, and the obstruction exploded into his lips, and seemed to burst there, and the dark and the pain broke forth with it; and that was all.

This was the manner of the death of Pak Yen Sou, a soldier of North Korea, on the 28th of May, 1953, on the west central front, a few yards from the body of Private Jack Parrish of the 4th Midshires, who had killed him, and whom he had killed.

CHAPTER TWO

THE SURVIVORS

Mrs Parrish worked mornings at the Grove Street cinema, sweeping out the toffee-papers and the cigarette-ends and all the complicated rubbish of the evening from between the seats, mopping down the tawdry marbled floor and facings of the foyer, polishing the glass over the vast faces of improbably beautiful and impossibly over-sexed film stars. What with the rising cost of living, especially the price of food, she had to do something to eke out her husband's money, and this was as pleasant a way of earning an extra pound or two as any. It wasn't far from home, so she had no bus fares to pay, and she liked the sense she had there of being surrounded by youth and excitement. The girl in the pay-box and the two usherettes were fresh little things of about twenty, the operators were boys not much older in years, and a good deal younger in sophistication; and they all went to a great deal of delightful pain to reproduce in themselves and their contacts with one another something of the glamour celebrated so hugely on the scarlet and gold walls.

The other cleaner was a large, taciturn woman with a baritone voice, who kept herself to herself; but Mrs Parrish followed the wrangling, posturing, innocent eccentricities of the young people with a warm artistic sympathy, and the zest of a contemporary. She needed youth, since Jack had been away. He was an ordinary enough young fellow, but she missed him, for he was the only child.

Mr Parrish was store-keeper at a small engineering works just outside Caldington, and did not come home to his dinner, so Mrs Parrish could walk home at leisure when she finished work at about half past eleven, do her shopping on the way, and sit as long as she liked over her makeshift midday meal and cup of tea, before she attacked the housework she had left from the morning, and began the business of getting her husband's dinner. With only two of them in the house there was not so much to be done.

They lived in the poorer and older side of the town, separated by all the shopping streets and the market from the new housing estates into which Caldington was lately blossoming. In their district the streets were lanes, and the shops narrow, irregular, old-fashioned frontages from the beginning of the century, their upper storeys hurriedly assimilated into flats, for Caldington like every other town was bursting with young, homeless families since the war, and there was good money to be made out of rents. But so strong was the period influence of the setting that even the windows of these new dwellings tended to feature looped lace curtains and potted geraniums.

The Parrishes lived, not in a flat, but in one of a terrace of six two-storey houses in red brick, shabby and mean and sixty years old, but still with some dilapidated pretensions about them, a painted white arch and a minute fanlight over every front door, a course of fanciful light fawn bricks between upper and lower windows, a name cut into every lintel, though the inhabitants no longer used them. Mrs Parrish's house-front announced itself, surprisingly enough for a back-street of a small Midland town, as 'Cromarty'; but all it ever said on her letters was 4, Hogarth Terrace.

She let herself in at the front door, taking the key from its hiding-place inside a spiky white shell which decorated the end of the step. The quietness inside never seemed chilling to her, never took her by surprise. Mr Parrish was never there at this hour, and the boy, even when he was at home, belonged to the weekends and the evenings. Here in the middle of the day she lived amicably with silence, disturbing it only with the small sounds of her own movements, and sometimes with bursts of sweet, reedy, preoccupied song. The dog from down the row, the cat from up the row, paid her occasional cupboard-love visits. They were always welcome, provided they did not come together.

She took off her hat before the mirror, and tidied her thick, greying hair. She was fifty-one, and still good-looking, a middling tall woman with an active, spare figure, and a kind of awkward grace about her. She had to make her clothes last for years, regularly furbishing them up into new shapes with an inventive but not always successful optimism; yet she had moments of elegance, when her clumsy tailoring achieved an illusion of style. In the gaunt asymmetrical face her large eyes, smoky-grey, looked young, gentle and unworldly, but her mouth and chin were wry, resolute and alert, as she herself had had to be to survive undamaged. Mrs Parrish was undamaged. The easy faith, the calm grace in which she had been reared had never yet been dented by any of the daunting things which had happened to her, in a life far from easy and seldom calm.

Over the mantelpiece in the kitchen, which was also their main living-room, there was a large framed photograph of her husband, from the days of the First World War, in the unreasonably archaic

23

uniform of the time, with a Kitchener moustache, a ramrod back, and a row of medal ribbons. It was there, in preference to the one or two later pictures she possessed of him, solely because he had a sneaking affection for it. The martial look, the breastful of glory, neither added to him nor detracted from him for her, unless the tiny derisive glow of affectionate mockery she felt for this version of her husband was an added delight. Sometimes she thought that it was, but sometimes it seemed to her that the sly smile she hid so carefully from him diminished him, and she would have been glad to put some other picture in the place of this one.

There was a picture of the boy, too, a new one, also in uniform. Under the insouciant beret with its cocked badge his thin young face looked oddly uneasy, and a little startled, as if the very speed of his metamorphosis worried him. He was like his mother, his features had the same irregularities, though hardly formed yet, with all the touching tenderness and newness of the boy just become man. Skinny young necks they have at eighteen, she thought affectionately, too slender for the weight of their heads—all Adam's apple in front, giving the show away when they're scared or embarrassed, and all tight, anxious lines at the back, where the tendons run up into their hair. She loved them at that age. But then, she loved young male things at any age short of tedious maturity. All Jack's friends had always got on well with her, and run in and out of her kitchen for support, or reassurance, or advice, just as freely as he had, all the time he'd been growing up. She was warming and safe, whether building them up or dressing them down; and she was liable to do either, as the occasion demanded, with the same freedom

24

and thoroughness.

Mrs Parrish was richly sexed, though she did not know it. All her life she had made bold and innocent use of her sex, and never once suspected what she was doing; and quite a lot of boys had budded handsomely as a result, without knowing any more about the process than she knew herself.

'Boys are no trouble,' she used to say cheerfully. 'I could have done with half a dozen of 'em.' It was one of the few notes of regret she ever sounded; for, after Jack, something had gone wrong and she had never been able to have any more.

She turned his photograph more squarely to the light, and made the fellow of her son's scared, wary face back at him. Six months more, my lad, she thought, and you'll be home, and having to settle down and do some work again, for a change, and we shall see how you like that. She liked to believe that the army was spoiling him and making him lazy; she'd been doing it, as a defensive measure, ever since she had begun to understand how much he hated it, and was longing to be rid of it.

She had no illusions about her only son. Any real boy, mixed and imperfect and pathetic and amusing, was a thousand times more fun than an imaginary perfection, so why cherish illusions? He was no better and no worse than many another, a nice kid, not very clever, not very industrious except in the ingenious wrong directions even dull boys seem to nose out by instinct. He had blundered in and out of the average number of scrapes, and been about as good and about as bad as most boys. Even being the only one hadn't unbalanced him unduly, and she had been able to give him his head, because his father, bless him, took parenthood very seriously indeed, and was well able to supply all the curbs necessary.

Tom's sense of responsibility was a nuisance sometimes, but on the whole he wasn't so hard to manage. It was only when the boy began to grow up, and his father failed to realise it, that she had had to take sides. She remembered the first girl, and all the attendant mystery and agony: the clean neck, the greased hair, the late return, the smart telling-off, the self-conscious rebellion, and the inevitable clout across the ear, appropriate, perhaps, to a cheeky kid, but not to the young lover still exalted and drunk with his newly discovered masculine dignity. What wounded self-love, what unforgiving sulks for days and days after the offence! And on the other side what obstinate self-assurance, what unrelenting paternal self-justification, covering what suppressed twinges of regret!

In his middle teens Jack had rather tended to sulks. He had taken to thinking and brooding more than most boys bother to do, but not so extravagantly as to cause her any great anxiety. All he needed was a bit of coaxing sometimes, and a bit of bullying other times, and he came round as sweetly as could be. There was nothing in Jack to worry about. Jack was all right.

She laid one corner of the kitchen table for her solitary meal, and put on the kettle to boil. Usually she merely ate up yesterday's left-overs, or boiled herself an egg, not because she was one of the self-sacrificing kind who accept it as their duty to eat what no one else wants, but because she had a hard-learned allergy to waste, and on the whole very little interest in what she ate. But today Maisie, from the pay-box, had brought her a fresh lettuce, and she opened a tin of luncheon meat to go with it, and made herself a

26

salad. She was just making the tea when the postman knocked at the door.

She had seen his hat pass across the corner of the window, and waited unmoved for the plop of letters through the front door, as usual. Probably the gas bill, or something just as unwelcome! She had received a letter from Jack only two days ago, and was still buoyant with the relief of it; for every long silence was a gradually tightening tension, since at any time, unknown to her, some bad thing could happen over there, and the days lengthen out into an endless quietness. There was no other letter for which she cared so urgently. She merely pricked an idle ear for the sound of their fall, ready to assess their possibilities by the noise they made; and instead of the flat, brisk smack of a circular, or the sibilant murmur of a slimy little note from some relative, came the rap of the postman's knuckles at the door. She went to open it, only mildly surprised, thinking it must be a parcel, though she wasn't expecting anything.

It was a telegram. The postman acted completely out of character with it, popping it into her hand with a hurried murmur, and withdrawing hastily down the short path to the gate, though he was known to be the nosiest old party in the neighbourhood, and would never normally retreat from a spectacle which promised to be interesting. But even without that fair warning, Mrs Parrish had recognised bad news. In her world neither telegrams nor relayed telephone messages meant anything but trouble.

She roused her senses quite automatically to encounter it, without any heroism, rather with an irritated but unhesitating reluctance. She was used to meeting unwelcome events, and wasting no time in

27

dealing with them, because she had never had any time to waste. She opened the telegram, and read it, still standing just within the closed door. Then she went back to the kettle, and turned off the gas under it.

They regretted to inform her that Private John Parrish was reported killed in action in Korea, on May 28th. He had been dead three weeks when his last letter reached her, dead already when her heart drew breath again to reassure her that he was still alive.

*   *   *

It can happen to anyone, she thought. My boy is only a boy like any other. I am no worse off than the rest. He's gone, and that's all there is to it. He was the only one we had, and it's just a pity; but our case is just the same as thousands of others, and we can't complain of it or alter it any more than they can. All the lamenting in the world won't bring him back. It's nobody's fault; the lot falls where it falls. Let's have none of this futile business of 'Why did it have to happen to mine!' She had never lost sight of other boys in hers while he was living, she wasn't going to start now he was dead. Rather had she been used to seeing every young man through the light of her love for her own, and feeling for their growing-pains with all the more acute and intelligent tenderness because she knew them so well in her own. They were all human. You couldn't feel for one without to some extent accepting them all.

She didn't try to eat, she knew it would be useless. But she sat by the table drinking cup after cup of tea, and then she got up and washed her cup, and put the

28

things away, with all the tidiness of habit she covered the bowl of salad with a clean, damp cloth, and put it in the pantry. All the practical motions came to her hands naturally. Her mind, uninvolved, proceeded apart from her body, upon its own involuntary path.

There was nothing new even about death. When you are poor enough, you have no buffer to fend off from you the earthy realities of dying, and on that account you perhaps mourn it less, certainly fear it less. Nursing the incurably sick is something you do yourself as a matter of course, and the details of their departure become matters of course in their turn. There is no mystery, and no horror.

But he was twenty, and healthy, and had before him that long and troubled and sturdy life that men have a right to expect, before they fade off naturally to make room for the next generation. And this time the mystery and the horror, as of something outside the cycle of nature, would not leave her mind. She knew the old, gathered after their due ripening, had not been cheated; she knew they were not lost. But the young and unfruited were another and a darker matter.

Her hands went on automatically with the business of the day; she swept and dusted, and began to peel potatoes for her husband's dinner. The chief difference the news had made to the arrangement of her time was simply that there was at least one extra duty to fit in. Renie Pollard would have to be told. She could not be left to come trotting in blithely here during the evening, with her bright affectionate chatter breaking over Tom's head from the doorway like a skittish wave, before ever she had time to see any change in him, and take warning. Better she should be in her own home when she heard the news.

29

Between preparing the vegetables and cooking them, say about five o'clock, Mrs Parrish thought she could make time to run across to Urban Gardens and get it over. Her hands, obedient as ever to the proddings of necessity, quickened their tempo to catch up with time.

No, there was nothing unfamiliar about death. Renie's sister's baby had died, a year ago, without ever tasting so much as the beginnings of a child's astonished consciousness. Do what they might, they'd never altogether get rid of the possibility of young things dying untimely. But that had been the result of an obscure disease of the blood, and all the resources of the family, and the estate, and the doctors of the town, had fought gamely on the child's side. She turned her eyes away from all useless speculation as to who had fought on the side of her child.

She knew all about the necessities of death. What was gone had to be relinquished, in an act of amputation upon her own mind; and the more cleanly and firmly it was done, the more likely were the living to go on receiving their due. She had no use for the widows who insist on creeping into their husband's graves, none for the obsessed mothers who turn their backs on the rest of humanity to worship the embalmed souls of their dead children. Moreover, she knew too much to attempt the exorcism with too much violence or in too great haste. All the time that she was tidying the kitchen she was feeding through her heart's memory, with a grateful, unresisting tenderness, a flood of recollections, inconsequent as fragments of dreams, out of the stored-up treasure of her life with Jack.

His father would take it hard, but he would get

over it. Only those who have never had to accustom themselves to getting over things, who have never had to learn acceptance, break down on the effort when the time comes. And Renie—well, she was not seriously afraid for Renie. That soft, ingenuous warmth would find another outlet, because it would have to, being unquenchable. The readjustment would be painful and pathetic, but the process was assured. Mrs Parrish dealt only with realities, because their hard shapes had always determined the development of her world; but she counted minds and spirits among the realities, and as firm and undeflectable as any. Nor did she blame circumstances or creatures for being what they were.

At five o'clock, when Renie would be just coming home from the toy factory, Mrs Parrish put on her hat again, and let herself out by the front door and locked it behind her, putting the key meticulously back into its shell on the step. She walked through the side-streets of the town towards the new housing estates, and spoke here and there to people she knew, and no one looked at her yet with that special and awful compassion she feared. It was enough that the centre of her life should have been torn out, leaving a great gaping hole, the edges of which she must somehow knit together again in her own way; it would be worse by far when the void became visible to everyone. She was safe yet; no one had heard. Give the postman one more day, and all the town would know it.

In the prim little semi-detached pink house in Urban Gardens she broke the news to Renie's mother in terms almost offensively brusque, glad to be there and have an ally before the girl came home. There was no time for the sympathy with which Mrs

31

Pollard, a stickler for the forms, would have liked to load her; the first light tap of Renie's high heels on the concrete path, and the two women drew together solidly, forgetful of themselves and each other, to spread the whole resources of their experience and calm about the defenceless young.

Renie came in blithely, swinging her white plastic handbag and swirling her cotton skirts under the short curl-cloth coat. She was small and rounded and fair, with a pertly serious face, and a long bob of hair artfully curled under at the shoulders. Jack had picked up with her when he was seventeen and she sixteen, and in spite of an occasional tiff they had stuck together ever since, though to the casual observer they might seem to have about as much in common as earth and air. Nor had they changed each other very much in those years. And if he had come back and looked at her again, after crossing half the world, he might well have realised their incongruity; he might even have been so enlarged with experience that Renie would have recognised it, too, and moved on in her ungrudging fashion to someone marked like herself with the charm of incurable and self-justified frivolity, leaving him free, absolved, and still dear to her. If he had come back!

'Hullo, Mum!' said Renie, glowing. 'Hullo, Mrs Parrish! I had a letter this morning! He's all right— only browned-off, just like always. I read it four times—every time I got a minute to myself. We've got some rush orders to get out this week, so we've been on the run every single minute, but never mind, we shall be shot of them by Saturday morning, with a bit of luck.' She hung up her coat, and turned to face them again, still shining with her own native content, whose life now was to be so brief. 'And, Mum, there's

32

the sweetest little nylon blouse in Taylor's window—pale pink waffle nylon, about twenty-three and nine. Can you lend me five bob till Friday? I've got enough for it if you will, and honestly, it's a bargain, the best I've seen for the money, and you know, it's getting scarcer again if anything.'

Her mother went close, and put her arm about the girl's waist. She said, in the slow, considerate tone which is itself a warning of bad news: 'Mrs Parrish has had news, too, Renie—since yours.'

Renie was quick enough to recognise the voice and the touch. The gaiety took wing from her face instantly, leaving her arrested in the lightness of her attitude like a dancer frozen into stone, her breath held, her dilated eyes fixed with sudden, intent questioning upon Mrs Parrish's face.

'About Jack?' she asked in a scared whisper. 'It's bad news?' Mrs Parrish nodded. 'I had a telegram, Renie. He's been killed in action.'

Renie braced a hand against her mother's side, and pushed her away. Her face was white as paper. 'I don't believe it!' she said, in a high, strenuous voice. 'They don't always know. Sometimes they're taken prisoner, and they think they're killed. It might not be true. They make mistakes. They made a mistake the other day, they wrote and told a woman her son was dead, and he really wasn't. It's happening all the time. They haven't a clue!'

'There might be a mistake,' said Mrs Parrish, shaken horribly with these useless convulsions of hope, 'but we daren't bank on it. They don't say killed if they think there's any doubt.'

'I won't believe it! They couldn't let it happen!' Renie was shouting now, her head back, her hands clutching at air in the frenzy of her despairing

33

optimism. 'Damn it, they're supposed to be making peace! They've been at it for months. They can't get people killed while they're pretending to make peace—nobody'd stand for it! *I* won't stand for it!' Her face crumpled piteously. She groped her way into Mrs Parrish's arms, and hung round her neck, wailing: 'Oh, Jack—Jack!' The rebellion was over, her tears broke like a flood, and rained and rained, gratefully, generously, peacefully, the blood of the past pouring out of her.

It was easy then. They half-led her to the sofa, and sat with her there between them, rocking and cradling her, and answering her few attempts at speech with the readiest, the most reckless reassurances. Her inexhaustible tears, her prodigal tears, full of sweetness and reconciliation, washed away all the revolt out of her, washed her into a coma of deep, drugged sorrow, not all painful. They put her to bed, and when she had wept herself out, she slept deeply, would sleep all night without any dreams, withdrawing herself firmly from a situation which was too much for her. When she awoke, death would have receded by a day, and already Jack would be far enough away for her eyes to focus him. She would come downstairs in the darkest dress she had wearing some brooch he had given her, pale and proud in her nobility, the widow of a war hero. The compensations would rise diffidently here and there in her day's work to touch and remind her. Mrs Parrish was glad to feel so sure of her.

'I shall have to be getting back now,' she said, 'to get Tom's dinner. But I'll look in in the morning, and see how she is.'

'She's young,' said Mrs Pollard. 'They get over things. They have to! You can't just stop living.'

34

She went to the door with her visitor. 'If there's anything I can do to help you out—'

'We shall manage,' said Mrs Parrish. 'We always have.'

They did not commiserate with each other any more; there was no need, now that Renie in her violent generosity, had satisfied the gods for all of them.

*   *   *

Tom Parrish sat about all the evening with the telegram in his hands, furtively unfolding and re-reading it every ten minutes or so, to see if by some miracle he could interpret its meaning this time in some different and less hurtful way; but it still wounded him with the identical significance, no matter how often he opened and examined it afresh. He could not grasp it. He drew his thick grey brows together in the anxious frown of the slow in reaction trying to overtake events. Tears gathered slowly in his bewildered blue eyes, and were blinked back again under the tired lids. She could not bear the hurt look upon his face, all the more because she knew it would not long remain there. If Renie was well-adjusted to losing a lover with the harmless, unrestrained violence of summer rain, so was he adjusted to relinquishing a son with patience and resignation. What was the use of kicking against what could not be helped?

His stubby brown fingers moved clumsily upon the folded paper. 'Well—we always knew it could happen. It's happened to a good many besides us.'

He was trying to sound like a soldier father making his farewell to a soldier son, but the blind, bewildered pain of his voice, fumbling along the phrases of resignation, frightened him badly. He looked to his wife for reassurance, and met the full, quiet stare of her eyes, curiously opaque, as if she had drawn a veil over them. She was writing little notes to the scattered groups of her family and his, to tell them what had happened; but after every line she looked up again at him, watching him as warily as if he had been a sick child in her care.

'Yes,' she said, 'we're in good company. It isn't only us.'

'It's funny,' he said, forcing his unwilling voice into a harsh loudness, 'it's always the best that go.'

She recognised an old lament, an old rite, the dressing of the grief to make it bearable. How can you endure the loss of the real, the ordinary, the insignificant, whose very littleness and intimacy makes it irreplaceable?

'He was a good lad. He'd have done well. I was talking to his foreman one of the days, and he says to me: "Tom," he says, "I'll be glad when I see your boy back. There aren't so many like him," he says, "workers *and* bright and quick to learn." He'd have gone far in his trade, our Jack would. Always picked up things so easy, even as a kid—remember? A fine, handsome little lad he was, too—everybody took to Jack—'

Mrs Parrish heard the vulnerable voice level out into recovered calm. She knew that she was listening to the beginning of a fictional biography of the dead boy, which would grow and root and flourish in the house, daily watered, nightly elaborated, until it put forth heroic flowers, as like the small but not unworthy budding of Jack Parrish as the sun is to a guttering candle. She watched with a steady, unreproachful smile her husband's florid face, struggling back from the unbearable to the bearable. He had already abandoned the cold and naked ground of truth, because to cling to it was to die. He was making himself a house of fantasy to keep off the killing wind. Others would help him to build it. Renie would enter gratefully into the merciful conspiracy, the hero's woman living up to the hero; and by this means she would survive the pain and the loss, until time turned her irrepressibly lively eyes outward again, and her nature settled them upon some other young man. The charade would have to last Tom longer than that, a whole lifetime; but the imagination, tenacious in self-defence, would have turned the legend into truth for him before the boy had been dead a year.

She smiled, tenderly watching the blurred eyes which met her own for no more than an imploring instant, and then evaded recapture. 'He was a nice boy,' she said.

She remembered obstinately the little faults, the less nice things about him, the occasional self-protective lie, the disinclination to wash, even at seventeen, the imperfect temper, the displeasing habit, the human and forgivable retreat from encounters with bigger boys, the regrettable and usually regretted impulse to take out his failure upon small boys; all the things he had had to contend with in himself, and which had made him a struggling human child in painful growth, and kept him now safely limited for her to the size of a man.

'He was making a good soldier, too. I know the signs. He'd have got a stripe before he came out, that I'm sure of.'

She listened to him thoughtfully, the pen lagging in

37

her hand; she did not abet or discourage his fantasies, but only regarded them with a sad analytical eye, watching the details build together, watching the legend grow. Soon other voices would be joining in the threnody, other defensive memories dredging up lost anecdotes of the boy's childhood, and dusting them from the littleness and ordinariness which alone made them unique and his own. Within the shadow and shelter of the creature they would create, this symbolic hero, above life-size, with the clear, beautiful, blank face of classic non-identity, Tom could hide from the reality of his loss. A man has to use what means he possesses of staying alive, of coming to terms with his world, a world without sons. But she sat silent at the kitchen table, her chin on her hand, and did not follow him in his retreat.

She, too, could have recalled out of the past many memories of Jack Parrish, but about her stories there would have been nothing heroic, nothing remarkable, nothing to provide consolation for anyone, least of all herself. She kept them shut within her own mind, the recollections of the times when she had failed him. Were they as frequent as they seemed to her now? She had not thought so. Yet all that came most clearly to her mind was failure and mild injustice, the occasional moments when she had blamed first and asked questions afterwards, the times when she had laughed at him and not succeeded in hiding her laughter, or when he had trusted her to meet the confession of his temperate little sins with her usual large gravity, and she had reacted bewilderingly with exasperation.

She knew that they amounted to nothing, that they had passed out of Jack's mind long before the extremities of cold and danger and distance swept greater grievances away; but the time was gone when she could balance better achievements against them, and undo them over and over. She was cheated of opportunity, as he was.

To reject bereavement is useless, to question it waste of breath; but she watched Tom edging his blind and painful way towards readjustment, and she did not take a step to follow him. It was unpractical, of course, to brace herself against accepting the loss. Or is it necessarily always so unpractical? The mothers of murdered sons, for instance, expect justice for the dead, and do not mildly reassemble their powers into the shape of resignation and leave all alone. Is that unpractical? The mothers of convicted murderers, for that matter, continue erect and in positive conflict, believing introduced innocence, believing in the right of a human creature to justice and his honest life, and vehement that justice has not been done. Sometimes they can prove their point. Is that unpractical? Is it more practical to let truth go by default, and infringe the image of absolute justice by which others have to live after us?

'One consolation,' said Tom, strenuously ridding his childlike blue eyes of the tears which slowly oozed and filled them, 'at least we know what he died for! That's something, at any rate. He died in a good cause, for democracy, for decency, to keep the world safe.'

She looked at him and said nothing. All manner of curious remembrances were going through her mind. She could read. There was a sergeant once who came back from Korea, from this mission in which he had certainly believed, and was asked by a reporter what the man in the street in that troubled country thought about it all. He said: 'There's no such person—there

39

are no streets!' There was also a photographer for a reputable magazine who came back from the recovered territory, and said to the public with terrible gravity: 'All I know is, if this is liberation, humanity can stand no more of it.' There were others, too, every one almost silent, uttering only one fearful phrase of doubt. Jack had not been even so articulate. Yet she thought of his letters now, those brief, homesick, browned-off letters any boy might have written, with the same awareness that they marked the edge of an abyss, into which she had never yet looked.

'Yes,' said Tom defiantly, avoiding her fixed and deliberate gaze, 'at any rate he gave his life for a great cause—he wasn't wasted.'

She said remotely: 'It could have happened to anyone. It has happened to a good many.' But it no longer calmed her to think of it in those terms, it merely multiplied by the number of the dead, by the number of the bereaved, the enormous disquiet which was beginning to eat at her heart.

She turned her head away, so that he should not see her unrelenting face, though she did not think he would read anything of her thoughts there. She got up from her place, and came round the table to him, taking the telegram out of his blunt, pathetic fingers, and leaning over him with her arm about his shoulders and her cheek against his greying temple.

'He was a nice boy. He didn't have all his life, but what he had was good, and he enjoyed it. We can always be glad, anyhow, that we got on so well together, the three of us.' Because she was so fond of him, and so far from sharing his attitudes, she could think of nothing more and nothing better to say. Instead, she held her husband gently against her heart, and kissed him on the forehead.

'And we can't even give him a proper funeral!' cried Tom, his voice breaking harshly. The tears broke out at last, and rolled down his russet cheeks, slowly and reluctantly, hiding in the hollow furrows which ran down towards the corners of his granite mouth. He turned his face into her shoulder, whimpering: 'We shan't even have that—not even his funeral! It doesn't seem right, Alice—it isn't good enough. Not even being able to bury him proper—'

*   *   *

Young Renie came to Hogarth Terrace three days later, when all the neighbours knew the worst, and many had already passed in and out of the house with their sympathy and their offerings, building their idealised recollections of Jack Parrish into the mausoleum Tom was busy erecting over him. It was already an impressive tomb; it dwarfed the dead boy within, but it gave Tom something to do. She understood its efficacy when she saw him open the little bureau drawer where his own old medals lay, and take them out for the first time in several years, and hold them in his hands for a few stolen seconds, as if they could re-establish a threatened contact.

'He was a fine boy,' said the neighbours, 'you've got every reason to be proud of him, Mr Parrish. He did his duty to the end.'

But Mrs Parrish said nothing at all. She had come to no conclusion, she had made no complaint; only she was not proud of her son as they meant the phrase, nor was she convinced that he had done his duty. To what end? If he had indeed done his duty, if she had done hers by him, the end might have

41

been different.

Renie came with ceremony, in a new and severe black costume, with touches of white at her throat. She had chosen it well, giving her whole soul to the selection, and put on with it her best black shoes and nylons, and a little black bonnet of a hat. She came with proudly raised head and soberly painted face, pacing sombrely like Andromache, so absorbed in the worthy staging of her grief that it had become almost a delight, fully a satisfaction. There was nothing false or small about her devotion to sorrow; she was paying the largest and most sincere compliment she could to the memory of Jack. She was made for living, and when other channels for her joy in it were temporarily stopped, she could take out that innocent passion in homage to a death, without insincerity or inconsistency.

Others came also, on the same propitiatory errand. The headmaster from the church school, who had taught Jack, and knew his qualities as well as Mrs Parrish did, paid a brief visit. It was odd to hear him talk of the boy now.

'A live wire, for all his quiet ways. I was never one of those who underestimated Jack. Whatever mischief was going on round our classroom, I could always be sure Jack was well in the middle of it. Not a bookish boy, no—he was far too busy using his ingenuity and enterprise in other directions to top any examination results. It wasn't any lack of ability, I was well aware of that.'

He sighed and smiled, shaking his head over some remembered scrape, probably ugly and unsatisfactory in Jack's eyes, which had somehow become transmuted into a dashing escapade for these people who survived him. As if a dead man had no

42

right to his own frustrations, but for their own comfort they must take even those away from him, and pretend that he was fulfilled, that he died satisfied of everything a man could get out of his life, and had no just complaint! Mrs Parrish saw that in its ubiquity this also was an admission. Only those who feel themselves to be in the presence of guilt set out to absolve themselves.

Some of his friends and contemporaries came too, those who were not themselves in uniform. There was Jimmy Seddon, whose eyes were too bad even for the Forces, and John Taylor, who was deferred because he was in the mines and setting out to be a mining engineer, and Freddy Baines, who had something wrong with his feet. They were subdued and inarticulate in her presence, but not awkward; they had known her too long and too well for that. They uttered a few bald phrases of sympathy, and sat for a long time with nothing more to say; but she felt their hurt as something nearer to her own, because they were too close to the same fate to make up any fantasies about it. There, but for the grace of God, they went, every one; and by their faces they were not too sure of the grace, nor that the election was God's doing.

So she was at ease with the young men, and comforted them by being more talkative than they were. It was after the first of them had left her that she really began to question her own heart.

The letters were in the bureau, the only voice Jack had now lay in them. She shut herself into the bedroom with them one afternoon, and read them all through again. The words had not changed; what she felt more acutely than ever before was the void of homesickness and bewilderment behind the words,

43

and between the letters the harassed, frightened, unhappy silences. She sat mechanically turning the letters down one by one on a new pile as she finished them. There were not so many of them; when they were all read, they made only a meagre little bundle in her lap.

'Dear Mum,
    'The stuff you sent came all right, and thanks for it, you don't know what a difference a bit of stuff from home makes out here. We are all right, barring the cold, which is something chronic. It makes you wonder how the folks here get on, living in the gutters and any hole the way they do. You see a lot of kids trying it on their own, but they don't last long. They beg off the Yanks, but there's too many of them begging in competition, there's no living in it. It doesn't seem as if any of them has a home or any family...'

'... couldn't move on the roads for all these folks going south. Everybody in the country on the run, only with nowhere to run to. Escaping from tyranny, our sergeant says, and heading out for democracy. You ought to hear him—he's a lad. I don't know what they left, but I know what they've come to. You should see the way their own police treat them...'

'... been a bit of a stink over some soldiers who went looking for women, only they went looking in a private house. Threw all the men out, and shut themselves in with the girls. They weren't our chaps. One man belonging to the house got shot dead because he stood by his wife and didn't go

44

when he was told. Some British went in and broke it up when they heard the women screaming. That time there nearly was a battle, a pity enough cops turned up to stop it. What they call an isolated incident round here, only they come pretty often...'

'... doing a fine job, he says. You know the usual line they hand out when they want something. Our sergeant says no kidding—a fine job of demolition, and some really classy undertaking. Wholesale terms, he says, distance no object. Cremations a speciality, he says...'

'... not used to traffic, they never seem to get any sense. You can't move for them down town, I never had a chance to miss him, but it was this policeman who shoved him right under my wheels. I told them that, but they just say, we don't want any trouble with the South Korean authorities, they're working in extremely difficult circumstances! I wish to God they'd get some of these people a place to live, and get them out of here, somewhere they'd be safe. Maybe somebody's doing something about it, I don't know. We never see any sign...'

'... I wish I was out of here. I have to lay off calendars, I get counting the days else. It isn't as if anybody's better off for us being here. They don't want us, they want to be left alone to make the best of it. They've had enough, too, they've had all they can do with. Imagine *choosing* this for a life, if you could break stones instead!'

45

Too clearly from the forward areas now, and all news, all writable feelings, reduced to this one unassuageable, frantic longing.

'I didn't get a letter by this post. I worry when I don't get a letter. You can't tell what's happening half the time, but I think some of them never turn up. Write as often as you can. It's bad enough, the things we have to do, even when we know it won't last for ever, but when we don't hear it seems like this is all there is. I wish I could give the days a shove, and hurry up out of it. It isn't the fighting! You get used to being scared to death, but there's things you never get used to...'

When she had read them, every one, she put them together again neatly, and tied the bit of tape round them, and put them back into the bureau, and went on with her work. They had to have time, they moved slowly in her mind, lame-footed, not to be hurried. There was no longer any need for haste, she had all the time in the world, since no manipulation of days or circumstances could bring back her son.

*   *   *

Dead for a great cause. Was that what he had felt? They had claimed two years of his life, and pulled up by the roots all the other years he should have enjoyed, to pay for something they no doubt thought worth the price. He had seen the crusade in action, and what had he thought it worth?

She did not want to do anything in haste. She wanted first to be sure of her own mind, to understand fully; because even if it was clear that a

46

wrong had been done, it was far from clear who was responsible. Somebody owed reparation. Somebody had either to produce the goods for which the price had been paid or be answerable for the betrayal.

If what they had bought with his life was not what it had been represented to be, he had a just complaint, and someone ought to follow it up, for it was a complaint which belonged not only to him, but to all the others, those gone before him, those just growing out of the schoolroom to follow helplessly along the same road after him, those condemned perpetually to purchase and re-purchase with their lives the same promised land which was to be heaven, and which he had seen, and on which he had turned his back in horror and disgust.

Mrs Parrish, peeling the potatoes and putting the onions on to fry, accepted the election of circumstances. She would never have any rest again until she knew to her own satisfaction who was guilty, and had confronted him with what he had done.

She did not think of Pak Yen Sou at all. She knew nothing about him, and if she had known, she would only have felt upon her fixed and resolute heart the burden of two young dead men, instead of one. Both betrayed, both humbly requiring an account of their lives, against the unidentified.

CHAPTER THREE

THE PRIEST

The reverend Charles Faulkner, Rector of Saint Michael's, Caldington, was in the late sixties, which for a man of his profession and habits is hardly even late middle age. Mrs Parrish, catching her first glimpse of him over his wife's shoulder, from the doorway of his study, was astonished and stimulated to see a body and face so vigorously and unmistakably male, and movements of such positive grace. He had come to the main living of the town only eighteen months ago, from an obscure but wealthy parish in the south-east of Midshire, and though she must have seen him occasionally in the street, or in mediocre photographs in the weekly paper, she had never been so close to him as this before.

Knowing his name and background, she had had in her mind some vague preconceived notion of a blend of small county aristocrat and conventional cleric, and had expected a cassock, and a sad gravity, and all the forms at their most rigid. The man who rose from behind the desk to come towards her had on a grey lounge suit of classic cut, and in his buttonhole a sulphur-coloured carnation tipped with red. He looked, perhaps, sixty. He had a thin, high-nosed face, deep-eyed and vehement, but a little worn; such a face as some musicians have, at the end of their lives, after the flood of their passion and experience has reached its plain.

His wife said, in the slightly portentous voice with

which she approached his more intimate duties: 'Charles, this is Mrs Parrish. You remember, I told you she asked to come and talk to you about her son.'

'Of course!' He offered her a lean hand, and gripped her with fingers as hard and well-exercised as her own. 'Come in and sit down, Mrs Parrish.'

She took the chair he set for her, and settled her handbag into her lap under clasped hands, watching the Rector's wife withdraw from the room and close the door with careful silence behind her. She wondered why men like this should attach their lives to women like that. A good soul, probably, thoroughly kind and charitable; but so obvious even in her virtues, of a consideration so inconsiderate that Mrs Parrish felt uncomfortable in her presence, and knew all the rebellious impatience of the nineteenth-century poor on being done good to. Such sweet unsolicited compassion gave her an itch to be away, and out of the atmosphere of indebtedness. She watched the short, thick, undistinguished figure recede, and heard the click of the latch, so discreet as to be embarrassingly obtrusive, with a wry sense of relief.

The man wasn't like that. He had resumed his chair behind the desk, as soon as his visitor was seated, and closed and pushed away the book which had lain open in front of him. He sat gazing thoughtfully at her over his linked hands, waiting for her to open to him whatever it was she had to say. He did not rush into words himself, nor seem in any haste for her to break the silence until she was thoroughly ready. And yet he must know, as his wife knew, who she was, and if he had not, therefore, jumped to conclusions about what she had to say to him, and what she wanted from him, then he was by way of being an exceptional

49

sort of parson. She began to think that perhaps she was in luck, that perhaps she had happened on a completely honest man. His face had a weathered look in more than its colouring and hard leanness, and the somewhat blunted aquilinity of his Red Indian nose; its expression was weathered, too, the deep, folded lines of experience grown into the bone, the eyes receptive and illusionless, and lucidly sad. He was no kind of parson she had met with up to now; not unworldly and ascetic, not hearty and determined to be of the world, not trying to level himself with anyone, either the saints or the common run of men. If he was what he looked, he was himself, and resolved to abide by that.

'You know about us,' she said, stating what was taken for granted. 'You must be wondering why I didn't go to our own vicar.' Hogarth Terrace was in St John's parish, over on the east side of the town.

'I was wondering,' he said, 'that he had not come to you.'

'Oh, he did. He came as soon as he knew.' Her voice was quite tranquil, even matter-of-fact. 'Mr Stokes has been very good, he tried to do whatever he could for us.'

It was clear that there had been nothing for him to do, and that she had suffered his visit and his efforts with forbearance rather than gratitude.

'But this is something else. I needed to talk to somebody for my own satisfaction, and I thought it had better be somebody who didn't know me, and hadn't known Jack. I didn't want any preconceived notions about us to get in the way. You know how it is, you can talk to a stranger straight out, somebody you never saw before, and need never see again unless you both want it that way.'

50

'Yes,' he said, looking at her steadily, his eyes only faintly puzzled, and willing to follow her to enlightenment, 'I know.'

'I go to church,' said Mrs Parrish thoughtfully, looking into her linked hands. 'Not every week, but pretty regular. I don't know as I've ever done much thinking about it, it's just the way I was brought up, and I've gone on doing it. I've never wanted to stop, or felt like changing. So when there's something I've got to sort out, something important that I can't altogether get the hang of by myself, it seemed right to me to come to one of you people, and see if you understand it any better than I do. I'm not asking for any miracles, I'm just trying to understand what's going on, for a lot of other people besides me; and if you can shed any light, that's what I need from you.'

'The only oracle,' said Charles Faulkner, with intent gravity, 'is the one you carry within yourself. All the rest of us can be no more than witnesses.'

'I know that,' said Mrs Parrish, raising her direct and handsome eyes.

'Whatever evidence I can give, I'll give, if you'll ask your questions.' He hesitated, uncertain of what was most needed from him. These were not the simplicities he had expected. He had expressed himself as to his own spirit, unguardedly, because of the surprising subtlety of her composure, and she had taken the point and made her answer with the same aplomb. Now it seemed almost false to put his sympathy into words, and yet all the more essential that so obvious a necessity should not be evaded. 'I am deeply sorry that you have lost your son.' He did not say that it was God's will, though in less hackneyed words Mr Stokes had said it. She was glad of the bareness of his expression of sorrow. 'That is

51

not what you want from me; it is what I want to say to you. I realise that you are engaged with something very much bigger than any comfort I could offer you.'

She sat looking at him steadily for several minutes, considering how to begin, her hands folded upon the black imitation-leather handbag. 'It isn't that I'm not grateful for your sympathy, or his. But there's something more important than that. My son was what they call a National Serviceman. He was just twenty. In a few more months he'd have been home, but it didn't work out that way, so that's over. But he's dead, and that isn't over. We've all got into such a queer way of thinking—no, maybe it's always been like that, and we're just beginning to get out of it—that these things are taken for granted. There's nothing special about our Jack's case to pick it out from thousands of others, nobody knows that better than me. But that doesn't make this case nor any of the others right. Jack never wanted to be a soldier. He didn't want to be put in a spot where he might have to kill somebody else or be killed himself. He never did anything to ask for that, nor to deserve it. He only went because he had to, because they're all taken by law, whether they like it or not. He never had any choice in the matter. And he's dead. Somebody did that to him, Mr Faulkner. Somebody's done this to his dad and me. Don't think I'm forgetting all the others in the same boat with us. Jack's just one boy to stand for the lot.'

He said gravely, seeking to understand before he searched his own heart, but already filled with an inexplicable uneasiness: 'You are bringing a charge against someone—something or someone—for the deaths of all of them.'

'I don't know yet what I'm doing. I'm only thinking, and asking. That's how it seemed to me. Somebody sent them where they didn't want to go, for a purpose they didn't want to serve, and they were killed. Is that murder? I don't know what else to call it. And over and above that, there's the making them kill other people. They never wanted that, either. What would you call that? Corrupting minors? Or offending these little ones? It's much the same thing, isn't it?'

Her voice was quiet, painstaking and slow, feeling its way through the meshes of prophecy. He had looked at her narrowly, during these last sentences, to watch for the gleam of intent self-consciousness, but she was not even thinking of herself except as a mine from which this arduous ore came up into the light. She had fixed her eyes beyond him, to have no distractions in her difficult search for a means of setting forth what was in her mind. Nothing would stop her, and nothing would turn her, but she did not know how formidable she was.

'You are not satisfied,' he said, watching her intensely, 'with the direct fact that where there is a war, there is an enemy?'

'Well, for instance—who would *you* say killed Uriah?' she asked, the focus of her eyes coming back quite mildly to his face.

'Yes—David.' There was no other answer, how could he even insult her by looking for one? And when it was said he was himself held by it, in a growing agitation. He got up from the desk, and began to walk back and forth across the bright sunlit space of the window, but the issue would not be evaded, it marched before him still confusing his eyes. If only she had come to him in the crisis of her

53

grief he would not have been short of words.

'So you are seeing the deaths of these young men—this appalling waste, as no one could disagree with you it is—as the result of a conspiracy of some creatures unknown, against humanity?'

She repeated patiently: 'Someone did it to them.'

'There is guilt. How can any of us deny it? We all share in it. There is guilt! And yet it is not so simple and clear a thing as it may seem. Our lives are not everything. They should not be undervalued, but they can also be overvalued.' He stopped, knotting the hard brown hands before him, his hawk's profile sharp against the window.

Mrs Parrish said reasonably, and without any indignation: 'Oh, I'm with you that we can put our own as low as we like but there's only one value you've got the right to put on anybody else's life, and that's the highest. The same as you can't spend other people's money—not honestly.'

He felt the sweat break on his forehead. It was like turning about in a nightmare to evade an undefined enemy, and being confronted every way with the same shape, which on waking could not be recalled or forgotten. She was watching him now more closely, with some wonder and concern, but without any judgment. When he was silent for a long time, shutting his lean cheeks between his hands, she suddenly opened the black handbag, and took out of it a little bundle of letters tied up with tape.

'I'd like you to read his last few letters from there. It's the only way you can get any evidence out of him, now, and it's only fair you should know everything I can tell you about it. They won't take you long—he wasn't much of a writer, nor that much of a talker, neither.'

54

He sat down at the desk with them, and in the act of untying the tape suddenly looked up at her again. 'You haven't a photograph of him? I saw the picture in the paper, of course, but it gave very little idea of what he was like. I should like to know how he looked.'

She gave him, without a word, a passport-sized print of the photograph she had, framed, in the kitchen at home; uneasy, obscurely disquieted by his uniform as by broad arrows, the boy looked up at him wide-eyed and defensive, fending off the future with that distrustful stare. His hand shook as he held the card, and he set it down on the desk before him, and let it lie there all the time he was unfolding and reading, one by one, the last letters of Jack Parrish.

While he was about this, Mrs Parrish waited, without impatience, her considering eyes weighing him in the context of his study and his vocation. She knew who he was, a son of one of the poorer branches of the Faulkner family whose history sprawled across the last three centuries of Midshire history, cropping up in every major military campaign from Marlborough on, and step for step with the generals, in the major livings of the Church within the county. The more brilliant and wealthy had gone into the army as a matter of course; she hadn't thought of that when she came to him. Such a family tradition might have coloured the whole of his thinking, but somehow she thought he had escaped it. Perhaps the day of the Faulkners was over. There were not so many of them now, only a few dwindling rivulets here and there left of that sturdy stream. What this one had got from them was more subtle and more valuable than a lingering regard for military reputation: the assurance of personal authority, and a fastidious conviction in movement and speech, the repose of those secure in their own personalities, who feel no need for insistence and emphasis. He had as a gift what she had to fumble for.

It was very quiet in the room. The rest of the house, so far as Mrs Parrish had been able to see it as she was led through, was lush and comfortable and excessively ladylike, as if the place were full of women. But here there was very little except the desk, and two or three chairs, a couple of rugs on the bare boarded floor, and a profusion of books all round the walls in haphazard shelves, which had obviously been built on to at need in any convenient direction. All the books looked well used, and the room, for all its bareness, had the relaxed look of a place constantly and serenely inhabited. The short, lumpy wife, with her housewifely hands, didn't come in here much; perhaps she wasn't encouraged.

On the end of the desk there was a broken wooden crucifix about a foot high, worn almost shapeless with age, and riddled with worm, the half-obliterated features of its Christ still markedly sorrowful even in their decay. On one of the bookshelves there was a little terracotta Madonna and Child, human and jolly and sparkling with an unexpected vivacity, Renaissance just trembling into Baroque. Mrs Parrish had never heard of either, but she was capable of weighing the qualities of both when she saw them. It seemed to her that when this energetic baby became a man it was possible to believe that blood would flow out of his wounds, and that he would feel, and cry.

The Rector read the letters to the end, with a courteous concentration for which she was grateful, his deep brows drawn low over the hollow settings of

56

his eyes, his hands turning the pages with measured, austere movements. Then he put them all together again, and looked at her over the meagre little packet he held between his palms.

'Not everything which is well meant is done well. How can I pretend to understand, or to be able to justify, things about which my own mind has often been divided? I am not sure that we are wise to look beyond our own personal losses. There is nothing final about death. It means only an ending to this world's part in us, and our part in this world. Oughtn't that to be enough for us? The dead are gone from this world, but that's all. We are right to feel our loss, but dare we feel theirs? Isn't it better to acquiesce, to acknowledge that they are gone, and cannot be recovered here?'

'I'm not trying to recover him,' said Mrs Parrish simply. 'All I want is justice. There's something due to all the others who're going the same road. I want to know where I must go to get at the people who did it to him. Somebody must be answerable. I know all about the law of the land, but there's another sort of justice above that.'

He said very gravely: 'I understand. You have given the Church the first opportunity of clearing itself.'

She looked back at him blankly, for no such thought had been in her mind in coming to him, and it seemed to her curiously irrelevant now that he had suggested it. 'I thought in a matter of right and wrong—real right and wrong, not just legal—you might be the one who could help me to get through to the truth. That's all. I'm in no hurry. I'm not accusing anybody. I only want to know.'

For whom, then, had he spoken, with that new and

solemn eagerness, if not for her? Was it possible he was about to deploy a reasoned defence in order to convince himself? Before the Church was accused, to deliver the Church? He recognised the most damning of all indictments, and recoiled from all that he had meant to say. She was looking at him with dark, level, questioning eyes, terrifyingly shrewd like the eyes of the saints. She was wondering about him, wondering if he was the man she had hoped for. He saw the burning brightness of doubt, as sharp and cold as a sword, fixed in the centre of her regard, but she waited, and did not prejudge him. It was as she had said, she was in no hurry; she only wanted and waited to know, to be sure of her own observations and the deliberations of her own heart. There was plenty of time for judgment, and eternity for damnation.

He was confused by his own sudden loss of words, the precipitate recoil from all he had meant to say to her; and grasping at almost any speech to fill the void, he made what he knew instantly was a fatal mistake.

'You are looking for human scapegoats. But is that fair in such a case as this? You know yourself that there may be greater considerations than the lives and needs of individual human beings. What a man dare not claim from us, what he has no right to claim, perhaps a nation may—' He had stopped, even before the quick, astonished flare of her eyes stopped him; the word in his mouth had appalled him, he did not need the flash of her derision to show him how unworthy it was.

'As far as I'm concerned,' she said, her voice lighter than before, and colder, as if the whole situation had somehow lost weight by the measure of his revealed lightness, 'there are no nations—only people. If a thing's wrong, none of the talk about nations will

58

make it right. Nations are people.'

She got up, and held out her hand for the packet of letters. She was going to leave him now, and he could not bear that she should, for he had done no justice either to himself or her. Justice was her passion, she would not wish to deny it even to him. He rose also, but kept his hold upon the letters, to keep in spite of his own stupidity his tenuous hold on her.

'I didn't express myself well. The word was badly chosen. But instead of a nation, let us say rather civilisation—or, better, humanity itself with all its truest values. That has taken a great many lives, and it has not always asked permission. It claimed a right. Was that justified? Sacrifice is always single, always poses the same problem of price and value. I have no easy answer to it. But remember that there was a precedent. God Himself so loved the world that He gave His only begotten Son—'

His voice was already low, almost a whisper, and because of the still, acute stare with which she faced him the words dried up in his mouth.

'God's the one who must answer for that,' said Mrs Parrish, 'not me. At least he gave only his own son, and with his son's consent, or so we're told. My son never consented. His dad and me never gave him. Jack was taken, not given, Mr Faulkner. Who was it took him? That's all I want to know. That's something you can't put on to God,' she said distinctly, opening her thin hand pointedly but gently for her property.

He put the letters into it, caught for an instant into a superstitious awe of her, for she had a terrible authority about her. He felt the bone in the middle of her humility, the steel inside her meekness; she knew nothing about her own resources, she was simply

59

going away from him in disappointment, with a resigned sigh, because he had not provided a single clue to her problem of identification. Or was it rather that he had answered her very clearly? Did she know the name she was seeking? Was it his name? Churches, like nations, are only people. Was he the man?

'So little of the purpose and the design are revealed to us,' he said feverishly. 'Don't question too closely. Trust a little, too. We all have to live by faith. Remember, and be charitable, that to most of us, fallible as we are, it does seem that there has been a purpose, a large purpose, behind the spending of these young lives, that the terrible decision to spend them *was* justified.'

She looked back mildly, without any hope of him or any resentment against him, still laboriously, doggedly, singly pursuing her inviolable truth. 'Then those who spent him ought to be able to show me what they got for him. If it had been really the salvation of the world, it'd take a bold mother to say a word against it. But was it?'

'It was the preservation of human and Christian values, or so they saw it—'

He stopped again, for she had smiled. The first smile, so slender, and sceptical, and sad that he had almost thought it no more than a reflected shadow from the branches of the laburnum tree outside the window. Her eyelids lowered for a moment, she looked down briefly at the letters in her hand. She said nothing about the discrepancy, but the glance had its own fearful eloquence. He remembered those human and Christian values which had confronted Jack Parrish in Korea, and his voice failed in his throat. What part had Christ had in all this, unless as

60

a victim?

'I'll be getting along now. Thank you for seeing me. I know you have plenty of calls on your time, without me bothering you.'

She was going, and nothing could keep her. He moved at her elbow, helpless to change anything now.

'I'm afraid I haven't been of any help to you.'

'Well, as you said, it isn't as if it was simple.'

He opened the door for her, and drew back with a sharp recoil from the sight which confronted him. On a straight-backed chair in the hall sat a very young man, upright, nervous and humble, clutching his cap tightly in his two immature and rather grubby hands, his feet placed neatly side-by-side before him, uneasily aware of their dusty shoes on the pretty blue rug; patiently, apprehensively, meekly, he was waiting for the door to open, for the Rector to be ready to see him. He had come straight from work, calling for his girl on the way, and though he had tried to smarten himself up as much as he could manage in his working clothes, the shaft of sunlight in which he sat found out the soiled weariness in his face, his nervous persistence in an errand which irked him and made him temporarily uncomfortable, but which was of vital importance to him. The girl sat at a little distance, and in shadow; it was not easy at first to see beyond the boy.

He did not look like a prospective bridegroom. It cost the Rector a conscious and convulsive effort to remember who he was, and why he was there.

'Good afternoon,' said Mrs Parrish, looking back for an instant from the front steps at the shadowy room and the bright, humble boy. She closed her bag with a snap upon Jack's letters, and walked away

61

down the curving drive without turning her head again.

*   *   *

At tea, in the chintzy morning-room, with his wife enthroned behind the tray and his two unmarried daughters making conversation over the cakes, he kept his silence, and it passed for normal. Often he had little to say after the world had been at him, and the women made it their business to fend off the irritating details of living until he should have shaken off the shadow of vicarious miseries. Their presumption was wonderful and in its way generous. He knew he had benefited from it in the past, in spite of his affectionate scepticism. They shielded him from the vexations of the world, he shielded them from the knowledge of the fragility and ignorance of the protection they spread about him. Now and again he saw, through the strong, believing security which enfolded them all, the immensity of the darkness at which they never guessed, and it appalled him. Then the boundaries of his experience cramped and hurt him upon every side, and he struggled, as he thought, to break them and be enlarged. Now he saw that the struggle had always, in reality, been to diminish himself again into the bounds of what he knew, and be rid of the unbearable pain.

He looked at his daughters, and threaded together in his mind the strands of their divided interests, and found almost every colour of the spectrum there. Florence was nearly forty, and cut out admirably for the single life she seemed to have chosen; emancipated, clever, a committee-woman of excellent sense and wide sympathy, active in his

62

parishes since her girlhood. There was not much she had not seen of human trouble. Elspeth was twenty-six—the married Anne came in between—and taught music at two local grammar schools; she was gay, and handsome, and engaged to be married. Sophisticated and of strong character, they had none of the narrowness and specialised outlook many people expect to find in women of the vicarage. But though they had ventured among the chaotic lives of all manner of people, they had never entered any but the lives of their own kind. He knew that. To touch, to lay the bright little bubble of their interest alongside, that was not to enter. There is no harder thing in the world than to break the membrane that divides one human creature from another.

He felt himself insulated, like them, from all real communion with the people he had passionately desired to serve and help. It was not a new feeling, it came upon him whenever he was presented with the opportunity of contact with someone of his own stature, and failed to achieve the longed-for union. All despairs, all convictions of failure, stemmed from this; he need look no further for the seed of his grievous disquiet. The conviction of guilt was only the extension of failure; the woman, the boy, were no more than the mechanism of his own inadequacy. Despair is a mortal sin, he said to himself, holding off the memory of the boy's face from him.

'That poor woman!' said his wife, manipulating the teapot. 'I feel so sorry for her. It seems even worse for a thing like that to happen when an armistice is already in sight. More wanton, if one didn't look beneath the surface of things. And I'm afraid it isn't easy for a woman in her situation to see beyond her own loss. I do hope you were able to comfort her a little.'

She was not asking a question, nor did he give her an answer. It was pointless to explain to her that Mrs Parrish had not come looking for comfort, impossible to express how little she needed or knew how to accommodate pity.

'Poor Charles!' She was sorry for him, too, in an affectionate, abstracted way, with as little need of comment from him. 'It's a terrible burden sometimes, justifying the ways of God to men.'

Particularly, he thought but did not say, when they are the ways of other men, not of God, and have no justification. And he wondered what centuries of the world's injustice and cruelty had been shrugged off in God's direction, and what lengthy agonies of submission and resignation preached successfully to the victims in God's name.

'I doubt if I did anything for her,' he said, 'but I don't think she was holding it against God.'

'She did seem very composed. And of course, it's two or three weeks since she heard the news, and I suppose she's had time to come to terms with the sacrifice that's been demanded of her. But even so,' she said gently, 'it's easier to admit the need of a sacrifice like that than to feel it sincerely. One always feels yes, the occasion made it necessary, but need it have been *mine*?'

They had three daughters, but no sons. He wondered if she could have given voice to these tender, innocent platitudes if they had had sons. Mrs Parrish had made it clear that not one dead young man, but thousands upon thousands, came with her in search of their stolen lives. That was why the boy's face was no longer quite so clear in his mind. He could see with terrible clarity the set of the nervous

64

young head upon the slender, immature neck, the shoulders not yet squared into soldierliness, the ill-fitting folds of the battle-dress, but the features melted and changed whenever he tried to fix them, and would not be limited.

'It makes it a little easier,' she said, 'that in this case the issue was so clear a one between right and wrong. It isn't quite so awful to have to make a case for the rights of a cause like *that* to take men's lives. You wouldn't have to hesitate, this time, to tell the poor woman her son died doing God's work.'

He sat gazing at her across the tea-table with his usual grave serenity, and gave no sign of the superstitious pangs with which her words transfixed his heart. He heard again all his own arguments paraded complacently in her mouth, deployed before him so that he might see them for what they were. He trembled to think of his own tongue uttering these horrible blasphemies.

Yet the woman had gone away without reproaching him. It was only the boy who would not go away.

*   *   *

It was the evening of his mid-week service; he held it, as usual, to an almost empty church, and a choir of two men and a handful of diminutive trebles. On such occasions they said the psalms, and ventured into song only for the two or three hymns, which could always be salvaged in unison if they foundered in too attenuated harmony. The Rector's family seldom came over on these Thursday evenings, and their absence severed one more thread which linked him with his private world, and left him marooned upon an island of dim Gothic stone, subtly lit from the altar candles and the sombrely coloured windows, an obscure and peaceful place which had nothing in common with the bright, busy, worldly church of Sundays and festivals.

He knew, none better, that the two elderly ladies and the one devout lay reader attended because attendance was a part of the public character they had constructed with care, and chose to sustain for their own purposes. The clerk came because it was his duty, and he was a conscientious man. The organist, because choir practice followed, and the competent performance of the church's weekly music meant to him all that the church should have meant. The choir boys came because they would have had to risk word of their absence reaching their parents in due course had they stayed away, and it was not worth making an issue of it except for a really sufficing reason. And the Rector comes, he thought, gazing between the candlesticks at his worn wooden crucifix in which the deep shadows bored like lines of grief, because it is expected of him and has become a habit. Even the stones are not here out of love. Even the light, burning and smouldering through the heavy Flemish glass with its rubies and its violets and its dark, bitter greens, visits us only coldly inside here. It might not be early July, for all the colour and scent of it that penetrates this place. There might be no motion nor choice nor response in man, for all the warmth it gives inside these walls.

He recognised the dungeon he was entering, because he had entered it many times before, and felt and heard the door clang to behind him. He watched the candles burn steadily colder and dimmer, the young roses in the two vases grow ashen and dry

66

before the bitter stare of his eyes. Doubt came round him like a freezing wind, sealing him from his own kind. All this, he thought, all the years of belief and dedication, however vain, were all we had; and how if we have laid them all upon the devil's altar, while we thought we were carrying them straight to God's door? How good have the signposts been? And where have they brought us? Suppose I am here, with my face fixed toward this little, unresponsive image, and all the while the God whose gestures could really enlighten me, whose very look could make my energy burn up and blaze into the right channel, is waiting in the dark behind my back, and cannot call me out of my delusion? And when the day comes, and we set eyes on the saints, will they look to us like a drove of seedy rogues and vagabonds, not fit for our company? Shall we turn away from them in dudgeon, and say: 'This wasn't what we expected of God!' and go away voluntarily to look for more respectable society in hell? Again?

We speak of the devils of doubt. But what if these are the despairing angels, fighting to turn us while there is still time? How if the light we are after is steadily dwindling in the distance behind us, and we are walking steadfastly, resolutely, with ears devoutly shut against the demoniac voices within, towards the final darkness? And how if those whose defection we are never tired of condemning are the few who have listened, and turned about, and are going gladly and confidently towards the light? Do archbishops and bishops never wake up in the night and wonder, and tremble to the heart because no man can *know*?

With this desert agony the Rector was very familiar, all the more because he himself had

67

sometimes been reckoned among the deserters. But familiarity never diminished the despair of the spirit which filled him when he confronted again the threshold of the arctic coldness of his own misgivings. He fixed his eyes upon the dim, soaring spaces of the nave, in which his little flock was lost as in a twilit sea, and the verses of the psalms slipped through his lips into the large obscurity with a lamentable, small, clear sound, lost slowly among the shadows where the few inclined heads floated ghostlike, without age, or sex, or personality.

'"Lord, how long wilt thou hide thyself, for ever: and shall thy wrath burn like fire?"'

'"Oh, remember how short my time is,"' besought the four shrill trebles cheerfully, little pagans with the whole of eternity in their pockets: '"wherefore hast thou made all men for nought?"'

The wavering candlelight conflicted with the subdued light from the windows, ageing their bland faces suddenly into a terrible, affrighted maturity. He saw that they, too, would soon be eighteen, and that their time indeed might be shorter than they knew.

'"What man is he that liveth, and shall not see death?"' argued the psalmist through the Rector's cold, shocked lips. '"And shall he deliver his soul from the hand of hell?"'

But he knew that it was no answer. He raised his eyes, and fastened them deeply into the shadowy receding spaces under the organ-loft, as one casting out a riding anchor in a sea which could be only weathered, not bested.

There was someone there at the back of the church, someone unaccustomed, someone unknown. Unknown, or too well known. He had made himself as inconspicuous as possible, in the darkest place

68

against the wall, but the figure was tall and slender, the head uncovered, a young man's head, dutifully bowed over a prayer-book. The Rector shut his eyes for an instant, but when he opened them again the figure was still there, the young head still tenderly inclined, a vague, lighter oval in the dimness, the features so faintly visible that he could make of them whatever he chose.

All the time that he was reading the Lesson his eyes strained after a better sight of the stranger. Sometimes it seemed to him that he discerned the slight, bewildered features of Private Parrish, fending him off with thick, girlish lashes now half-lowered over defensive eyes. Sometimes the face seemed broader, the bones thicker, with a blunt American shaping about the jaw and cheeks. Sometimes the figure shrank together into a slender, compact shape, with a small, smooth black head, and fine tilted brows above oval dark eyes, a closed oriental face. He had only to thrust vision a little beyond its strength, and he could assemble the dissolving shadows into any face he had ever seen or imagined; any but an old face.

Young men did not come to mid-week evensong at St Michael's. No young man had ever attended, apart from the rare chorister, since Charles Faulkner had come to the parish.

'"Whoso shall receive one such little child in my name,"' read the Rector, in his beautiful, alert, unclerical voice, '"receiveth me—"'

'"Woe unto the world because of offences! For it must needs be that offences come, but woe to that man by whom the offence cometh!"'

The young head was lifted as he closed the book, and he was aware of the grave regard of eyes, though the shadows swirled before him as he strained to see more clearly, and the face remained elusive and undefined. What he felt was the tentative but very serious touch of an intelligent and questioning innocence, in which he swung as in a balance; and he was pierced by a sudden brief frenzy of pain because he could not sense whether he weighed firmly or lightly in the scale to the mind behind those still unconfronted eyes. He turned to the altar with the convulsion of distress still bitter in him.

When I rise and turn again, he thought, my eyes will be rested from the effort to see, and then I shall see. I shall meet his eyes fully, and I shall know if I am the man, the guilty man, the man who has seen all these things happening, and looked the other way, the man who has been an apologist for the murderers, the man who is himself among the murderers. I shall know whether I have my face turned towards the light or the darkness, heaven or hell. He was modern enough to disbelieve in more of hell than a man can carry in him and live, but he knew that that was enough.

While he said the prayers he looked upward at his old, worn Christ, the German fragment he had rescued once from a sale in Bavaria, and brought home, and grafted so lovingly to the new oaken stock on which it now rested. It was very old, and of the same descent as the terrible and beautiful Calvaries from the eleventh and twelfth centuries in the Rhineland cathedrals, but without the extreme expressionistic agony. A lesser hand but still a skilled one had made it, and within its slighter grace all the human pain of the Crucifixion lay softened but present still, waiting only the unexpected flicker of a candle, the fall of a slanting light, to transfix the heart

70

afresh with the conviction of death and suffering repeated and repeated without respite through all the experiences of man. The Patripassian heresy, the doctrine of the continual suffering of God, was in this crumbling sliver of wood.

The face was subject to startling change with the draught that made the candles waver, and with the angle of his vision. Looked at thus, from his knees, the conventional slight fringe of beard faded into the deep shadow, the face lost in years, and gained in fear and distress, the hollowed cheeks and drawn mouth achieved in their contortion of pain a revelation of youth. This Christ was newly a man, would not live to be fully a man, could not dic pure of awareness of manhood. Pierced on the threshold of maturity, with the widening horizon already in sight, he died endlessly the bitterest, the most deprived of deaths. Was it possible, he thought, trembling, that Christ himself was a conscript?

He closed his eyes to cut himself off from thoughts so terrifying and so unprofitable, and with the darkness he was calmed. But when he rose from his knees, and turned to announce the last hymn, another and subtler change had come upon the young man at the back of the church. The Rector's eyes, rested, should have been able now to distinguish colouring and form; instead, he had looked too long at the bruised face of wood, and it hung before his vision still, and would not be blinked away. It lay like a mask over the face of the young man, and melted into his features its own sorrow and outrage, and the Rector could not stare it from him. It had become of intense importance that he should see himself at last in the mirror of those eyes which had measured him from the shadows. He was a man without

71

superstitions, yet he had made a superstition of this. He had to know whether he was damned, for the state in which he hung now seemed to him very like damnation.

He knelt again, hearing as in a dream his own voice saying the final prayer. This time his eyes were closed; he would not look up again into the convulsed face above him, with its sudden blinding youth which impressed itself so corrosively upon his eyes if he let them dwell there. This time he would turn back to the fading light of the nave from the darkness within his eyelids, and there would no longer be any veil of illusion between him and the young man who had been sent to him.

But by the time he had turned to bless them and send them away, the young man was already gone. He was too late to see that silent departure, he heard only the soft clink of the heavy latch relaxing into its socket, and a light step leaving the muffling mats for the flags of the porch. To intercept or pursue was impossible. He followed the ungainly little recession of choristers out into the vestry, and as soon as he had received their last prolonged 'Amen' he excused himself, and went out into the green and whispering evening among the trees and the graves, and hurried round the corner of the church to watch the few worshippers going decorously homeward.

The sun was still on the road, and July in the roses which arched against the grey wall. He saw the two old ladies going gingerly and gently down the sloping path to the lich-gate, dangling their inevitable umbrellas and fluttering with mauve scarves. Then the lay reader, brisk but grave, and the clerk trotting like a terrier after him. But the young man was not to be seen in all the bright, bald length of the road.

He went back slowly to the vestry. The memory of the dead waited for him patiently as he moved within, putting away his cassock, checking the list of hymns for practice, fending off, even as he desired it, the moment of loneliness. For though it fled him when he pursued it, he knew that when he fled from it, it would follow him, the young figure with the shadowy face and the veiled, assessing eyes, the oracle, the angel.

CHAPTER FOUR

THE POLITICIAN

William Dallas, M.P. for Caldington, East, was one of Labour's bright and promising young men, one of the new Socialists who had come to the party after the war, complete with a burning awareness of social injustice, so recent and startling that it had shaken him clean off his course.

He was Caldington-born, the son of a local solicitor with a good standing in the county, and he had moved serenely through the successive stages of prep. school, minor public school, provincial university and an irreproachable county marriage, to take over his father's practice at the age of twenty-five, when the old man died. He was comfortably settled in, with an older partner who could do the work for both of them without the least trouble, when war broke out, and he left his wife and three-year-old son, on the crest of a wave of not particularly difficult or painful patriotism, to volunteer for the army.

Until then his preordained passage through life

had never taken him into any but ordered and harmonious surroundings. There was plenty of poverty and misery to be found in Caldington, if he had ever suspected its existence, but it was a balanced town which suffered less than most from the depressions of the late 'twenties and early 'thirties, and its darker aspects were far from obvious, and had totally escaped him. But the industrial north through the blitz was quite another matter. For Dallas it was like seeing the earth torn open before his feet, and finding himself staring with horrified eyes into an underworld of cramped and undernourished misery, where creatures compressed and distorted but unmistakably human struggled to live decently without the most elementary materials for the job. He grew hot with the undirected indignation of all the newly-enlightened, and began to overturn systems wholesale in his mind.

It was not his fault that he found himself attached to a backwater of a staff job, and spent the first five years of the war in various parts of the British Isles, and even in 1944 got to France only well after the real excitement had moved on towards Germany. He never saw anything which could be described as action, but saw plenty of the miserable chaos left behind by occupation, and had his share of the mess to clear up after the tide of action had gone by. The violent readjustments which were being made locally in the social set-up, by Resistance men in too much of a hurry to wait for law, could not entirely deflect his attention from the injustices which were receiving no readjustments from anyone. Once he had set his horrified eyes upon the social anomaly, it confronted him wherever he turned.

He came out of the army in 1947, burning with zeal

and impatience, and joined the Labour Party. He was a strong asset locally, with his connections, and it was not long before he was chairman of a local branch, and then chairman of the constituency. He took these offices very seriously indeed, and spent all his spare time reading up the past history of the movement, and the lives and utterances of all its pioneers, until he could out-quote the old men on their own struggles, and set them straight on their own principles. With a little practice in public speaking, and his own native fluency and confidence, which every experience of his life had had the effect of reinforcing, he was soon moving from meeting to meeting in a wider sphere than merely one constituency.

As for his wife Ginnie, she was young, amiable, and extremely pretty, so that though she was incapable of making a speech of more than one line without committing some irresistible *gaffe*, she came in handy for opening bazaars and judging baby shows, for crowning May Queens and auctioning cakes at sales of work. She had no politics of her own, and was even a little vague about his, but she grasped as much as she could of what he said about them, and professed herself staunchly in agreement with his conversion to social responsibility. She was very fond of him, and it made good sense to her that two in a house should be headed in the same direction.

East Caldington habitually voted Labour by a modest but fairly steady majority, being the industrial side of the town, and having, even in its country districts, several large, scattered factories. West Caldington as regularly elected a Tory, for equally cogent reasons of self-interest. The member for the west side dying in 1949, Dallas was

75

approached to contest the seat, and while he did not succeed in taking it from the enemy, came within a couple of thousand votes of accomplishing the feat, which was nearer than anyone had come to success before him. So it was natural that at the general election which followed he should be considered the right man to hold the east side, which was losing the services of an extremely popular idealist by his refusal to go on any longer fighting down his disgust with the whole grubby business of government. His attitude, of which he made no secret, did not improve the morale of the constituency party, and in view of the generally turning tide in the country even this traditionally established seat was regarded as precarious. They wanted a safe man, a local man, an attractive presence and a persuasive and persuaded tongue, to stave off defeat, and appealed to Dallas to transfer his attention from west to east. Of the west they had given up hope for that occasion, the east they retained with a slightly lowered majority, but still by a reassuring margin. And William Dallas went to Westminster with pleased expectation, and a sense of having embarked on his true career at last.

After he was established there, and becoming gratifyingly vocal on a level of articulacy somewhat above the usual standard of the House, he lost, or at any rate modulated, his fine indignation. The weight of responsibility on his shoulders checked the first resplendent impetus very efficiently; he had to admit it to himself when he sat down to take stock at the end of his first year, and because it disquieted him, he began to invent all kinds of personal crusades for the under-privileged people who had first driven him into politics, to make up for his failure to launch a general crusade on their behalf.

He undertook a certain amount of legal work free for people who needed it and could not pay for it; and he established a regular monthly audience at his office, on Saturday evenings when everyone could take advantage of it, so that constituents who had any personal problem or grievance could bring it to him direct. Then, even if he could do nothing whatever to help them, the outlet provided by his sympathetic attention gave them at least a feeling of being justly valued here; and he was aware, though that was not his reason for inaugurating the service, that their easy and warm gratitude did him no harm among the neighbours.

Action on these many and varied requests and grievances was so often impossible that he sometimes felt a bit of a humbug, but having begun the service he could not back out of it, and the rare occasions when there was really something he could do came to be almost rapturously welcome to him. It grieved him sincerely that he could do so little, but the world could not be altered in a day, or perhaps in a generation, and in the meantime these poor creatures had to live, and alleviation was surely better than nothing.

The difficult truth was that although his life had brought him belatedly in contact with some minor phases of human frustration and deprivation, he had never shared in any, not even in imagination. He had not enough imagination for that, not by any means enough to break out of his background and enter into the skin of these people whom he conscientiously regarded as his brothers. He had a sense of fellowship, but none of equality. He wanted ardently to do something *for* them; it had never occurred to him to slough his security and get down among them

77

and do something *with* them. But the difference was so subtle that neither he nor they noticed anything wrong.

Taken by and large, East Caldington was proud of its bright young man, and inclined to be cocky about his chances of minor office if ever his party should get back into power. His lively qualities in the House were becoming known, his legal knowledge was the kind of asset a young Socialist needed to get anywhere in 1953, and he had proved, was constantly proving, in his solicitude for the tender individual rights of his least influential constituents, the goodness of his heart.

But what they were inclined to preen themselves on more complacently still was his social background, his cultivated and fluent voice, his well-groomed good looks, and the excellent cut of his clothes. Nothing pleased the Caldington Labour Party so much as to get him on the same platform with his neighbour Member from the west side, who was remotely connected with the peerage, and to observe how much more elegant and urbane was their Bill Dallas than the Tories' Ronald Crozier. It did something for their lingering inferiority complex.

Only the colliers of the older generation, who had lived through times which left them in no doubt of their equality with anyone on earth, dared openly look askance at this modern modulation on a well-marked theme. It was not the Savile Row suits and the manicured hands and the school tie that caused them disquiet on behalf of their movement, but the suggestive gratification and relief of their fellows at having achieved such a symbol. They had nothing against him, he was a decent enough chap, they considered; but only a very sick movement indeed could mistake him for a saviour just because he was socially accomplished, and wave him triumphantly in the faces of the enemy in this far too revealing fashion. But the old colliers were in a minority, and Bill Dallas was human, and subject to the flattery of exaggerated esteem; and he was beginning to enjoy being flaunted, and to become as supple when waved as any silken banner.

It was not his fault. Circumstances had conspired to thrust him into a difficult and corrupting position, and his own temperament, agile and responsive, spread like a sail to catch the breath of encouragement, and furled nimbly to evade the sudden cross-winds of disapproval. He could not help it; his sensitivity to these shifting breezes produced an almost automatic reaction, adroit and infallibly accurate, which his mind had thereupon nothing to do but rationalise. But he was not at all aware that for him adhering to his socialist principles had become the same thing as keeping the confidence of the electors. It was simply something that had happened to him, unrecognised, and to which he had instinctively adjusted himself. After all, to antagonise the electors was to lose the opportunity of doing these disinterested personal services for those who most needed them.

There were, for instance, the few but significant injustices he had been able to smooth out of the housing list, the misunderstandings between local bodies he had cleared up happily, the probation cases in which he'd been able to give some practical help, as well as advice, the muddle of that young farming apprentice's deferment, the grievance of the gypsies at the closing of their old camping ground, the very harsh sentence on that practically halfwitted young airman, which he had succeeded in having reduced. Surely these were something to be able to offer. He took comfort in them, and they held off with gratifying success the disease which had driven his predecessor into the wilderness.

He was pondering the list of his small achievements, modestly enough, as he came down by train on Friday, the 10th of July, to spend the weekend in his constituency. He still kept his household in Caldington, and thought of it as home, though Ginnie divided her time between the minute flat in London as her wifely duty drew her, and the country house as her devotion to young Edmund lured her back into an enchantingly earnest posture of motherhood. She was there now with Eddie, and it was pure joy to be hurrying back to them both, even though he would have to snatch his moments with them as best he could in the intervals of meetings.

It was the weekend of the Caldington Miners' Rally, and on Saturday evening Dallas was to be one of the speakers at the gala meeting with which this event always closed, late in the dusk in the arena before the pithead at Fallow Deep, with torches, and singing, ending with the unerringly fine hymn tunes which were so loved in the district, and expressed so strongly the strain of Welsh in the Midshire blood. Before that, he had to open the traditional Fair and Flower Show in the afternoon, and between these duties he must and would fit in his session at the office, that chastening hour and a half of little people's distresses. Whatever he shelved, he refused to shelve that.

He wondered what there would be for him this time. He was always both eager and reluctant to approach the office on these occasions, sadly aware of his too frequent helplessness, but still hopeful that for someone, at least, there would be something he could do. He thought of the usual little row of silent people waiting in the outer office, hushed and constrained, caps on knees, the women with hands nervously knotted in their laps, exactly like patients watching the door of a doctor's surgery. Sometimes his heart failed him when he contemplated their immemorial, their uncomplaining endurance, sometimes he grew irritable in his weariness with their moments of self-assertion and aggression. Always, at the bottom of his heart, he felt guilty towards them, as if he himself had created the very knots he was trying to undo.

*   *   *

'I hate war,' said Dallas, very suddenly and quite violently, but still in that pleasant, low-pitched voice which set no harsh echoes jarring in the room. 'I hate hurting people, I hate seeing people hurt, and above all I hate seeing human beings tearing one another. I daresay I hate it as much as you do, Mrs Parrish—I know no one could hate it more. I only wish I knew how to get men to give it up for ever as a subhuman game that never has been worthy of them, but I don't, and that's the truth. Only I beg you not to think that we're reconciled to it, just because we don't yet know how to prevent it.'

He sat close to her, in front of his desk. It offended him to have a symbolical barrier between himself and his visitors on these occasions, and he always moved his chair to the open part of the room, putting his professional self behind him. If he had reached out his hand he could have touched the woman's hands,

81

linked upon her knee; and had the gesture been called for, he would not have been too shy to make it, for his physical impulses were sure-footed and candid, and he knew how to trust them. But the mother was as calm as he, and on safer ground, for she had not to grope for the right words or the appropriate tone, since the initiative was with her.

The long, worn oval of her face, slender-boned and asymmetrical, confronted him steadily with direct, smoke-grey eyes of a beauty and intelligence which singularly daunted him. Usually people came in here cloudy and misshapen with their own grievances, and the labour of giving them expression, but this woman had a shape and a motion as defined as classical music. The authority and composure of her commonplace body, the contained and aloof sadness of her eyes, these were the only things that set her apart from any other middle-aged woman in his waiting-room. They all had a sort of family resemblance, dingy in unfashionable black or dull dark colours, their clothes worn shapeless with long service, their hands dried and lined with work, with enlarged joints and flattened nails. He thought of them as being almost old. He was assuming that there must be at least fifteen years between Mrs Parrish and himself; in fact, there were just six. And the illusion of distance was one which she shared with him, for he seemed to her a shiningly young man, untouched by life, smooth with confidence.

'I never heard of anybody in your position,' said Mrs Parrish, 'in this country or any other, who didn't claim to be a man of peace. It makes you wonder how war's managed to survive so long, with all the governments against it.'

He felt this speech sting him as if it had been

delivered bitterly, and yet, on feeling back gently along the level thread of her voice, could find no bitterness there. The control she had on her tone was natural and forceful. He was not even sure that the smoky eyes had not burned clear for an instant with a faintly satirical, smiling light which did not at all mitigate their composed sorrow.

'But there have always been governments,' he said, frowning down into his linked fingers, 'which make the same profession, but keep in reserve the idea that as a final means of getting what they want, war becomes legitimate enough.'

'I lose my bearings a bit,' she said, 'when we begin to use words like governments. Let's stick to people. At least we know what a man is. A man of peace, like yourself. You hate violence, but you think if someone uses it against you that justifies you using it back against him. Double measure, if you can manage it. As long as someone else did the first killing, it's all right for you to do the last and the most. Is that what you mean by not believing in violence?'

They seemed to him to have strayed far from her son, that poor lad whose photograph lay on the desk among the fanned-out sheaf of his last few letters. And he did not know where she was going, nor how to turn her back. The strangest part of it was that he had heard vaguely similar arguments before, but delivered with furious, distressed conviction, usually by knotty little delegations of pacifist women who clung together fiercely as they delivered their angry broadside, ready to repel the expected counter-attack. But Mrs Parrish explored the significance of his replies with a civil and patient grace, confronting him alone and without any haste or anger. One would have thought she had the whole of time at her disposal. Nor did she put to him the issue of absolute pacifism as if she thought there could be only one right answer, but rather as if she were interested only in the movement of his mind among its inmost convictions.

'I think,' he said, 'it would be a bold man who could seriously, thinkingly, put an absolute ban on *any* act, and say: "This *must* be wrong in *all* circumstances, this I'll never do upon any consideration." I do hate violence, but I can conceive of circumstances in which I should feel justified in using it. I do loathe the very thought of war, but I am *not* prepared to say it can *never* be right for a country to resort to it. What really matters is that one should maintain the right to judge of a situation as it arises, and to do what one finds to be right in that situation.'

He brought out these words with real care, conceiving that it was the honest answer to her, and for an instant he was quite blind to the more fearful question with which he had trapped himself. He raised his head, and met her eyes fully.

'Yes,' she said, 'I'm with you. That's exactly what matters. How much right to judge did my son have?'

There was nothing in her voice of triumph or venom, no indication that she had anything to gain by scoring points over him; and he had to remember, with shame, that indeed her only stake in the matter was already lost, past recovery. No, it must be he himself who had turned that quiet question flaming across his path like a sword, barring him off from the immune peace of Eden. He felt its heat and brightness cross his eyes, and flinched from it; and then he saw that he had left himself a loophole yet.

'I've said that there may be circumstances in which we have to contemplate and accept what would, in

84

almost any other context, seem to us wrong. You object to our talking in terms of governments and nations, but both are the sum of individual human beings. And as a man may, in some terrible circumstances, find it his duty to kill, so a state may occasionally be forced to find it justifiable to arrogate to itself the right of choice of its members. A crisis can't wait while every human creature involved makes up his own mind. It's for that very reason that a government, at least in a democracy, must have the weight of public opinion on its side, through elections—to give the maximum authority possible to these enforced choices made on behalf of everyone. Nobody pretends it's a perfectly just system—it's simply the best approximation we've been able to evolve yet. In the future we may do better—I hope some day we shall.'

'You forget,' said Mrs Parrish, 'that my son had no vote. Nobody in your government or opposed to it represented any voice of his.'

The flash of the sword turning was far too swift and violent to be the work of her hands. He had surely closed the loophole against himself. He linked his long, smooth fingers tightly round his knee, and kept his eyes lowered intently upon them, because her eyes confounded him too deeply, and he no longer wanted to meet them.

He began to be voluble, and was appalled at the disorganised sound of his own words as he deployed them. He admitted the anomaly, admitted it was an injustice, regretted it; personally he would have preferred to see young men called up at twenty-one, when they already had the vote, both for the sake of fair play, and because it was a far maturer age, and one at which they were more likely to weather the break successfully, without allowing their whole lives to be set adrift aimlessly and beyond recovery. But simple numbers and facts made a change impossible at this stage, wherever the right lay. Consider what would happen if the age was changed to twenty-one now; for three years the wastage of twenty-year-olds finishing their time would go on, while no new recruits could be drafted in to fill the gaps. Why, the army would dwindle down to half strength, the forces in Malaya and Kenya and Hong Kong and a hundred other places could not be maintained, the whole Commonwealth would be laid wide open to attack and disruption. He regretted bitterly the terrible necessities which were robbing not only her, but many other mothers, of their sons; but they were necessities.

'And not of our making,' he said warmly, growing indignant because of the ineffective sound of his own voice, and its feverish, insistent repetitions.

She said with almost indifferent calm: 'Oh, no, they're never of our making.' She said it as if it could be taken for granted and understood, even forgiven, that countries, like children, could never acknowledge their own guilt; as if this was something about which she was not prepared to argue, so far aside did it lie from her purpose, which was with the uniqueness of man rather than his common limitations. She sat looking at him for a moment in considering silence, memorising the aristocratic oval of his face, with its smooth, fresh skin and clear, assured lines, out of which that faintly hurried and harassed voice came so strangely.

'So, when it comes to the point, you think they had a right to my son's life? You stand by their right to take him and have him killed?'

86

'God forbid!' he said, genuinely appalled. 'You make it sound like murder.'

'Yes,' she agreed, 'God forbids it, but nobody seems to take any notice of that.'

'But we—Members of Parliament, Government, people, all of us—we're caught in this world, we have to live in it as best we can. Compromise is forced on us. It isn't we who have made this unbearable situation in the world, but we have to live in the results of it, and we have to defend ourselves and the things we believe in. Yes, even at the cost of injustice and conscription, even at the risk of certain losses of liberty, and at a price in young men's lives. We *know* these things are not right—we contemplate them only because we have no alternative.'

'If you contemplate them,' said Mrs Parrish reasonably, 'obviously for that case you accept them as right. Anything else is just playing with words. Of course there's always an alternative.'

'But what can we do? The weight of the forces opposed to us is something we've got to take into account. We can't stand off Communism with our spotless reputation—'

'You won't stand it off without,' she said simply.

He heard himself running on and on, saying no more than he believed, and had always believed; but he had never quite had to say it before, and it all sounded incredibly shoddy in his ears. Yes, he would vote to keep the two years of National Service at eighteen, whenever the principle was challenged. Yes, he would stand by and defend his position as justified. Yes. And all the time she sat there watching and listening to him with a sceptical face, thoughtful, not arguing, only her eyes quietly, slowly, parting him nerve from nerve, probing the causes of his

87

vehemence before he himself could turn and examine them.

He knew he was beating at air which had done nothing to offend him, that she was opposing to his insistence nothing more than her simple statement that there is always an alternative. For whom, then, was he straining his heart and his beliefs? For himself? There was no one else to hear him. Why defend himself, if he really believed he was justified? She had accused him of nothing, except a choice which she did not deny was his to make—a voice for the acceptance of the idea that you are justified in preparing to kill someone who just conceivably may be thinking of killing you; and, worse, justified in causing others to be forced to do the killing for you.

'We are not alone in finding it a necessity,' he said indignantly. 'Other countries have forms of national service. The Communist countries also resort to this violation of individual liberty, you know.' He felt for a moment really vindictive, as though she had denied it, as though she had taken the opposing side in criticising her own. He heard his own voice with horror, remembering her loss, struggling to return to the immediate sympathy he felt with her grief. He was behaving abominably, and in a manner quite unlike himself. It was as if the affair had turned into a fight for his life.

'Do we have to do what they do, then?' she said mildly. 'It's what *we* do that's going to save or damn us, not what the others do. In hell—supposing there is hell—what sort of comfort do you think there's going to be in telling ourselves we're no worse than the rest of the inhabitants?'

She put out her hand, and folded together the handful of letters. He watched her in a sudden and

88

helpless silence, his mind returning into the detail of those half-articulate pages. What was new about it, after all? Who had supposed that the behaviour of an army in the field, however benevolent its original intentions, kept infallibly the level of virtue at which it had aimed? What was surprising in the lapses which had caused that poor boy to look again at his cause? There was napalm, and the methods of getting labour to the plantations in Indo-China, which by all accounts were pretty sickening, and the gentle nature of South Korean justice, and the reversions, no doubt to some extent encouraged, of the Dyaks in Malaya, and now these very nasty rumours which were beginning to seep out of Kenya—all the spots on all the idealistic enterprises in the world, what was secret about them? But he had kept his eyes firmly upon the reverse of the medal, observing and hugging to himself the wrongs committed by 'the others'; and now she had taken that probably rather infantile consolation implacably out of his hands.

And the boy was dead, and he had had no choice. Dallas watched her gather up the pathetic photograph, following with his eyes the defensive stare of those wary young eyes, which had been fixed intently upon the photographer, and therefore clung as tenaciously now to whoever confronted him. Less handsome than his mother, and more ordinary; but then, he had never had the chance to develop beyond the beginning of maturity. The most he had was no more than a promise, and unfulfilled now, incurably. But there was something memorable there, all the same. It burned in his mind after the black handbag had closed on the pasteboard copy. It accused him because it was only the shadow of a quality, remote behind that half-formed face, and because it would never be anything more.

'I'm sorry,' he said, passing a hand confusedly across his forehead. 'I seem to have been concerned more with defending my own views than with understanding yours. I didn't mean that. I really am profoundly sorry! I'd do anything I could to alter this state of the world, to bring the broken pieces together, and spare other women what we couldn't spare you. Couldn't—or wouldn't—I know you must blame me among the rest.'

'I haven't blamed anybody yet,' she said, rising. 'I only wanted to understand where you stood. I'm not in any hurry.'

'I wish I could help you. I wish there was something I could do.' He wanted to find a better note on which to close, something on which their minds could meet and agree, but he knew that wherever he looked he would find nothing. If she was not looking for sympathy in her bereavement—and she had shown no sign of expecting any reconciling word from him—then what was she looking for? He didn't know what she wanted from him. He felt nothing except a sense of injustice, as though she had opened a door to him, found him to be seriously short of the person she had expected, and closed it again gently but irrevocably in his face. Only that, and somewhere deep within his mind a kind of superstition about her, a conviction that from this day on he would never be rid of her, that she had left with him a token, a touch on the flesh, invisible, indelible, by which to know him again when the time came.

'It's good of you to give me so much of your time,' she said quite practically, moving towards the door, to which he sprang before her, hunting still for some final word which should break the spell. 'Things aren't exactly easy for you.'

'Are they for anyone? It makes me ashamed, to think how hard they've been for you. But I can't throw away what I believe.'

His hand was at the door-handle. Desperate with frustration, he hunted darkly through the forest of his misgivings, straining after one gleam of unmistakable light, but the lost day did not revisit him. It was so unfair, so impossible of solution. If you held fast to the inflexible standard, half the world might die for lack of a little ruthlessness, die for one scruple. If you made concessions, and it survived maimed, it might some day turn round and curse you for betraying the very cause you thought you were saving. Was it right that a man should have to carry that choice himself? Was it right to take the onus from him? He himself had stood up for the right of every man to make his own decisions, and the next moment had recoiled into the reservation that in times of crisis such freedom must be restricted. But except in times of crisis, what need was there for a choice so fatal and so solitary?

'Good night!' said Mrs Parrish, giving him a last calm look as the door opened.

She had left the waiting-room empty, and they had been too completely absorbed to hear the footsteps leaping lightly up the stairs and crossing the rubber-composition floor. The door simply opened upon a tall young body, a vivid, glowing face. She walked into the quickly flung circle of a long arm, was held steadyingly against a bounding heart, and heard a breathless little gasp of apology explode over her head, complicated a little with laughter, and still more with instinctive but painless shyness.

91

'Oh, I say, I'm *awfully* sorry! I thought everybody'd gone—seeing nobody waiting out here, you know—so I just crashed in. I haven't hurt you, have I?'

He still held her, politely withdrawing his arm by slow degrees, in case he had upset her balance. The impact of his body, the embrace of his arm, had felt as wild and mettlesome as the movements of a young colt, and his withdrawal had the same exuberance. He moved back a step, lightly and swiftly, on his toes, and it was like a lively colt's leap out of range of touching. But the wide, hesitant smile, half-diffident, half-arrogant, softened readily to the responsive light in Mrs Parrish's unastonished eyes. Young men were no great mystery to her.

'I came to fetch my father. I didn't realise there was still someone in with him. Sorry I butted in—I'll wait out here.'

'I was just going,' she said.

Dallas stood there behind her, his hand still at the door, watching them draw apart rather warily. He said nothing for a long moment. How was it he had not heard Eddie's feet on the stairs? He certainly took no great pains to be inaudible. He saw the hand which Mrs Parrish had flattened against the boy's sleeve to steady herself at the first shock, watched it withdrawn slowly, wondered that it left no mark of her fingers behind. The apparition had been too apt for accident, or despair and his own sense of being misjudged had turned apocalyptic within him.

The boy was seventeen, without brothers or sisters, dearly loved. From the moment her hand was laid upon his arm, his father had seen him dwindle in an instant, wide young shoulders rounded a little into ill-fitting khaki, bright, confident, heedless face

92

dulled into bewilderment and suspicion, keeping a wary distance about him against the assault of too much experience. Like that other boy, the dead one, shrunken with the recoil into disillusionment and disgust, as if he, too, had come back to hover humbly at the door, wanting to ask who had really held the gun that killed him.

'I brought the car,' said Edmund gaily, 'if you're ready. We'll have to pick Mummy up at the hall, she's still admiring flowers.'

'Give me just five minutes, Eddie, d'you mind? I must clear up one or two things here. Would you see Mrs Parrish out for me, please?'

He turned from them hurriedly, shaking the ridiculous vision out of his eyes, wanting the door closed between them while he composed his face, while he put by him the absurd moment of panic. Until it was gone, he couldn't face Edmund's much too alert and solicitous eyes.

'Good night, Mrs Parrish!' His haste was almost indecent, but at least the door closed in time, and he was safe and trembling within, and the soldier, the dual-faced petitioner, the fruit of a day of overstrain and nervous tension, of course, shut out on the threshold. He sat down, trembling. It was just what he needed tonight, after this, the resounding hymns of the rally, the roused, uncritical collier-voices, more Welsh than ever with fervour. Depression couldn't survive that. A few minutes, for decency's sake, and then he would go.

On the outer side of the door, Mrs Parrish and Edmund Dallas stood looking at each other; and in a moment, with suddenness and complete conviction, they smiled.

Edmund spoke as soon as he had made up his mind
about her, simply because his nature was turned
serenely outward, and it came naturally to him to
speak to anyone with whom he found himself. Only if
the other person had something about him so
forbidding as to stop the birds singing was Edmund
likely to hold his tongue. He could be happily silent
with people he knew well, but was incurably, shyly,
childishly talkative with those not yet known, about
whom he felt always a warm, impulsive and
unoffending curiosity. Particularly was this so when
he found them in intimate conference with his father,
and deduced, and was instantly concerned about,
some personal trouble clouding their horizon. He
took a great interest and pride in his father's work,
and wanted, at the first touch of it, to add his own
weight to the balance.

On the other hand, what was duty and service in
his father might be held to be merely impudence in
him; and though the words were quivering on his lips,
it took Mrs Parrish's smile to charm them out of
hiding.

'I hope there was something he could do? He feels
so awful when there isn't.' Then he flushed and grew
quite grave, for it sounded as if all that mattered to
him was his father's gratification, and that was not at
all what he had meant. 'That is, I didn't really mean
to ask—' He met her eyes, and sighed with relief,
because she was looking at him with such a
reassuring shrewdness and placidity. 'Yes, I *did*! But
if you mind, I won't. I didn't mean to be rude, at any
rate.'

He knew by then that she did not think him so, and

his voice, though still a little shy, had stretched out into a soft and friendly ease.

'I don't mind,' she said, studying him with the respectful friendliness of a contemporary, aloof and yet warmly personal, as though his uniqueness had been the first thing she had seen about him.

She stood, composed with that angular distinction and almost-grace of hers, in her shabby dark clothes, glossy and confused with age and repeated alteration, looking at him with reassuringly open curiosity. She had to look up to study his face, for he was tall, within an inch of his father's impressive height already, though youthfully slender yet, without enough flesh on his fine long bones. The way she looked at him made him feel taller still; it was an effect that Mrs Parrish's grey eyes often had upon young men, and at this moment she was launching upon him something more subtly flattering than even the impulsively confiding revelation of her invincible femininity. That was there to be felt, certainly, mirroring his new and pleasing manhood, in which she took frank delight; but deep within those gratified and gentle eyes her distress stood gazing at him, uncovered, trusting him on sight, charmed into showing itself tamely where it was assured there was no enemy to fear. He felt the sadness pass into him, and trembled, and was enlarged to receive it eagerly and gratefully. 'I came to talk to him about my son,' she said. 'He was killed in Korea. He was a National Serviceman, near the end of his two years. That's all. I knew there was nothing your father could *do*, before I came.'

The words made it sound almost as if she had been parading her sorrow for the sake of a little distinguished sympathy, but the tone did not sound

95

like that, and the woman did not look like that.

'I'm sorry,' said Edmund, for the moment leaving his father out of it. He could not think of anything else to say, but the silence did not worry him, any more than it appeared to worry her. He was too busy receiving impressions which came crowding in upon his senses to notice how long the quietness lasted. His broad, freckled forehead pleated itself into a thoughtful frown, and from under the thick, levelled-out line of fawn-coloured brows his blue eyes stared intently at her, wide-set, full and decisively oval in shape, with firmly-drawn lids and long boyish brown lashes.

He had probably been a very pretty baby, thought Mrs Parrish, and like many such had grown into a comparatively plain youth without losing the debonair confidence of prettiness. Rather elegant in his dress, too, in faithful compliment to his father, no doubt, but with a saving carelessness about the way he had assembled the copy. He said: 'I'm sorry!' with awe, but firmly and finally, as if he expected it to mean something, and felt no need to scrape round the embarrassed corners of his mind to find a few decorative words to blur its nakedness.

'Whoever ought to be saying that to me,' said Mrs Parrish, 'it certainly isn't you. At least it's none of your doing.'

She had identified him at once as an ally, though every echo of his father in his face and his person might well have caused her to wonder. The mark of the victim was plain on him; she guessed his age as seventeen, but set him only at the very beginning of his eighteenth year, an error of four or five months. Well-cared-for young creatures of his kind, fair-complexioned and candid by habit, frequently look even younger than they are. It made no difference. The same mystery which had deflected Jack would soon be dissuading this boy's life also from its pole. The invisible half-god who had eaten her young would as indifferently eat the young of William Dallas, M.P. Her eyes softened upon him, resting gratefully upon one clear face in whose absolute innocence she could believe without question. Nothing he could say to her, no manner of echo of his father, could alter that certainty. She was even prepared for the echoes, and ready to let them go by her unarrested, keeping her eyes upon the more poignant truth of his brightness, so soon to be dimmed.

'It seems such a terrible waste,' he said, feeling after his words delicately, but still with a suppressed force of feeling which took her by surprise. 'Not even as if anybody was the better off for it. Nobody can have wanted it—not even the—the other man, the one who did it. I don't suppose he ever even saw him, really.'

'No,' she agreed, 'he can't have wanted it. He was in the same boat himself, I daresay, wishing he was home, and they'd all let him alone. But somebody, somewhere, must have wanted it. It happened.'

He did not seem to know any of the orthodox things to say. It was as if he had never really turned and looked at it before, or stopped to wonder where he was going at eighteen, when he surrendered himself voiceless to the direction of some other, and inaccessible, hand and mind. He stood looking at her with his face faintly clouded with wonder, and deeply concerned for her. Nor was he hunting for words to scatter about the silence. He seemed content to be inarticulate, and to stand there wondering and considering, and feeling her sorrow.

'Did he hate it very much?' he asked. 'I mean—having to go?' There was no easy way of asking the things he suddenly wanted to know, but he felt reassuringly that she would know how to interpret what he might say. For answer she opened her shabby handbag and showed him the photograph of Jack, and the little sheaf of his letters. She unfolded the last of them.

'That's the last word I had from him. Read it, if you'd like to.'

It was all there, the whole betrayal to disillusionment and disgust, compressed into the few laboured lines. And if it was anybody's business, it was surely his. She could see by the curious, still quiver of his face, like the shudder of clear standing water, that he wanted and did not want it, but he put out his long, shapely, tentative hand, and took it, and read it, holding it with fearful delicacy between his fingers, as though he knew he was holding his future, and that it was as fragile as glass, and might shatter if he handled it carelessly.

'It isn't as if anybody's better off for us being here. They don't want us, they want to be left alone and make the best of it. They've had enough, too, they've had all they can do with ...'

'It isn't the fighting. You get used to being scared to death, but there's things you never get used to ...'

Edmund refolded it with the same fastidious gentleness, as still as an animal watching danger, and as wildly shy. His eyes, turned almost purple in the shadow of the dropped lashes, burned bright blue again as he looked up into her face, and handed the letter back to her.

'You see,' she said, 'why I couldn't just let it go by.'

'Yes.' But he was still troubled and bewildered, because so many had let it go by, because it seemed so hopeless to try to do anything else, and he could not see for the life of him what she was attempting. His forehead knotted itself again into the deep, considering frown, anxious over his own helplessness.

'It doesn't seem right. Even if it *had* been for something worth it—'

'Don't worry about it,' she said, closing her bag. 'I shouldn't have told you, it's no fault of yours.'

'No, I'm glad you did. Only I wish—I mean, it doesn't seem right that he didn't have any *say* about it. Does it?'

'I must go,' she said, 'your father will be ready in a minute.'

As soon as she took a step towards the door he remembered that he had been told to show her out, and attended her punctiliously across the outer office. She was not used to being squired, it raised a slight flush of pleasure in her cheeks, and a deep spark in her eyes. The small, vigorous wind of his movements as he leaned past her to open the door had a fresh, faint scent of tweed and young foliage and sunlit air about it. He was like an impulse from all the youngness and hopefulness and tough resilience of the world, but he was seventeen, and within a year they would be after him to stop up another gap in the leaking barriers between men of this kind and men of that, as though neither he nor those beyond the frontiers were humankind. And he would have as little choice as any of the others about

99

going or staying, and his uniqueness would soon be knocked out of him.

She hesitated on the threshold, and half-turned to look up into his face, a last, thoughtful look, memorising what she probably would not see again. It did not seem to her to matter very much that she had made him wonder a little before his time; what moved her to a curiously personal compunction was that she could do nothing to preserve him intact from the misappropriation which had overtaken Jack. He was just one like all the rest, and like the rest he would go where he was thrust, and take on the shape they had in mind for him. What else was there for him to do? The law of the land, for which the responsibility seemed to flow like flood water to every door, had seen to it that any resistance on his part could be easily broken.

'It's because you think it wrong, too, that you came,' he said, because she had not answered his last question.

'Yes, I suppose it is. But you mustn't take it to yourself. Whoever had a hand in it, you didn't.' She thought also: 'And whoever might have a chance of altering it, you haven't,' but she did not say it. He would come to that realisation only too soon, he was feeling his way towards it at this very moment.

'Good night!' she said firmly, turning from him.

'Good night, Mrs Parrish!' He had remembered her name, and the neat, boyish politeness had come back into his voice with the formality of leave-taking. He stood quite still in the doorway, and watched her go down the single flight of stairs, and she could feel no uncompleted protests or unasked questions of his trailing like broken threads of gossamer after her skirts. He had no threatened inner place of his

100

personality to defend from her, he did not, like his father, ache for the moment when she would disappear and leave him free to forget her, nor, like the Rector, feel agitatedly about the corners of his mind for some gift with which to propitiate her. The boy was clear as crystal, and all his doors were open. She could go or stay, and he would remain undamaged and unfrightened, because his conscience was clear, because he had never done her any wrong. Neither her nor anyone. Only the innocent could afford to listen to her, only the innocent dared understand.

He was so quiet that from the covering darkness of the turn of the stairs she looked back for an instant. He was still standing where she had left him, looking down after her with a wide unfocused blue stare beneath that level frown of his, his lower lip caught thoughtfully between his teeth. His face was full of a trouble and anxiety which had little awareness of his own predicament in it, but was all for her and Jack.

She felt his warmth follow her like a sweet impulsive wind, down the stairs and into the evening street, the gala Saturday evening street that led to the park and the bands, and the hymn-tunes, and the speeches, and all the hypnotic smoke which covered from sight, decently and gracefully, the deaths of reluctant and inarticulate young men who had had no say in things. She wondered as she walked homeward through the still gold light of a cloudless sunset, how long he would remember. It was not a bitter thought to her, and it did not diminish him; he was seventeen, and if his memory could protect him by turning his eyes away from discomforting things, so much the better for him. Everybody has to get through the world as best he may, and spare a hand for somebody else when he's steady enough on his own feet to see his way to the gesture. Nobody can do more. To keep his own balance, before long, he might be forced to amputate his recollections of her and her son. She wished him luck with his forgetting; he was a nice boy, he deserved to be lucky.

She smiled with pleasure, thinking of the delicate way his arm had steadied and drawn back from her, and of the attentive, proudly adult way he inclined his head when listening, and above all of the uncompromising directness of his eyes as they had measured and mutually trusted each other. It was the first time she had smiled in that way since the telegram had arrived. He was one person who quite certainly owed her no amend whatever, and the only one who had freely offered a rounded and guiltless regret.

CHAPTER FIVE

THE PARENTS

Ginnie Dallas was still scintillating among the faithful in the Weavers' Hall when her son came looking for her. It was past time for the Flower Show to close down, and many of the exhibits had already been taken away or sold on the spot, but there were still a number of attendants and enthusiasts discussing the judging, not always charitably, and relaxing with a little gossip after a heavy day. There remained the rally at Fallow Deep, which would probably go on until midnight, and before tackling this final exhaustion of the day they felt entitled to a smoke, a drink, and a rest.

The hall was eighty years old, and solidly built, good for another century or two yet; which often seemed to Edmund rather a pity, because it was shockingly ugly outside, and dark and dispiriting within, with high, prison-like windows and an air of being unsure whether it should be considered a sacred or a secular edifice. It had the worst of both worlds, with elaborately arched chapel doorway and aimlessly vaulted roof, and no focus for its half-suggested piety but a large bare platform and a vast vacancy of boarded floor.

But the flowers, even in their late disarrangement and with many gaps, effected a radiant transformation. Their colours, slightly falsified and flattened now under the electric bulbs, had yet an exuberant beauty and gaiety. The few blooms which had suffered from the long day's confinement to the point of exhaustion hung tipsily out of their wires, swaying too-heavy heads upon enfeebled necks, and shedding iridescent hair upon floorboards already spattered with water and leaves. A sweet, soft, melancholy scent hung upon the air, and below it like a tidal undertow a second and heavier scent, vegetable and green and lush, the smell of earth and growth.

The cluster of women moving importantly about Ginnie's corner had a floral appearance, too, especially about their hats. Hats were coming back lately, at least for social occasions like this one. Roses, forget-me-nots, anemones, camellias, nodded upon wisps of white straw that gripped the head like finger and thumb closed upon a chocolate. Half-hats, they were intriguingly called. Ginnie was wearing one herself, a fluff of ice-blue tulle and a languid blue feather that curved clean round and under her chin, and stirred agitated light fronds along her left cheek when she laughed, which she did whenever it occurred to her that the remark on which she had embarked had inconvenient connotations for some member of her court. It happened fairly often, and the little, gay laugh was the defensive reaction she had developed to deal with the emergencies resulting. Into that charming trill of sound all the indiscreet words were deflected, and disseminated into silver notes. At this, her one subtlety, she was exceedingly adroit, for her kindness, her desire to have everyone about her happy, acted as a kind of Geiger counter in place of intelligence, detecting by instinct the mines she was about to set off.

She was sitting on the edge of a table now almost cleared of its flowers, and he had to edge his way to her side through a taut circle of militant Labour wives. There were a few men, too, members of the inner councils of the constituency party, and effective, no doubt, in their own setting, but reduced to insignificance here among so much female plumage.

The women tended to be smart, sharply-spoken, alertly practical, with lively, defensive faces, and they made Edmund feel like a regimental mascot with their pleased smiles and proprietary greetings. He returned both, slipping apologetically from one contact to the next with a faintly uncomfortable grin and reddening ears, trying not to get caught up anywhere into more complex inanities. Women in the mass made him restive, and when they were these particular women, who regarded him rather in the light of another banner to be waved in the faces of the enemy, he found them discomfiting in the extreme.

He was no fonder of feeling a fool than most boys of seventeen, and generally speaking he preferred to steer clear of too intimate participation in party occasions. But his principles, confidently and enthusiastically inherited, demanded that he should make an ass of himself with good grace now and again; he liked his colours publicly nailed to the mast, in fairness to everybody.

Ginnie in the middle of so much clear-cut professionalism looked more than ever a deliciously incompetent amateur, willing but bewildered, as though she had, in all probability, drifted into quite the wrong gathering, but had not a sufficiently definite idea of what was expected of her to be put off her stroke by the mistake. She was quite used to groping her way through dreamlike irrelevancies in a great many contexts, and could abandon herself to that kind of breath-to-breath living better than most people, being of an airy lightness peculiarly well adapted to riding the wind. She was small and slender and invariably dainty, sleek in a blue shantung suit and white nylon blouse, as immaculate as a crisp newly dressed shop-window, with that distracting feather just brushing her throat with its fronds, and her slim nyloned ankles crossed and swinging gently. Her arms were full of roses. She had fluffy golden hair cut short, and clustering in curls like those of a cherub on a Christmas card, and eyes of a blue two shades darker than her son's.

She was talking to the women, earnestly and sympathetically, about the prices of food and the general cost of living, a subject on which she could speak with so little authority that it was doubtful if she even knew the current price she was paying for butter. She simply paid the grocer's bill every week, without querying or even considering the items involved in it. She had never been rich, but she had never in her life gone short of anything for want of the price of it, and she did not at all realise to what a struggle for existence she was assenting with so pretty and concerned a warmth. Edmund, worming his way through to her side, heard the vehemence of her affirmations, and could not help smiling to himself at the thought of his mother hanging anxiously over her purse, wondering how to stretch its contents to the end of the week. He had a secret and silent compact of affection with his father about Ginnie, who was never to be teased, laughed at, suppressed or enlightened.

'Oh, here's Edmund!' she said gladly, as he penetrated the inmost circle about her. 'I suppose that means it's time we all moved on. Good gracious, it's turned nine o'clock! I'd no idea! Councillor Evans, do you know my boy Eddie? Don't you think he's the image of his father? Come and shake hands with Mr Evans, darling!'

Edmund, withdrawing into his most severely adult manner, which made him appear rather younger than usual, obeyed the injunction gravely. He never had time for more than a few banal remarks before Ginnie ran on gaily like a brook, so he had given up trying to think of anything sensible to say. He smiled into a weather-beaten elderly face, distributed the remnant of the smile vaguely round the rest of the circle, and added a few quick glances and murmurs of recognition.

'Have you brought Bill from the office, darling? What have you done with him now? You didn't let him get away from you again, did you? Poor lamb, he's forgotten how to relax; as long as anyone gives

106

him an anxious look or pops a word into his ear he'll go on slaving till he drops. But we *must* be on time at Fallow Deep, it's their biggest day, and it wouldn't be kind to be late, even for a good reason. Where is Daddy?'

'He's just talking to Mr Trent, in the little room—about the arrangements for next weekend, I think. But he's ready, whenever you are, he said. Can I take anything for you?'

'Well, there's a basket of vegetables there that I bought, but I think we could leave those at the caretaker's cottage, and fetch them to-morrow. It's rather big. But my roses—Look, aren't they *heavenly*?'

She held them up to his face, and he curled his fingers round one of the golden half-opened buds, and caressed it without embarrassment, smiling with pleasure. Everything with Ginnie was heavenly or ghastly, her vocabulary consisted largely of expressions from the extremes of feeling into which by her very nature she was unable to penetrate, either upward or downward.

'Come here! Hold them for me a moment! That's a good boy! Now, keep still—' She broke off the bud he had touched so gently, and threaded it into his buttonhole, spreading out its leaves and patting all delicately into place. 'There, now you look really festive.'

He could hear behind him the indulgent murmurs of the women, sentimentally a little drunk, like the disembodied voices of thousands of ponderers over royalty in the picture papers, going: 'Aah!' and 'Sweet!' and 'Isn't she lovely!' as if both Ginnie and he had been dolled-up children doing a precocious turn. He didn't seriously mind it, but it never failed to

107

surprise him. Sometimes he thought that if *he* had been a worried mother of a family, genuinely at a loss how to pay the weekly bills, all he would have felt about Ginnie and her well-dressed indignation would have been a desire to beat her over the head. Which, as he very well knew, would have been grossly unfair. The party women were much nearer to a truth with their verdict that she was absolutely sweet.

'Now we shall *have* to go, I'm afraid. It's been a simply wonderful show, and I wouldn't have missed it for anything. Shall we see you all later, at the rally? Mrs Davies, *do* let me know how that business of your daughter's goes on. If she really doesn't like it there, I *might* be able—And I won't forget the twenty-fifth. I'll come down for the whole week before, and help you to get things ready. I do hope it'll be fine! Such a nuisance if we have to take the event indoors, and it never pays so well. Oh, thank you, Mr Luce, I'm always dropping them! If it isn't my gloves it's my bag! Goodbye, everybody! It's been lovely! Thank you for my *exquisite* roses, I *do* love them.'

Edmund, still nursing the roses, followed her royal passage to the door, pink with composed shyness, dropping half-articulate politenesses into the laps of any new devotees who confronted him. This kind of wholesale good-fellowship tired and depressed him at such close quarters, because he could never be sure exactly how much of it was genuine, even on his own part, and for that reason distrusted it perhaps more than was justified. But he was never put out of countenance by it, because he had learned to balance the social duties of honesty and kindly compromise very early in his life. As soon, in fact, as he had begun to realise that his mother was a very silly woman,

108

which had happened when he was about nine. He didn't regard it as a fault, merely as a fact, and it was no sooner acknowledged than it made logically necessary the enlargement of his own scope to supply her limitations. He began to take his share of responsibility for her at ten years old, and enjoyed and adored her all the more for the protective warmth he felt towards her. By the time he was fourteen it was a hard job to tell which of them was looking after the other.

Dallas was in the little ante-room within the doorway of the hall, talking meetings, printing and local policy with his agent. They haled him away, the conversation still earnestly entangled in compressed details of time and place and price, out of the doorway and down the steps to the street, where the car stood waiting for them. Two or three women came out on the steps to wave them away. Mr Trent reached for the handle of the door, still talking.

'Are you going to ride in front with me, Ginnie? I'm driving this time—there'll be a lot of traffic on the streets just now.'

'No, I'll take my roses in the back, you have Eddie. You see so little of him, and I have had him for the last two days—except that he never seems to be in,' she added, installing herself with a flash of slender, honey-coloured legs, and reassembling her roses carefully as Edmund placed them in her arms. 'I can talk at you both from behind.' She waved a hand to the agent as the car slid away from the kerb, and then leaned into the rear window to bestow a last flutter of a lace handkerchief upon the women. 'There! I've done my duty!'

Her soft, relaxing sigh was one of pure enjoyment, not at all of weariness. She installed the roses in the

109

opposite corner of the seat, making a fenced bunk for them with a rug, and giving them her husband's briefcase to lean against.

'Are you never in?' asked Dallas, smiling along his shoulder at the boy as they threaded the High Street, chronically prolific at this hour on a Saturday night of suicidal strollers with a preference for the middle of the road.

'Mummy's hardly been in the house since she came on Wednesday, how would she know? Yesterday she stayed to tea at Mrs Hartley's, and left me sitting at home like an idiot, waiting until after five for her to come in. Didn't even 'phone. And I was dying for my tea!'

'Darling, I thought I'd told you I might—honestly! And who went out on Thursday evening, and left *me* all by myself? And goodness knows what happens when I'm not here to keep an eye on you. I know you have Mrs Windsor round your little finger. You probably forget to come home at all.'

Edmund laughed, looking at her quickly over his shoulder. 'I told you, Thursday was quite a mistake. I went into St Michael's to have a look at the place where they're proposing to put that memorial stone, and I got interested in a rather nice brass they have, but it was getting dark down in that corner at the back, and I was on my knees to it, and all at once in came the old boy and his choir and all—well, a bit of a choir!—and I couldn't get myself out of there. Not gracefully! They never had a voluntary, or anything, or I'd have taken the hint. I had to get up off my knees and join in. If I'd *known* it was the night they had a service—'

'Wouldn't do you any harm,' said Dallas.

'No, I liked it—I don't know why. There was

110

almost nobody there. He's an awfully impressive-looking old boy, the new Rector, I was quite awed.' The word came off his lips lightly, but was not wholly unintended, though he often let words off their chains in a manner half-extravagant, half-experimental, to see how high they could fly. 'I hope you're both in good voice tonight? You've probably got about two hours' singing to do.'

'Oh, that's the least of it,' said his father, swinging the wheel as they turned into the straight, seedy Victorian stretch of Munslow Street, and the dazzle of shop-windows fell behind. 'You be thankful you haven't got to talk, as well as sing.'

'You sound awfully tired, darling,' said Ginnie from the back seat, with anxious sympathy. 'Did you have many people at the office tonight? And all hopeless, I suppose! Oh, dear, it does seem a mishandled sort of world.' She had no idea that she had said anything uncomfortably true; it was just one of those things one says. 'They kept you a long time.'

'They had a lot to say, poor devils.'

'Hordes of them? What did they all want? Houses? Or is it the food prices? They do seem frightfully concerned about those just now, I've heard nothing else all the evening. Who was there?'

Names would have meant nothing to her, he enumerated instead some of the grievances they had brought to him. He did not at first mention Mrs Parrish or her son, and it seemed to him that there was a slight tension about Edmund's silence, as though he were a shade too intent upon leaving her unmentioned. He had let the boy drive from his office to the hall expressly because he had not yet become sufficiently at home when driving to talk at the same time, and it had seemed well to avoid, for the moment, a conversation which could hardly begin anywhere but with Mrs Parrish.

Curious, thought Dallas, how those two had fallen so naturally into conversation as soon as they were left alone together. From his own office he had been quite unable not to hear their voices, though with much needless shuffling through papers and shaking up of the contents of drawers he had evaded hearing what they said to each other. They had stayed there together, with notable silences, for almost ten minutes before he had heard the outer door opened, and after a long moment closed again. Something in the quality of the two voices, quiet but unconstrained, had not been as he had thought it should be; and of all his visitors that night, this was the one he would least willingly have brought to his son's notice. He had expected immediate questions and confidences as soon as he emerged from his room, and had gone to some trouble to divert both; and now, when he was ready for them, and had even come to the conclusion that it would be better to get them over, and have the fervour of the rally in hand as a cathartic, Edmund had nothing at all to say.

It was too late to leave the woman out of his recital now; if he omitted only her the gap she left would merely confront Edmund the more sharply. If the boy wouldn't talk about her, it must be because to some extent, however innocently, she was on his mind; and if his father made the same hypersensitive deletion, it would only too clearly be for the same reason. Whereas she was not, she must not be, she must not even seem to be, on his mind more than the others. What was there special about her case? She was one among thousands.

'And that unfortunate woman who lost her son in

Korea,' he said, braking behind a battered old van to let a Munslow bus go by. 'And with a cease-fire practically in sight, too.'

'Oh, I remember! Poor thing, how dreadful! But what did she want from you?'

'A miracle, I'm afraid,' said Dallas, deliberately probing towards the rapt centre of Edmund's silence. And his mind reproached him for a moment with the minute insincerity, for he knew very well what Mrs Parrish wanted, from him or another, but even if he could have brought himself to answer simply: 'Justice!' it would only have sounded false and theatrical. And the next instant it seemed to him that in fact he had merely made the same answer in different words, for justice, whenever one stumbled over it in the world, had the absurd, astonished inappropriateness of a miracle.

'How awful for you! And for her, of course, poor woman, but what can *you* do about it? I know you don't grudge them an outlet for their grievances, but, Bill darling, it does seem so *unfair.*'

'It seemed unfair to her that he should be taken. And after all, I am her M.P., she's got a perfect right to come and tell me when she thinks something wrong is going on and someone ought to protest.'

'Oh, I know—and really, it isn't for me to blame her, when something so terrible has happened to her. But it just *happens*! It's the same risk for all of them, it's just chance which of them comes through safely.'

Edmund sat with his shoulders flattened well back into the curve of the seat, with his eyes absently watching the unrolling ribbon of the road, and his hands playing with a pair of linked keys in his lap. Stealing a sidelong glance at him, Dallas could find nothing greatly wrong with the picture. The boy's

113

silence was not at all brittle, nor his withdrawal too wary and intent to be normal; his serenity was no more than faintly clouded with thought. He was not talking simply because on this subject, as yet, he had nothing to say. It was impossible even to guess whether his preoccupation was with Mrs Parrish, or his next examinations, or merely his next meal.

It would, Dallas acknowledged, have been the simplest thing in the world to turn on him and say: 'What did *you* think of her, Eddie? She was talking to you afterwards, wasn't she?' But for some reason he did not do it. He found himself afraid of the look which might replace the meditative placidity of Edmund's face if he should be forced to confront the subject of Mrs Parrish squarely. He knew just how the blond-brown head would turn towards him, and the exact quality of the suddenly lifted eyelids, their unresentful alacrity, the way they rolled loftily back into their high-arched settings whenever he was challenged directly, even if it meant having to own up to something loaded with penalties. He had always been the most open creature breathing. If you asked him point-blank, he would always tell you. *Ergo*, if you did not wish to risk knowing, you took devout care not to ask him.

Ginnie's imagination, thank God, never made the obvious connections. She was not at all likely to be startled by the implications of her own dictum that it was the same risk for all of them, and to suffer the sudden horrifying vision which had confronted Dallas in the doorway of his office. Yes, they all had to go. That was precisely what conscription meant, and though no doubt there still existed obscure possibilities of evading service, given enough influence and assiduity, there could never be any way

114

out like that for them. Dallas would not have considered it, and even if he had been brought to that degradation, Edmund would never have consented.

But there were honest considerations which might delay matters for a few years. Edmund was in his last year at school, and looking forward to London University, and he had made up his mind years ago that he was going to be a doctor, and was heading towards his chosen vocation with all his might. And surely there would soon be a cease-fire in Korea, which removed one of the most appalling possibilities. Unless the negotiations broke down, and the whole indescribably bloody business broke out again, which God forbid! God forbid! Everything he said or thought tonight had dismaying echoes. But surely, surely they couldn't let it flare up again. Surely there was human feeling enough in the world to prevent that disaster. And if his studies would only hold Edmund safely out of uniform for four years more, who knew how many trouble spots might have been burned out, or dwindled down into an exhausted peace of satiety and disgust?

But there was an answer to everything he could say to comfort himself, and through the evening air, as he drove out through the ebbing streets of the town, the thoughts came pulsing like gnats to bite him. Who knew how many more trouble spots might have burned up by then, either? Who knew whether Egypt would be in flames, or some other bit of the long-silent Empire suddenly erect and reaching for a gun? These things happened overnight. That was how Korea had happened. A mad gallop through the United Nations, like a steamroller amok, and before people could realise it, before they understood that anything had happened which might touch them, their sons were on the sea. You don't have any warning, you can make neither preparation nor protest, they are just snatched out of your life as the wind snatches a hat from your head. All the same, four years' delay might bring them to a better time, and there was no sense in throwing away such grace as was offered. It might even be possible to cut the call-up period to one year by then. There might be another Labour Government. Not that that fact alone could necessarily alter the burden of events, but still, one could hope—

Or, of course, there might be a general war.

'Listen!' said Ginnie. 'I can hear the band!'

They were at the edge of the town, where a ribbon of high-road uncoiled into the west between rows of semi-detached houses, with over-decorated fronts and prim little lawns. Before them the green of fields melted into the dusk, becoming the darkest of smoke-grey and olive-dun, and cast up against the saffron afterglow the occasional sharp outline of a tree, full-leafed and solidly black. Crouched low into the lap of twilight, the houses dwindled to doll-size. The sky, unimaginably lofty and clear, separated itself utterly from the world, shook off the touch of matter and man. But out of the bewildering distance between that shrunken shadowy littleness and that luminous height the brass bands of Caldington sent forth unabashed snatches of brazen music, fitful with the vague gyrations of the breeze, but persistent and pervasive as breath. Man had no intention of being silenced.

Edmund sat up straighter, and put his keys away, sniffing the air ahead with a kindling face. Already he could see the flat cut-out shapes of the spoil-heaps against the solid gold of the dusk, and the sharp

116

surrealist erections of the pitheads. A shifting glimmer and glow below them, faint and small, marked where the torches of the colliers were massing. There was a large oval space, common ground, hemmed with copse on one rim and heath on the other, and on the edge of the neighbouring field, just screened by the trees, there would be a small fair, with Dodg'ems and roundabouts and shies, and a little steam-organ piping merrily in competition with the bands. A few gypsy-wagons, too, on the heath, for all the hangers-on of local festivals gathered for the Miners' Rally.

'I'm hungry!' announced Edmund. 'Do we all call in at the canteen for sandwiches, or have we left it too late for that? Because if you don't want anything until afterwards, you won't mind if I go and forage on the fairground, will you? I'll be there before they get to your speech, honestly.'

'Aren't you coming to sit with us in front?' Ginnie was reproachful, but not greatly surprised.

'What, all through old Jarrett's usual rigmarole? Mummy, have a heart!'

'He wants to go and throw at coconuts,' said Dallas indulgently. 'All right, suppose I drop you off at the gate, and you can go and stuff yourself with sausage rolls, or chips and peas, or whatever's going. But don't spend too long with the girls on the Dodg'ems, because I'm going to need your moral support when my time comes.'

'I'll be there! Wouldn't miss it!' The smile he gave his father as he jumped out of the car was half-mischievous, but half-serious, too. He waved his hand, and hopped over the ditch, and they saw him for a moment against the garish coloured lights of the fairground booths, striding across the grass with

117

lifted head and happy, appreciative gait. Even his back view looked hungry, intent and charmed.

Fairs by night have a real glamour, their voices breathy and hoarse with outdoor living, their colours jungle-bright and yet mysterious in the context of the darkness they defy. Edmund detected even a special scent of excitement in the breeze that met his lifted nostrils, compounded of the cooling foliage of the summer night, the hot, oily smell of machines already some hours in use, gingerbread, sawdust, paint and canvas, frying fat and human exertion; as motley a collection of ingredients as the pandemonium of music and shouting and shrieks of laughter that went to make up the characteristic utterance of the fair. He himself began to smile as he approached the glittering rim of the trodden ground, the infection of other people's gaiety parting his lips and brightening his eyes. Soon he would be laughing aloud.

The smile was perfectly implicit in the back view of him as he loped up the field towards the whirl of lights; it was in the blithe way his heels left the turf, and the eager forward lift of his head and thrust of his shoulders. They sat still in the car for a long minute, watching him go, and Ginnie was smiling, too, with all the fond indulgence proper to a mother. It was the very face with which Edmund sometimes regarded her, when she was not observing him.

'*Nice* child!' said Ginnie.

'Very nice! So like his mother, don't you think?'

She reached for the door of the car suddenly, and hopped out, and climbed into the front seat beside him. The breath of the roses came with her. 'The image of his father, most people say.' She touched his cheek lightly with her soft, kind, impulsive fingers. Every now and again, when she did things like that,

118

for no reason in the world except that she was still rapturously in love with him after eighteen years, he felt a tremor of disquiet. It was a terrible strain on a man, to be thought as wonderful as Ginnie thought him, to be expected to know the answer to every question, the counter-spell to every threat. Suddenly he had a nightmare vision of Ginnie bereaved, Ginnie stunned beneath the hammer-blow of unrealisable loss, confronting him with the questions to which he had failed to find any answer, pointing him to the evil he could not undo.

'How much right to judge did my son have?'

He drove on, almost abruptly, drawing his cheek away from her touch, tramping hard on the accelerator as though he believed the voice could be outrun; but it went with him all the rest of the way, whispering in his ear, in Ginnie's accents: 'So you stand by their right to take him and have him killed! If you contemplate it, obviously you accept it as right. Anything else is playing with words. There's always an alternative.' And again, clear and peremptory: 'It's what *we* do that's going to save or damn us, not what the others do.'

But what could he do for Ginnie more than he had done for Mrs Parrish? What for Eddie, better than the nothing at all he had done for Jack? In a man of principle it ought to make no difference when the victim is his own flesh and blood, but it does, it does! It makes all the difference in the world. It causes you to see the living as already dead, and to feel the dead treading close on your heels, and plucking with insistent fingers at your sleeve. It mates the living face with the dead face until the two are indistinguishable, and, wherever you turn, in all young eyes you meet the accusation and entreaty of these eyes, until you

119

cannot even watch your son walk away up the slope of a field without being aware that you are watching him walk away to his corruption and death, from which you have not lifted a finger to deliver him, nor meet him face to face in a doorway without foreseeing the last meeting, and the making up of the account outstanding between you and him.

'Darling,' said Ginnie, laying a soft, anxious hand on his sleeve as he stopped the car in the rim of the arena at Fallow Deep, 'you *are* looking a bit strained and overworked tonight, I'm sure you're driving yourself too hard. I won't have you cracking up— you can't carry *all* the cares of the world, you know, let someone else do a little bit of the worrying, too.'

The wind at that moment took the music of the band, and cast it over them in a great, gaudy gust of sound, like a burst of brazen laughter.

* * *

Edmund walked through the fairground with a bag of sausage rolls in his hand, eating his way steadily towards a pleasant repletion, while his eyes roved contentedly over penny-rolling games, rifle range, coconut shies, and half a dozen other ingenious devices for extracting the small change from his trousers pockets. Children and dogs darted about knee-high, complicating his progress with their abrupt eruptions and vanishings. Mothers and fathers of families steered their offspring, with the caution of experience, round the worst temptations, and parried with long-suffering calm such demands as they thought unreasonable, enjoying their own tolerant scepticism as acutely as the children's immoderate joy, and rousing the gaudy ghosts of fairgrounds of their childhood, when kids got real value for their pennies. Boys and girls, linked two and two or strung in bright trailing necklaces of summer colours, roamed from booth to booth, their faces sharply illuminated in the flashing crosslights from the merry-go-rounds, their voices pitched shrilly to penetrate the bronchial roar of the steam-organ. When he had eaten the last sausage roll, Edmund topped off his ambulatory meal with a bag of ginger snaps, and shared at least half of them with a lean but sleek bull-mastiff who came from under one of the wagons ringing the glitter, and attached himself by melting eyes to the paper bag.

The dog accompanied him round the field again afterwards, and stood looking on benevolently and waving his tail in slow, approving arcs while Edmund tried his skill at the rifle range, and the skittle alley, and rolled a few pennies to see if his luck was in. He won a small plastic doll at the quoits stall, and lost three times its value trying to work a movable grab inside a glass case. He rode a tiger on the outermost ring of the merry-go-round, trying all the balancing tricks he knew, and adding a few more extravagant ones when he found himself the object of the admiration of a shrieking girl of about his own age, who was clinging for dear life to the horse abreast of his mount. Edmund was not averse to being admired, nor to showing off a little, without too serious self-adoration, when the occasion and the general mood were right for it.

He leaned to give her the solid support of his arm and shoulder, and her yellow hair blew out and whipped his face, and her shrill, excited laughter rang wildly in his ear, and he was altogether enchanted. He held her tenderly until the roundabout began to slow

121

down, and the noise and the whirl of lights subsided gradually about them, and left them drawing apart shyly, body from body, arm from arm, dazed, smiling face from face. He helped her down, and their hands also separated slowly, and they went their two ways back into the bright little labyrinth, their eyes disengaging last of all, without either of them having spoken a word to the other.

It was almost time for him to move on, but he could not go without just one ride on the Dodg'ems cars. They were in mid-career, spitting sparks from the netting overhead, and jostling one another into wild, revolving skids, and the attendants were hopping from the barrier to the fenders to disentangle the worst scrawls, and distributing advice among the inexpert and threats among the reckless, all with that large, strident imperturbability which chiefly fascinated Edmund about fairground folks. He had to wait several minutes before the current was cut out, and the cars slithered slowly to rest.

There were plenty of other people waiting, too, and as soon as the cars emptied there was a rush for them. Into this competition he entered with zest, darting across the steel-grey floor and leaping into the nearest driving-seat like a greyhound, and was immediately visited by abashed compunction to see that several people were left plunging from car to car, and everywhere frustrated. Two disappointed little boys, the elder no more than nine years old, the younger not yet too old for oozing tears, drew back forlornly to the barrier, and stood there wistfully gazing. Edmund's heart, like Nelson's, roundly refused to stand it. He waved them over hastily.

'Like to ride with me? Hop in then, quickly, and keep your arms inside. You next to me, Tich—that's it! Hang on to me, if you want something to hold on to, don't hold the edge of the car, or you'll get your fingers pinched. Now, everybody settled? Right, we're off!'

A sturdy, shrill, and probably disapproving mother had just appeared at the edge of the floor. He waved a propitiatory hand in her direction as he drove off, indicating between his gesture and his smile that he would be personally responsible for the safe return of her imps. He was glad he'd resisted the temptation to turn over the wheel to the elder boy, as that ambitious child had certainly been willing him to do; she would emphatically not have approved of that.

Then he forgot her in the instant infection of evasion and pursuit, whirling the squat little tub round and round the track, in and out among the others, nudging one out of line here, swinging another round there with a flip of his tail, side-stepping a third by an inch, missing his aim at last, and getting tangled in a heaving mass of wedged cars and shrieking people, from which he ducked out backwards to swirl about in a dizzy circle and take off again. Not too hard, not too roughly, except when he miscalculated a little, but hard enough and fast enough to have the children ululating wildly with delight, and bouncing and shrieking at every bump. Edmund was too old to squeal, but his face was flushed and fixed in a broad grin of joyous mischief, and he wasn't prepared to swear that he hadn't let out a squeak or two of devilment before the ride was over. When the din subsided and the cars glided to stillness he hoisted the children out and followed them demurely to the barrier, composing his features into the winning gravity which might placate

123

their mother.

'I invited them—you didn't mind, did you?'

'The little tykes gave me the slip,' she said warmly. 'I'd told 'em they were too young to go on them things, so they nipped off behind my back.'

'But they wouldn't have gone on them, if it hadn't been for me,' said Edmund, diplomatically forgetting the unsuccessful dash they had made for a car of their own. The almost-spent shilling must still be clutched in the small fist buried so deeply in the elder boy's trouser pocket. 'I didn't know they weren't supposed to go—and you couldn't expect *them* to tell me, now, could you?'

She smiled, and flushed in a reassuringly feminine manner, and patted her side wave more accurately into place. He seemed a very nice young fellow, pleasant but respectful, she thought; but these suitable words did not contain quite all her thoughts.

'Oh, well, I'm sure they were quite safe with you.'

Edmund extracted the slightly crumpled doll from his pocket, and smoothed its feather skirt. 'Haven't you got a little girl, too? I don't know any little girls myself. I won it.'

Startled, and gratified, she said: 'Well, as a matter of fact, I have!'

He added the rose, plucking it suddenly from his button-hole. 'And this is for you!' He smiled, patted the boys companionably on the shoulders, and went off along the alley between the wagons. Striking attitudes again, he said to himself, half-tickled and half-vexed with the thought. Well, not deliberately, really. It just seems to happen. Anyhow, she liked it!

He ducked through the wire at the edge of the field, and threaded the thin belt of coppice which screened the east side of the arena. Waste ground, self-sown with silver birches, a few hawthorns and an occasional small oak, this ribbon of woodland separated light from light and sound from sound with a mysterious completeness, so that only when he was winding his way between the trunks did he begin to see the diffused glimmer of the hundreds of torches; and already, when he looked round towards the fair, its many-coloured, strident brightness was almost lost to sight. He came out at the crest of the bank which surrounded the arena, and halted there in the shelter of the trees, looking down on the scene.

Now it was night, and the dusk had become the true, clear dark, achieving the miracle, as always, while his eyes were turned away. The vivid light had all faded from the western sky, leaving upon the rim of the night only a faint, lambent stain, against which the significant shapes of the pithead stood like cut-outs of black paper, and the spoil-heaps were a saw-toothed ridge of mountains. Between this silhouette of enormous energy charmed into stillness, and the gradual rise of the grassy bank on which he stood, the wide, shallow amphitheatre opened, an oval of smoky, wavering points of light, and in the glimmer the hundreds of heads, all with their faces turned in one direction, reared blackly individual from a mass of shadow.

There is something awe-inspiring about an assembled silence and stillness of human beings, when they are motionless and quiet of their own will. Their oneness has the daunting quality of that massy, more-than-human shadow down there, but the awareness of their unique, individual, consenting intelligences superimposes itself like the vision of the lit faces rising from the dark. Edmund could feel their intentness, and his heart was caught up into the silent

125

tide of their emotion. The hidden force of their eyes burning all alike upon a single objective drew his eyes also.

They were looking at his father. In front of the modern baths there was a concrete ramp, with space enough at the top for a few chairs for the speakers and their women-folk, and an improvised rostrum with a microphone. Edmund could see Ginnie's profile and her fluttering feather in a shaft of light from the doorway, and the solid attendant shapes of two or three local officials whom he knew by sight. His father was already speaking, though by some trick of distance and air his voice came up to this solitude only as an indistinguishable thread of sound, fitfully received, frequently lost. It was to him that they were looking for a revelation, for whatever it was they awaited with all the force and readiness and longing of their unmoving silence, of their braced bodies and demanding eyes.

They were waiting, then, he thought with a slight shock of unforeseen understanding, for something from outside themselves. His father might almost have been a revivalist, and these the threatened souls waiting for salvation. But no, it was not really like that. They were not vessels waiting to be filled, they were full already, tensed and charged and ready to explode into action as soon as they should positively know what they ought to do. They were waiting for something with which they could align themselves, and their aching over-fullness of will and passion and intelligence. Edmund felt an unaccustomed brief tremor of disquiet; even right and wrong had become so muddled that it was all any man could do to find his own way. And for people like these, deeply aware of the urgency of action, it was unbearable to go on

126

for long uncommitted. Those who didn't think or care about the way the world was going didn't come to the Miners' Rally at all, or if they came, got no further than the fairground. It was a sort of portent of the modern world, this wandering in the wilderness, waiting for a sign.

He caught bits of the speech as he moved quietly down the hill. His father was talking about social justice, about the fight necessary to protect the rights of the weakest in a crisis economy. This in which they were living was a more or less chronic crisis economy, and for that state of affairs neither the electorate nor the Government of Britain need feel itself responsible. The ills of the world, this desperately divided world, were not of our making. Edmund was nearer now, and he could hear clearly the vehemence of passion that went into the disclaimer. *We had not made* the disastrous division which split the world in two. But we had to live with it, and be ready to face its threats, and to accept as necessary evil, involving us all, the war economy into which it had forced us. So far, he ventured to say, the overwhelming mass of the people were in agreement; where the Labour Party stood apart from the Government was in its assessment of how the necessary sacrifices ought to be distributed.

Edmund came down close to the edge of the crowd and stood, a little withdrawn in order to avail himself of the slope, watching the tall figure at the microphone, with its few and taut gestures, and its handsome, ardent face, which was flung by the flickering cross-lights into urgent relief. He felt no disrespectful amusement when his father raged against economic injustice, though Dallas's experience of the bitter side of things was no greater

127

than Ginnie's or Edmund's own. Of the genuineness of this indignation there could be no doubt.

'We all have to give—yes. But some of us, as you know better than I, have already given too much, have always been forced to give, whenever difficult times have hit our economy. Forced to give, when they had already barely enough to keep them and their families alive. *That* is what we stand against, and what I personally will combat with all the energy I possess. The sacrifices must come from those who have enough and to spare, not from those who are living on the borderline of poverty. The economies must be made in luxury spending, and among the higher dividends, not at the expense of food subsidies, and by refusing consideration to even the most modest of wage claims. *That* is where we differ from the Government, and that is the part of their policy, a vital part, which we shall certainly reverse as soon as we get back into office.'

The crowd surged softly, and sent up a murmur of approval. This audience rarely applauded until a speech was completed; they had heard so many that they assessed none until it ended. But the deep, throaty sound, wordless in acknowledgement, was what Dallas had learned to listen for and to need. His face, flushed and strained in the quaking light, softened momentarily into a smile.

'Couldn't we, some of you are asking, do more than that? Couldn't we to some extent reverse this country's whole advance into a war economy, and so solve, or at any rate very greatly relieve, our industrial and production problems? Since the risk of taking to a competitive rearmament is obvious, might not the opposite risk, of diverting our efforts from military to economic salvation, be worth

128

taking? That is a question that every man will answer for himself, but my answer would be a convinced and emphatic no! I only wish it could be otherwise, but we are living in a real world, and facing an explosive situation for which the blame—I say it again!—cannot be laid at our door. With the implications and dangers of that situation we have to live. I would like a world without conscription, a world without soldiers, even, as well as any of you. But as yet, let's face it, it must remain a distant dream.'

Why had he returned to harp upon Britain's national innocence? He'd stated his position once, it wasn't like him to hark back to ground on which he felt completely sure of himself. Edmund stood watching him with all the critical affection of a son who has always been encouraged to speak his mind. He thought, to be candid, that his father was weakening his case, making his very security look insecure.

'Let me say that I think the Labour Party has lost popularity partly as the result of its courage in facing the facts of life in the Defence sphere. And no less clearly, that I am sure they have been right to accept that loss. Defence is not something which ought to be made the subject of cheap, vote-catching manoeuvres. It's easy to demand the end of conscription—provided there is no risk at all of your demand being met. But any thinking person knows that to be honest such a demand must be linked to a demand for total revision of our commitments, and such a revision at this moment would be suicidally foolish. Western defence is a matter of life and death to us, and we dare not, in duty to ourselves or our allies, shirk any part of our responsibility there.

'But within the reluctant acceptance of continued

National Service, perhaps some more reasonable demands might indeed be made. Could not the period of service be cut—not merely without harm, but even with advantage—to eighteen months? Some of us at Westminster are beginning to think so, and I believe that the Labour Party is moving towards a demand on those lines. That adequate training *can* be achieved in less time than two years we have seen whenever the need arose. That the six months saved would lessen the divorce of young men from their ordinary life and jobs is plain to be seen, and it is also clear that industry would benefit very considerably. Our contribution to western defence would not be impaired, for we should have a quicker build-up of trained personnel. What must be cut out are a number of those far-too-heavy commitments in all parts of the world, where troops are being used in wasteful and ineffective police actions, brought about in many cases by the interminable hangover of nineteenth-century policies. The present Government *cannot* reduce these, because it has no policy which can relax local tensions and make policing unnecessary. But *we* have, and *we can*! We have a policy which can transform the Empire into a genuinely free Commonwealth, which will no longer have to be held together by force!'

This time the murmur of agreement did swell into a volley of applause, still as measured and thoughtful as the poise of the watching heads; but coming from them it was much, and he valued it. He went on reassuring them that the human problem was always in his mind, that they must not think it was not being considered. He put his head back with a sudden violent movement, outside his usual elegant self-discipline, and said: 'National Service has at least this

130

one enormous virtue, that it puts all young men on an equal footing. It's one game in which there can be no cheating. To anyone who doubts my deep concern with its frequently bitter implications, I can only say that my own son will be eighteen at the end of this year.'

Not applause this time, not the deep, devotional murmur of agreement, but a sound like a concerted sigh, accepting his membership in this burden of their kind.

Across the intent heads Dallas swept his straining glance, suddenly frantic to be sure of what he had perhaps been taking too easily for granted, Edmund's absence. He had begun to speak half an hour earlier than had been expected, because the Trade Union official due to speak before him was indisposed; and he had been scanning the rim of the arena throughout his speech without catching a glimpse of Edmund returning from the fair. At first he had missed the boy's acute and critical nearness, then he had found the lack becoming a freedom, and his tongue exploiting it by unloading from his mind arguments he would have hesitated to express within Edmund's hearing. This last furious bid for full membership in the troubles of his generation had startled Dallas himself with a pang of superstitious dread, and for reasons he wished passionately not to explore he found himself hoping with all his heart that Edmund had not heard. It was as if an attempt had been made to buy something—approval? peace of mind?—with the offer of Eddie's life.

He flashed an apprehensive glance at Ginnie, whose erratic understanding might well have chosen this very moment to transcend itself, and grasp what it should not have grasped; but she was smiling with a fond, untroubled pride, lost in her wifely dream. He looked out again over the intent audience, taking comfort from their uncritical eyes; and on the hillside above the extreme edge of the crowd, bright in the sudden flare of a disintegrating torch, he saw his son standing.

The gleam lit the boy's face for an instant with a startling urgency, and drew one intense flash of answering light from his eyes before it burned out into darkness. One moment he was there, gazing straight at his father across the waste of strange faces; the next, vanished, and nothing left to fill the dazzled eyes that searched for him, except the faint, slender, abrupt shape of the emptiness he had left in the air, hardly perceptible, soon dissolved into the unity of the night.

* * *

It was long past midnight, but Edmund was not asleep. He was sitting on the sill of the open window, his shoulder turned upon the soft darkness of his room, his face towards the luminous blue of the sky above the garden. He looked round when the door opened, and the lighter oblong of the window behind him made clear to Dallas the quick, slight stiffening of the back and shoulders, the wary and even faintly offended lift of the head. Nothing personal about it, in all probability no more than an instinctive reaction of annoyance because he was caught with an experimental cigarette between his fingers, and resented being watched at rehearsals.

Eddie had a few perversely sensitive spots scattered incalculably through the fabric of his blithe common sense, to make daily life with him more

132

complicated, and prevent that easy complacency which afflicts the parents of totally sunlit children. Normally he would attempt anything, with the happiest disregard for the exact degree of his success or failure; but there were certain things he couldn't bear to be seen doing until he could do them well, and most of them, reasonably enough at seventeen, were things connected with the dignity and elegance proper to finding himself a man.

At his age one must have a perfected suit of behaviour appropriate to the complete man of the world, whether one cares to wear it all the time or not. Until just over a month ago, what with football, and fencing, and one or two other athletic interests of the kind, it had never occurred to Eddie to want to smoke. Then he had decided that this, too, was an adjunct of the complete adult personality which he must have at command, in case he wanted it, and the bedroom rehearsals had begun. Now he was expert enough, in his father's respectful eyes, to pass muster anywhere; but Eddie was hard to please, and meant to master every gesture of the game before he played it in public.

So that was probably why the long young back stiffened. One should not walk in upon one's children before their party pieces are word-perfect. With Ginnie, of course, the boy practised assiduously and without self-consciousness, but that was different, because Ginnie was too innocent to realise that the charming flourish with which he presented his lighter or his case was aimed, ultimately, at some hypothetical girl of the future, and not at her. She was lovely material for experiments, because she herself was so accomplished socially that her limitations seldom even showed, and she partnered him with

133

conviction because she was utterly convinced.

'Hullo!' said Edmund in a perfectly natural voice. 'I thought you'd gone to bed.'

Why hadn't he? It would have been infinitely wiser. Ginnie was already asleep, her nose burrowed deeply into the pillow, and he would have done better to join her. Certainly there was something he wanted to say to Eddie; the only question about that was whether it could ever be said without doing more harm than good. But was there anything Eddie wanted to say to him? Or was this merely a state of hypertension due to the persistency with which that woman's son haunted his mind? He was so sensitive now upon any facet of this subject, so sore to the touch of any young man's hand, that Eddie had only to frown at some obscure speculation in his own mind to send indignant pains raging through him.

What if the boy had been unwontedly silent and thoughtful all the way home? Very likely he was simply too tired to be talkative, and pondering over some preoccupation of his own, nothing whatever to do with tonight, nothing whatever to do with his father. Very likely he had never wasted a thought upon the capital that had been made out of him. Eddie didn't bring all his problems home for solution. It never even occurred to him that his parents might be better at that sort of thing than he was; Ginnie so obviously couldn't be expected to help much, and his father was a busy man. Eddie fended for himself; the whole trend of his nature and his training was towards self-reliance. No, it was he, Bill Dallas, who was aching for a clearing of the air between them. Eddie didn't even realise that it needed clearing.

And, good God, what was there to be said? 'I

didn't really mean that I'd throw you in as a makeweight to buy their good opinion! I didn't mean that it was worth two years of your life, and the risk of losing you altogether, just to keep my job!' He shivered at the thought.

'Too wide awake—stimulation, maybe!'

He knew he was doing something Eddie didn't want him to do, but all the same he lifted his hand and switched on the light. He had to see the boy's face; that curiously wild, slender, chaste outline against the stars was too elusive to be of any help to him. He was straining his eyes fiercely upon it as the light leaped up, and it seemed to him that the aloof, shy creature sprang backward into the darkness from the touch of it, and left another, a changed boy in his place.

Eddie sat blinking beneath a slight frown, his body reassuringly solid and ordinary now that it had three dimensions; blinking at the sudden illumination, or at the smoke which sometimes he could not keep out of his eyes, frowning at the interruption of his dark solitude.

'You don't seem in any hurry to get to sleep, either. You suffering from nervous stimulation, too?'

'I was just sitting thinking,' said Edmund simply, and let the conversation fall out of his hands so abruptly that Dallas could not restrain a leap to catch it and keep it from breaking, as though it had been something fragile in glass. It made him sound almost garrulous in his own ears, but the boy was already half-withdrawn from him again into that inner preoccupation of his, and might not see anything wrong.

'Thinking about what? The dissatisfactions of a political career? Or my shortcomings as a speaker?

135

Or your own future?'

He couldn't let it alone. All he could do was inflect his voice against the grain into a bogus heartiness and comradeliness which appalled him as he listened to it, rather than let it fall into the abject anxiety in which his heart was held.

'I've been doing some thinking about that myself, as a matter of fact. With that eighteenth birthday of yours coming along in January, I expect you'll have to register before the end of this year—some date early in December, most probably. It's a big leap for a boy to make, I know, but there's no reason why it should interfere with your plans as yet. A chap like you, heading out on a medical career—you've every right to deferment, of course. All you'll have to do will be apply for it when you register.'

He went on and on with it, he couldn't stop. The invading silence would close in so coldly and deeply over the false briskness of his words if he once stopped talking; and yet there is a limit to the talking you can do upon one note.

'You won't have any trouble. Your job is to go ahead and get through your exams, and there's time enough to think about other responsibilities when you're qualified. Doctors are far too valuable to be allowed to get away.'

Self-hypnotised, trying to exorcise his own demon, he spread out before Edmund's eyes, naked and recognisable, the very fears he was intent upon concealing. It was done now; nothing could have held it back for ever, nothing could now undo it. The only remaining hope was that Edmund would be too innocent to understand, that the picture he had of his father would be still so absolute and inviolable that he would not realise the implications of what he was

136

hearing now.

The boy had turned back to the open window, though its starry spaces were now only a flat plane of darkness. He sat gazing out into it, and exhaling smoke slowly between parted lips. The back of his head had an intent and listening look. What was he thinking? Was he referring this reassurance back to the promise his father had made to the crowd at Fallow Deep? Two faces for two occasions—to them you promise that there'll be no escape for your son, any more than for theirs; to me you promise an easy way out without actually cheating. Was that what was going through his mind? If only he hadn't come back to the meeting quite so promptly tonight, there need have been no such heart-burning. It had always been understood that he would be deferred, there was nothing underhand about it, nothing to be ashamed of. It wasn't a question of privilege; he had the same rights as all the others, no more, and no less.

Edmund turned his head suddenly, looked full at his father with wide, alert and deeply troubled eyes, and asked: 'What was that boy, the one who was killed?'

So they were back to her! Dallas had known in his heart that the road would bring them face to face with her again and again, from this night on. Back to her, and to the young man she had left on their doorstep, back to the khaki which had never fitted, and the quietly desperate eyes which had found no way out.

'That boy? Which boy?' He was parrying for a few seconds of grace rather than hoping to sound convincing in his forgetfulness.

'The Parrish boy. What was he? What did he do?'

'Oh, young Parrish! He worked at one of the tool

137

factories, I believe. A metal turner, or something like that.'

He knew that he was trying to look as if he did not know where they were going, and he wondered, with those large, fierce, clouded eyes frowning intently at him through the smoke of the neglected cigarette, why he went on with the attempt. But he kept the laboriously casual, thoughtful expression upon his face, warding off the blue stare with superstitious insistence. For if the fiction went, his ascendancy went with it.

'Then there wouldn't be any deferment for him?'

'No, not unless there was an apprenticeship involved, and I don't suppose there was. After all, they can't very well defer everybody, there has to be some sort of selective process. But where the community might be losing a doctor, merely to gain a soldier for two years—well, it wouldn't be practical politics, would it?'

'No,' said Edmund in a polite, deliberate voice, 'it wouldn't, would it?' He crushed out his cigarette against the window-sill, and dropped the butt into the garden, and all the while he never took his eyes from his father's face. Dallas has seen him look at schoolmasters like that, with the same respectful, impenetrable, resistance, when some inner certainty, such as most intelligent children have, had erected its hackles instinctively against their pronouncements, and yet he had not experience enough to know why they were wrong, and he was right. Unable to out-argue them, but secure in his own rejection of their version of the truth, he would keep this civil but unconvinced silence, the implications of which they came to understand very well. More than one teacher had lost his temper and foundered on that rock, but

Dallas wasn't going down after them, not after seventeen years' experience of his own child.

'I didn't make the rules,' he said, with firm but careful lightness, 'but like all the rest, I have to play by them. So have you. We do if we accept the responsibility of belonging to the team, that is. Those who don't, of course, have a choice—of a kind, I suppose.'

He had brought the whole thing down purposely to a simple point which could be argued, but Edmund did not rise. He sat still, impregnable within his suspension of belief, staring steadily, thoughtfully into his father's face and waiting to understand. He was in no hurry, the urgency which possessed him and held him so still was something quite separate from haste.

'If we do agree that we belong to the team, we accept the position we're told to play in.' Dallas could no longer maintain his own stillness; he began to move aimlessly along Edmund's bookshelves, plucking a book here and there half out of its place, and thrusting it back again, listening to his own voice making meretricious middle-school sermons in a falsely casual tone, and dauntingly aware that they impressed that listening mind not at all. 'If you're more valuable as a doctor, and somebody else is more valuable as a soldier, and that's the way they want it, my boy, you've got no reasonable complaint, and neither has the other fellow. It would be the opposite of patriotic to make an unholy fuss about it on the grounds that you've got an easier deal than he has. Even supposing it were true!' he added, turning a restless, compelled smile upon the silent boy.

Edmund's eyes met him with the same alert and intelligent look, intent upon their own observations,

139

not in the least distracted by the words he was deploying so strenuously between himself and them. All those absurd analogies with the sporting boy's world snapped like gossamer before the uncompromisingly direct march of Edmund's eyes. And now Dallas recognised the look, and knew where he had seen it before. But for their blueness they might have been the eyes of Mrs Parrish, resolute, sceptical and patient, shearing through his defences argument by argument, justification by justification, without seeing them, breaking them like the cobwebs they were across the path to her decision.

He could not go on with it, he had been a fool ever to begin it. The sense of his own danger made him draw back with a haste which was almost ludicrous, though he tried to make his retreat as presentable as he could. A sudden shake of his shoulders, a laugh and a yawn, both false where he had been used to having only truth between them, and then the minute chime of Edmund's little clock striking one helped him to take the first step backward.

'Well, we've time enough to think about all that. I suppose we'd better get to bed. I didn't realise it was quite so late.'

'I suppose we had,' said Edmund obligingly, making the perfunctory suggestion of a movement to indicate his willingness to close the interview.

'Don't sit up too late.'

'No, I won't. Good night, Dad!'

'Good night, Eddie!'

He got out of the room in a fair imitation of the desultory manner natural to a man still wakeful but purposeless at one in the morning. Nevertheless, it was a retreat. The eyes followed him with their inflexible blue glance until the door closed between father and son.

CHAPTER SIX

THE EXORCISTS

It was an Under-Secretary from the Colonial Office who said to Ronald Crozier, when the autumn session was several weeks old, and the prolonged but grudging summer weather was burning out in an unexpected glory of golds and reds in the London parks: 'What have you been doing to your opposite number on the left, down in your town?'

Crozier looked up in vague surprise from his half-empty pint pot, and thoughtfully round the dingy little riverside bar which was habitually his refuge from both the social and the Bohemian among his fellow-members. He was wondering how the Under-Secretary had discovered it, and what attraction it could possibly have for up-and-coming young parliamentarians of his type, and where a man could find another even less frequented, and with equally good beer, if junior Ministers were beginning to make use of this one. He said with mild interest: 'Nothing, as far as I know. His stock's high. Why, what makes you think somebody must be riding him?'

'Oh, there's more of his humanitarian act pending,' said the Under-Secretary petulantly, and reached for his glass. 'Haven't you seen the Order Paper?'

There had been a great many questions from that

141

quarter since the session had begun. The member for Caldington East had never before been so vocal in the House, nor harped so aggravatingly upon one note. His own leaders, hypersensitive to the faintest suggestion of criticism of themselves, even by oblique implication, had been the first to notice the phenomenon and frown upon it; but Dallas had continued to raise that clear, warm, civilised voice of his with a curiously passionate persistence, as if he could not see their displeasure, nor feel the blood ebbing from his chances of office, when, if ever, they had gifts to give again. He had been in a very good position until he began acting like a Bevanite. Now he was headed for the wilderness with the other cranks and idealists, unless he watched his step. And being a popular man with the party rank-and-file wouldn't help him, as he must know very well from the experience of others. Only on polling day, reflected Crozier cynically, is it imperative to be popular.

'Your official nerves are becoming as tender as a pilgrim's feet,' he said. 'What is it this time?'

'He's got a question down about the use of bombers in Kenya, and another about some fairy story that C.O.s are offering cash prizes for kills among the Mau-Mau gangs. God knows where he got his information, nothing like that's come out, as far as I know—'

'There's something to come?' asked Crozier with interest.

'Good God, no! Is it likely? Oh, we shouldn't have any difficulty in squashing him over this particular issue. But what on earth's got into the fellow? He used to be reasonable enough. We never heard any of this humbug about inhuman methods until these last

142

few months. I used to find it middling comic, myself, but under steady repetition the nerves fray. First it was the broadside about the new French move— before the session was a week old, at that! "Is the Minister aware that the French Parliament has announced its intention of using only volunteers in Indo-China as from July 23rd of this year, and will he consider employing the same policy in Kenya and Malaya?" Would *he*, if he had this mess on *his* hands? He knows damned well he'd use everything he'd got! If he's given us a week of peace since, that's the most he has done for us. When it isn't the Foreign Office it's the War Office, and when it isn't the War Office it's the Colonial Office—lately it's been us most of the time.'

'I don't see that you've any complaint,' said Crozier reasonably. 'After all, putting it no higher than a policy level, his job is to chivvy us all out of power if he can. If his objections to the methods you're using are real, it's twice his duty to give you hell. Unless, of course, you hate him worse than the rest because he's more effective?'

He looked up from his beer with a bright, beguiling smile into the offended eyes of the Under-Secretary, whom he disliked with a single-minded candour he could not have indulged in the case of an opponent. Earnest junior officials he found tedious, and this one perhaps more than most; and being himself without ambition he could afford to enjoy his own prejudices. He could not remember any phase of his life, from school onward, which had not, after the first eager, idealistic enthusiasm, caused him to recoil gradually into the same half-amused, half-rancorous revulsion from its hierarchies and its organisational meannesses. It never drove him fully into revolt,

143

because he could not really identify himself with the misfits and outcasts either, since they also had their pretences and their affectations; but on the whole he always preferred them to the well-adjusted. And everywhere, at school, in the R.A.F., and in Parliament, the spectacle of success had been sufficiently repulsive to him to absolve him from ever wanting it for himself. He was lucky to have money enough and family enough not to need it. He would have been the first to admit that had he been born without these aids it might have changed his attitude very considerably.

'Because he's a bigger hypocrite,' corrected the Under-Secretary hotly. 'He objects to using bombers in Kenya, he objects to crop-spraying in Malaya, he objects to turning loose Dyaks against the terrorists, he objects to napalm—he objects to any methods that may have any effect. But he doesn't object to the policy itself! If he does, he never says so.'

Even an Under-Secretary, reflected Crozier, with faint, surprised pleasure, occasionally makes an accurate observation; and for the first time he began to wonder in all seriousness what lay behind these incessant sniping attacks, since it was true that they limited their range always to the methods, and offered no alternative to the strategy. Only the more obvious barbarities of colonial warfare, apparently, offended the senses of Bill Dallas; he let the comprehensive barbarity of warfare itself pass unreproved. All weapons come much alike to a man with his mind set on killing; taking a grenade out of his hand and leaving him his machete isn't going to afford much comfort to the man whose head he eventually slices off with the latter. Yes, thought Crozier, yes, Bill Dallas, what is it that's got into you?

144

You used to be a pleasant, amenable sort of chap, willing to go along with the rest and believe that the big boys in front knew where they were taking you. Now, it seems, you've somehow got to hear about another world, of which you naturally also want the best. So much energy laid out in indignant questions, so much per cent of your bright future staked in Christian rage, buys—what? A quiet mind? Half-measures never buy that, but maybe that has to be learned by experience. A conscience at rest? It used to seem easy enough, up to this summer. What went wrong?

'His own front bench are getting moderately annoyed with him,' said the Under-Secretary with satisfaction. 'If he gets his knuckles rapped a time or two perhaps he'll draw in his horns a bit. Most of what we're doing they started themselves. What difference, for God's sake, does the size of the bomb-load make?' He wiped his lips, as if his own annoyance tasted bitter to him. 'And what, anyhow, *does* he want us to do? Patch up a makeshift sort of agreement in those pestilential places, and then get out? The really crazy ones stand up and say so, and we know where we are. But not Dallas—oh, no, he isn't as mad as all that! He wants us to stay there, and fight all his little battles out for him, and never budge an inch. But with both hands tied behind us! That's what I can't overlook—the total irresponsibility of it! He's setting out to make himself a high moral reputation at our expense, with his tongue in his cheek every minute of the time.'

'No,' said Crozier, putting down his tankard with a careful quietness, and spreading his elbows along the bar. 'No, it can't be that. If he thought that could be a shortcut to fame, and wanted it as much as that, he'd

145

have opened his campaign long ago. No, Bill was all the foreseen and the expected, he came in like a lion, and dwindled gradually into a lamb. They were getting him shrunk nicely to size, and he went along with them dutifully, and never even knew what was happening to him. He didn't reverse willingly—something turned him in his tracks like Saul, my boy, like Saul on the Damascus road, only, as far as I know, Saul never tried to strike a bargain with whatever it was that hit him.'

He lifted to his companion's affronted and suspicious face a long, dark countenance lit by surprisingly light silver-grey eyes. Clearly the argument from St Paul had seemed to the Under-Secretary in rather bad taste; it was to be expected that it would. He obligingly compressed the sum of his wisdom into a few words, impeccable in their functional appropriateness, something even a junior Minister could fold up and put into his pocket without distaste. 'Give him his head. Don't attempt to stop him. He won't go too far.'

That was all, and he devoted himself to his beer again with a directness which suggested that the oracle had closed for the night. The Under-Secretary did not know what to make of him, but there was nothing new about that; and the man knew his fellow-townsman well, appeared even to be reasonably friendly with him, so there might well be sense in his verdict, and it might be wise to act on it. Only privately did Crozier cultivate this aloof, eccentric neutrality; in the House he was a sound man enough, and of excellent judgment, and could have found favour easily had he cared to please. Better trust his discernment in this case, as often, though without trumpets or acknowledgments, in others.

Give Dallas his head, then! See how far he would go unchecked, and it would soon become clear whether he had that fiery morality of his well in hand. And if he had, and knew enough not to trespass too far, let him fight it out with his own leaders, against whom, handled well, he might easily provide useful ammunition. Score any effective points off him, leave the rest well alone, keep the heavy artillery out of it. That was the line to take.

'I suppose you'll be going to your constituency for that memorial service this weekend,' he said.

'I'm reading the Lessons.' A wry smile curled for an instant in the corners of Crozier's long and pensive mouth. It was the beginning of November, the recognised season for unveiling memorial plaques to celebrate the decimation of county regiments in heroic, pointless stupidities. A year ago the 4th Midshires had been sliced to pieces in Korea without giving ground, in the kind of action which is hailed as a victory in Britain, without respect to the preference heroic young men naturally have for living. This year a stone panel to commemorate the event would be unveiled at the annual Armistice service, with all the trimmings of bands, banners, uniformed veterans, jingling medals, the halt, the lame, the maimed and the blind, in St Michael's Parish Church at Caldington, with Ronald Crozier, M.P., to read the Lessons.

'He's got a speaking part, too, no doubt?'

'Practically star billing. He unveils it.'

'It? What is it? I haven't had time to catch up on the details.'

'A carved stone panel, showing, in a formalised modern style, guaranteed painless, three steadfast young men in a slit trench, waiting to be obliterated.

147

It was the winning design in a nationwide competition—it must be good. It has the additional rather unexpected Chinese merit of necessitating the removal from the block of—I should say—the scrupulous minimum of stone. But I'm not sure if that excellence in this case should be counted as artistic or functional. Are you having another?'

'I've got to get back to the House,' said the Under-Secretary, gathering up his briefcase. 'You'll be travelling down with him on Friday?'

'Don't you think we should? Peculiarly appropriate to the occasion if we made peace for two days.'

'A strictly non-party event, in fact,' said the Under-Secretary with a smile.

'Precisely!'

*   *   *

Edmund was in London for an interview, and had prolonged his stay at the town flat by a day, in order to travel back to Caldington with his father on the Friday afternoon. So they were five in the first-class compartment on the Midland express that day, Mr and Mrs Crozier, their daughter Stephanie, Dallas and Edmund. Invitations were being manipulated before they were half an hour out of London. Edmund saw that this was to be a thoroughly social weekend, and might have been disposed to regret it, but for the presence of Stephie. If she was to be of the party, the prospect of having the Croziers to dine at home tomorrow night, and dining with them at the Unicorn on Sunday, was one that he could face with equanimity.

Just now Stephie Crozier was changing at such an

alarming rate that meeting her after an interval of six weeks was like meeting an unknown young lady for the first time. The last encounter had been early in September, when he and his mother had snatched a belated weekend at Bournemouth, to remind them of summer holidays once again before the sun was lost, and had run into Mrs Crozier and Stephie on the beach. The mothers had sunned themselves in deck-chairs while the children had bathed; and that time Stephie had been a willowy nymph in a white one-piece bathing costume, with a skin of honey, and wet, brown, boylike hair, and a paler mask round her eyes, tilted upward at the outer corners, from the sun-glasses behind which she hid when she was out of the water. She had a mouth which was short and firm when she was serious, and large and animated when she laughed, which she did often and unaffectedly; and her body, which had never before bothered him in the slightest, had acquired, since his last glimpse of her, totally unexpected subtleties and felicities, like an amateur sketch which had suddenly and amazingly come out right. Edmund had found himself hurriedly reckoning up his own few graces, and rendering hasty but devout thanks that he still had his Adriatic tan.

Today she was quite another person, and a much more daunting one, the fashionable *jeune fille*, of a more than insular elegance, in a slender town suit and flowing, cape-collared coat of ice-blue cloth, with short hair arranged in carefully careless wisps over her forehead, and face immaculately painted about the centrepiece of a cherry-red mouth. She wore an expression of sophisticated boredom, through which her lively eyes glittered alertly upon everyone who came within their range, and upon Edmund longest

149

and most thoughtfully of all.

She was one month past her seventeenth birthday, and full of surprises. Edmund, installing her in a corner seat, procuring magazines for her, offering her a cigarette and then a light with all the assurance of his long practice on Ginnie, saw the changes time had achieved in her, but could not guess at the transformation she was finding in him. She had known him from a gangling boy of thirteen, and had been a little dazzled, to tell the truth, even by the russet-brown youth of the Bournemouth beach; but this composed young man of the world, in his best town suit and most chaste and aesthetic of ties and socks, with his lordly command over inanimate things like cigarette-cases, and luggage, and the awkward straps of train-windows, might have been a changeling for all the promise she had ever seen of him in Eddie Dallas. She allowed him to cut her off in a corner from the conversation of their elders; and she looked at him from under her arched eyelids when he was not observing her, and thought: 'After all, this might be quite fun!' She had her father's eyes, pale grey-blue, but brilliantly full and deep.

Edmund rather liked Mr Crozier, with the kind of easy liking for which one seldom troubles to find a reason. There was something nice about his bright, incalculable, fox-like looks, and his almost universal mockery, which seemed to be intact within itself, and never looking for or needing an audience. There was a niceness about his frank and disrespectful liking for his impressive wife, and his refusal at the same time even to attempt to live up to her. Beside Bill Dallas, of course, he looked rather dishevelled, but even his untidiness wandered off along an alley of its own, and instead of affecting long hair and corduroys, or caps

150

and well-worn tweeds, identified itself firmly by an expensive and well-cut suit worn with no respect whatever for its cut or its tailor. His womenfolk had grown used to him, and let him alone, barring an affectionately managing gesture now and again to remind him that they had rights, if they cared to demand them. And he teased them gently and distantly as he teased everyone, but never attempted to turn or alter them.

Mrs Crozier made up for her abdication of any control over him by manipulating everyone else who came within her reach, but her authority was so serene, and taken so simply for granted, that people were usually too obliging to resent it. In a few years, if Stephie's eyes and chin, those clear legacies from her father, were any indication, there might be a collision of wills in which time would no longer be on Mrs Crozier's side; but for the moment she made a throne of her corner seat, and distributed her attention like largesse, unchallenged.

Stephie and Edmund had been talking animatedly about films, about the almost forgotten holidays, about the London shows, about their respective futures. Stephie planned to spend one year, or perhaps two, in France to perfect her French, and then come back and teach it. Only for a while, probably; she had plenty of other plans, so many that the real difficulty was going to be to fit them all into one lifetime.

'You're going to be a doctor, aren't you?'

'Yes.' Edmund reached out and rapped with his knuckles at the wood of the window-frame, and looked up at her with an unabashed grin when she laughed.

'What's that for? Don't you believe in yourself?'

'Enough for all practical purposes,' said Edmund. 'But it might not depend on me.'

'What on earth do you mean by that? What's going to prevent you from doing what you want to do?'

'All sorts of things might. How do I know? I'm just not counting any chickens unhatched.'

'That's a defeatest attitude,' she said, her light eyes glittering; and for no good reason that she could see, she was glad to have this tiny point of conflict with him.

He laughed, kindling in his turn, and that also was pleasing to her. She would have been disappointed if he had been either annoyed or discomfited, even though she was trying her best to provoke him. He did not even offer her one more word of explanation, but only laughed and wrinkled his nose at her, and was silent.

'I wouldn't let anything stop *me* from doing what I set out to do,' she said, jutting her attractive chin at him, 'and neither would you if you were really sure of yourself. I'm going where I decide to go, whatever gets in the way.'

'Such as the French railway strike?' suggested Edmund remembering the five days of penniless wanderings she had herself described to him in September with so much thrilling detail.

'Who was *trying* to get past that, I'd like to know? If they'd struck when I was on my way out, you'd have seen whether I could beat the deal or not! But it was five extra days of holiday to me—and they had to find us some money to live on, so what fools we'd have been to batter our way through!'

'That wasn't the way you told it last time. Remember the queue at the consulate? Seven hours of it? Was that all in the plan, too?'

152

'It was worth it to have the extra time in France,' she said defiantly, 'and anyhow, it was fun, too. I was telling a good story when I made such an ordeal of it. Everybody's allowed to exaggerate a little in holiday stories. I bet your Yugoslav adventures got a trifle tall, too.'

But she was a real woman, she shifted her ground as soon as she felt herself to be on a losing field, and came back at him obliquely and treacherously with: 'I suppose your Socialist principles made you decide to be a doctor—you wanted to be useful to humanity.' And she opened her astonishing eyes at him with a joyous flash, waiting for him to flare into glee or indignation, and not greatly caring which.

'Hey, you!' said her father, detaching himself from a discussion with Dallas over *The Times*. 'You're infringing the terms of peace. Lay off Socialist principles—lay off all principles, if you know of any others, they're all equally dynamite.'

'All right,' she said obligingly, 'I'll put it another way. *What* made you decide to be a doctor?'

'I thought I might like it,' said Edmund meekly. 'And it's a safe sort of living—unemployment seldom hits the medical profession.'

'Especially now it's nationalised,' she said wickedly. 'And of course, you'll enjoy working for the Government.'

'Stephie!' It was her mother this time, reproachful but amused. 'Slap her, Edmund, if she keeps breaking the rules.'

'He doesn't need any help,' said Dallas. 'Let her go ahead, he might convert her.'

Edmund knew better than that. Even if he had been disposed to try, he would never have made any impression upon that wildly confident certainty she had that her father's side was the right side. What her father observed with detachment, and presumably on the whole accepted, she embraced wholeheartedly, and vaunted to the world. Edmund supposed that children must very often embarrass their parents rather painfully by believing too much too easily, and on the whole he thought that might be worse than having them parade too many and too aggressive doubts. But then, Stephie was made in so positive a mould that all her geese had of necessity to be swans.

He thought that if she were given her head he would very soon have to quarrel with her, and no longer playfully, and the quickening of his pulse at the thought felt curiously pleasurable to him. It was not that he could enjoy quarrelling for its own sake, but rather that in this case it probably represented a phase which would have to be accepted and survived, if they were ever to arrive at any closer understanding. He did not examine more exactly what he meant by that, it was something beckoning brightly but vaguely in the future, not to be meddled with yet, for fear of complicating the way to its attainment. He was not even sure that he believed in it as a possibility; but when he let himself imagine it for an instant his heartbeats quickened, and he felt the blood rise warmly in his cheeks.

'You'll be at the service on Sunday, of course,' said Stephie, going off at a bewildering tangent. 'Or don't you believe in celebrating the heroic virtues any more?'

'I believe in it all right,' said Edmund, 'if only I could be sure what they are.'

He was no longer quite certain that he was not trying to provoke the promised conflict, and get it over. She, of course, was always sure of everything, and knew a vice from a virtue and a sheep from a goat at the first glance.

'I honestly wondered. Your father seems to have developed a down on soldiers lately; he's always asking queer questions in the House, trying to make out that our troops are the villains of the piece, all over the world. I was rather surprised that he wanted to be involved in this business of unveiling memorial tablets to some of them—I thought maybe he'd think they were better forgotten.' The eyes of her elders were off her for the moment, and she was being careful to keep her voice low, and herself well withdrawn into her corner, so that Edmund had to lean attentively towards her to catch every word of what she said. But this time her puzzled indignation was real enough.

She had no qualms at all, she saw still an Empire of perfect benevolence, and generation after generation of chivalrous soldiers and selfless administrators, every one devoted, not one corrupt or venal, sustaining with uncomplaining fortitude the calumnies of envious men like Edmund's father. Plainly she was disappointed in Dallas; she had not thought him that kind of person, and would even be glad to clutch at any palliating explanation that Edmund might be able to offer. She fixed her half-hopeful and half-hostile gaze upon his face, and waited for him to defend his father with the same hasty heat with which she would have flown to the rescue of hers.

Edmund, his shoulders spread protectively between the girl and the disapproval, however tolerant, of her elders, sat looking down quite gravely into her face, his tawny brows drawn together into a

155

slight, thoughtful frown. In a voice as low as hers he said: 'Maybe he thinks they'd be better alive.'

'Oh, as if that's any answer! You might as well go all the way back through history, saying they ought all to have lived to be ninety. There always have been wars, and we've always fought them without any calculating about the length of life that's due to us, and there've always been men with the spirit to go into them gaily, and get killed if they had to, and not whine about it. And I think that's a good thing, and what's more, I don't think a few people like your father, with this new little fretful preoccupation with letting everyone live to old age, are going to change things much. Every time there's a need for them, the young men will still go—all the best of them!' she said in her passionate whisper, and with flashing eyes. 'I suppose you find that awful!'

'Not if that's what they want,' said Edmund. 'I'm not too sure, myself, that rushing head-down into a fight and getting yourself killed is the best and finest thing you can do for the world, but those who like to spend their savings that way, can, I suppose. What I don't like is that they're so keen to make the same decision for other people.'

She gaped up at him in a curiously young and vulnerable stupor of astonishment at his stupidity. 'But don't be silly! ... Do you suppose there's a country in the world now that can defend itself just with *volunteers*? How *childish*! Of course there'd never be enough of them!'

Edmund's small frown melted into silent and delighted laughter. She was so pretty and so fierce, and so splendidly, illogically feminine. He couldn't have thought of a finer answer if he'd been trying to make up a column of howlers for her father's party.

156

And at the glimmering eruption of his mirth she flushed angrily, affronted even before he spoke.

'A minute ago you said they'd always be there, ready to come forward whenever they were needed. You can't have it both ways. Which *do* you mean?'

'They *are* there,' she said, furious now at having to whisper. 'It's just that war's grown so wholesale, it's outgrown the natural soldiers, and involved everybody, whether they like it or not. And countries have still got to defend themselves, haven't they? They've got women and children to be looked after, they *have* to have armies. The only thing to do is to make everybody do his share. Are you against justice when it means everybody going into danger together?'

'I'm not against a fair distribution of the danger,' said Edmund, with a sudden, quiet violence, 'but events have taken care of that for us, not forgetting the babies, as the people of Coventry could tell you—or the people of Dresden, for that matter. But I'm against a man being forced into being a soldier when he *doesn't* think that's what he's for, and *doesn't* choose to spend his savings that way. I'm against his being forced into it by law, or by unemployment, or by feudal custom, or by any other mortal thing outside his own conscience and his own will. You asked me,' he said, staring back into her amazed and horrified eyes, and feeling her shaken by the sudden rigor of passion which had convulsed his body while his voice remained so quiet and restrained. 'I didn't want to talk about it. We'd better stop there.'

Stephie sat gazing at him in fascination and almost in disbelief, and her rage had flowered strangely into alien buds of unwilling concern for him, and

157

awareness of his unsuspected difficulties. She forgot the need they had both acknowledged for discretion, and said suddenly aloud, in a voice shocked into mildness: 'But you're due to register for service very soon.'

Edmund said: 'Yes.'

'What are you going to do?'

He understood her perfectly, and was grateful for this acknowledgment of the momentous nature of the decision that faced him. She could not have asked that, in that direct and respectful way, if she had not understood. He wanted to put out his hand, and shut it warmly upon hers in her lap, in the smooth folds of the ice-blue coat. He wanted to bend his head and kiss the soft, rounded lips which hung apart in dismay and wonder, forgetful of their austerely painted bow, and the fastidious composure they had rehearsed before the mirror. His heart leaped and burned with a sudden hot, gushing spring of exultation and tenderness. But the lift of their voices to a natural level had drawn the elders back into their world, and all he could do was answer her simply and truthfully:

'I don't know.'

'Yes,' said Ronald Crozier, taking up delicately the thread of this ambiguous exchange, 'what *are* you going to do, Edmund? What's your fancy? Bill's old service, or mine? Or haven't you thought about it yet?'

Edmund's face turned to him abruptly, still flushed from the sudden heat of his awareness of Stephie, his eyes brilliant to fever. The voice had a deliberation which suggested more than the words conveyed. They looked at each other for a moment intently.

'I hadn't much, as a matter of fact, up to now. I'm

158

thinking now, though.'

'But you haven't decided yet?'

'No, I haven't decided—not yet.'

Everything was double, everything ran on two levels, the look, the question, the answer. The light assumption that he was merely debating with himself what service he should choose, if a choice was allowed him, was for the benefit of Mrs Crozier and Edmund's own father. Crozier knew very well that there was more in it than that; he understood it so well that he could even pitch his own interjection in the same dual key, a casual, kindly enquiry on the surface, this deep, mysterious confrontation beneath it. Edmund looked warily at the others, to see if they had not caught the second echo which rang so clearly in his ears, but Mrs Crozier was smiling easily on him, with no disquiet or suspicion, and if his father's face expressed anything more than the proud self-consciousness even intelligent parents feel at seeing their offspring receiving the attentions of others, it certainly escaped Edmund's eyes. A slight possessive anxiety was there to be seen, perhaps; fathers are involved in their children, whether either party likes it or not. But the future was what might be done to his son, not at all because of any misgiving as to what his son might do.

'He has plenty of time to consider it,' he said quickly and confidently. 'By the time he's qualified, he'll know his own mind. And by then the Government may know theirs.' The note of jealousy was there, but it was not directed against Crozier, it was merely arching its back against the general uncertainty which plays dubiously with the fates of boys just becoming men.

'True!' said Crozier soothingly. 'Doctors are

159

valuable people.'

'Edmund will make a charming doctor,' said Mrs Crozier, a trifle patronisingly, but with benevolent intentions. 'His bedside manner will probably get him to Harley Street in no time.'

The tight little moment of danger was disintegrating into small-talk, and all the significant crossings of glances had disentangled themselves again, like a complex figure in a square dance sorting itself out without mishap. Edmund could turn back to Stephie now, with no more acknowledgment of her mother's pleasantry than a polite, perfunctory smile before he abandoned her.

He could not afford to waste any time, for the greyish autumnal fields of the South Midlands were sliding past the windows, and in an hour more they would be in Caldington. He had known Stephie, in a desultory way, for years, and never really seen her; and now she had suddenly let fall all her delicate, mannered masks, in the shock of seeing him truly for the first time, and shown him her own face ardent and angry and sympathetic, altogether the mirror of a woman. And all they had left of this momentous journey was one hour! He shook from his shoulders all thought of his father's natural anxiety and her father's unnatural penetration. He wanted to forget everyone but Stephie.

Every man hopes for understanding, and she had checked her high, self-confident rage in respect for his perplexities, and looked at him with friendliness and concern tempering her hostility. He had at least a little ground for optimism, besides the simple fact that he was a natural optimist. He leaned forward once again to cut her off from her elders, and she lifted to him a face still doubtful and angry with thought, and said in a low but obstinate voice, for fear he should have misunderstood her restraint:

'*Patriots* are important people, too—to me.'

He smiled, but in his heart he knew then that as far as she was concerned there would never be more than one right attitude upon that point, and in the same moment he was a step nearer the realisation that he would never share it.

'All right, let's leave it at that. I told you, I haven't made up my mind yet.'

Crozier sat back thoughtfully in his corner, considering with detached curiosity the back of the boy's head, the wide shoulders flattened resolutely against any further interruption of this precarious little idyll. He thought: 'Yes, that could explain the propitiatory fervour—why didn't I think of it before? He has a hostage to buy back!'

Well, there was nothing new about that. Many an influential father had edged his boy quietly out of the draft under cover of a cloud of humanitarian concern for those whose fathers had no such influence. Yet it was not entirely satisfactory as an explanation of Dallas's crusading frenzy. The boy was in it, yes, most certainly, in it at the heart, but it appeared that he was not alone there. Dallas's conscientious qualms were such that Edmund alone could not account for them.

Fathers of prospective conscripts naturally set their faces against conscription, and become indignantly vocal about the denial of the individual's right of choice, and may very well keep up the outcry just as violently while they are taking advantage for their own of all the available means of evasion. Do they also grow passionate against the oppressions and injustices of which the less lucky young are made

161

the instruments? Only the excesses, mark you, not the policy! On the principle of: 'If a man ask thee to go with him two miles, go with him one, and hope to be let off the second.' As if an avenging spirit were hard on his heels, demanding the allegiance of the father or the sacrifice of the son, and Dallas hoped by these half-services, by this half-acceptance of his fate, to placate the demon and keep both his son and the better part of his career, too.

Parents forget, he reflected, looking from his own daughter to the other man's son, that their children are also people. There was more in the affair than the anxious father suspected. Crozier himself did not understand it yet, though he had caught a momentary glimpse of it in the double meanings of that pregnant brief exchange between the young people. What he had seen was the beginning of a journey, but he could not judge the road it would take, nor how far the pilgrim would pursue it. All he was sure of as yet was that Dallas might find he had lost his hostage by recovering him, just as surely as by letting him go unredeemed.

*   *   *

The bills announcing the Memorial Service, large and striking in red and black, with a cross and a wreath of poppies, were scattered about the shop-windows of Caldington almost as thickly as advertisements for rival detergents. It was impossible to walk through the streets without being brought face to face with one of them, and confronted, as in a magic mirror, with the challenging spectre of your own frivolity.

Renie Pollard, strolling home through Market
162

Street on the arm of her new young man, dragged him to a halt to look at the dance frocks displayed in Harpers' window, and found herself staring at the cross and the encircling poppies, affixed at eye-level upon the plate glass. The iridescent beetle-greens and burning-coppers of the latest taffetas were dulled for her, as though ashes had been thrown over them. She allowed herself to be detached from them at the first tentative urging of Chris Blakeway's arm, and as they threaded the High Street she sank into an unwonted silence and thoughtfulness.

'What's up with you tonight?' asked Chris, giving her an experimental shake as they reached the end of the lighted shops.

'Nothing! What should be up with me?'

'What's come to your tongue, then? Can't hardly get a word out of you to save my life. Have I done something to you?'

'No, course you haven't! Can't I think sometimes, if I want to?'

'You ought to sound your horn, or something,' he said, bluntly and cheerfully. 'We ain't used to it.'

She smiled, not without pride, for his robust self-confidence gave her considerable pleasure. He was a good-looking youth, a farm-worker from one of the big dairy-farms outside Caldington, and he knew his job, his own mind, and how to get on with girls. He had been after Renie Pollard ever since the death of her former boy-friend had left her free, and he had bided his time like a decent fellow, wanting no unfair dealings with either her or her bereavement. She was alive, wasn't she? Some time she'd need to look round her and see him, and he wanted her to like what she saw of her own free will, and not because it filled up the unbearable gap left by Jack Parrish. This was the

163

third time he'd been out with her, and three times makes the connection respectable. Give him a week or two longer, and he'd be in the house, and on the right side of her mother. He was doing nobody any wrong, nor was she. The other poor devil couldn't have her now, and she wasn't meant to live on her memories.

'Chris,' said Renie, in a small and solemn voice, 'I don't think I want to go to the pictures tomorrow night, after all.'

'All right,' he said obligingly, 'if you don't want to see it, I don't mind. What d'you fancy instead?'

'I don't think I'll come out at all, Chris—not this weekend, if you don't mind.'

He walked beside her for a moment in concerned silence, and then he asked practically: 'Are you going to tell me why? You promised me tomorrow night yourself. Is it something I've done?'

'No, I keep telling you! You're ever so nice, Chris, and I'm ever so fond of you. Only I don't feel like going out dancing, or to cinemas—not this weekend. It's because of that memorial service for the Midshires,' she said, raising her grave, fair face to look him in the eyes. 'I'm going to church!'

He almost opened his mouth to say outright that that was on Sunday, and that if going to the pictures with him was a sin on the eve of her one rare visit to church, it was a sin, anyhow; but he remembered that logic was not for women, and was magnanimous enough to allow her the innocent hypocrisies which did no one any harm. His disappointment was genuine, his position with her not yet quite safe, but he knew how to gamble intelligently, for he was an unusually able young man.

He said, in a voice as serious as hers: 'You won't

164

want me to go with you? I will, if you say the word.'

'Well—no, I don't think you'd better. It's awfully sweet of you, Chris, really. I knew you'd understand.'

'I suppose I couldn't just come along and be with you for an hour or so tomorrow evening, either? Just in the house—I wouldn't ask you to go out. No—forget it!' he said with a sigh. 'I see it wouldn't be the same. All right, I'll let you alone. The whole weekend!' he said ruefully. 'I don't know how I'm going to get through it, I tell you straight I don't!'

'I'm sorry, Chris!—Honest, I am!' she said, hugging his thick young arm in a transport of appreciation and sympathy. 'But I *owe* it to him. It's all I can do for him, now. You do understand, don't you?'

They had reached the darkness of a half-lit new road, and between the inadequate lamps the high hawthorn hedges shadowed them. Their walk slowed, they swung inward breast to breast.

'I understand all right, lass. You go, and I won't get in your way.' He put his arms round her with brusque gentleness, and kissed her in a manner which began as brotherly, and ended, after the passing of seconds, in white-hot ardour, as though the experience had over-taken them both unwittingly. 'No,' he thought contentedly, releasing her slowly from his arms, 'I won't get in your way—much! You forget that in a weekend, if you can!'

'I could see you on Monday,' said Renie faintly, 'if you like—I mean, seeing as I promised you tomorrow, and now I'm letting you down...'

Chris took her home with no more halts, well content with the establishment of his case. Let her have her two days of retreat, let her get that black suit of hers out and clean the collar and cuffs with lighter

165

fuel, and iron her plain white blouse, and get herself up for the last time like a little widow. Let her work all that nonsense of tragedy and romance out of her system in one glorious orgy, and after that she'd be satisfied to get back to the comfortable, solid pleasures of everyday, with a man alive. Jack Parrish, Chris thought, would be glad, if he could see what was going on, to know that she wouldn't be wasting her life mourning over him.

Renie did exactly what he had imagined her doing. The black suit had been undisturbed on its hanger for over a month, but she fetched it out from the wardrobe on Saturday afternoon, and brushed it well, and sponged the few shiny places, and pressed it with a hot iron and a damp cloth, and left it dangling near the kitchen fire to air. The original hat, with an eye-veil, had lost its charm for her now that she looked at it again after so long an interval; she decided to wear her new, plain black beret instead, the one that sat flat as a pancake on the top of her upswept blonde hair. The effect would be at once less worldly and more becoming.

Early in the evening she went round to Hogarth Terrace. The town band was practising in the Methodist school-room when she passed, the flag was already flying on top of the tower of St Michael's when it swam into her sight at the end of the long vista of Glebe Street, and it seemed to her that the whole town, with solemn countenance and bated breath, was moving intently towards the morrow's homage.

Mrs Parrish had cleared the table, and with her little hand sewing-machine almost swamped in waves of white twill, was turning a sheet sides to middle. From the pictures on the wall Jack looked into

166

Renie's eyes, wary and distrustful, the light of the kitchen fire reflected in flickering glimpses from the glass in the region of his forehead. Renie looked back at him steadily, lifting her head with that dedicated look that Mrs Parrish had not seen for several weeks now. She recognised it, and guessed at its source. It did not surprise her, or offend her; she felt no impatience with it. People had to live as best they could, helping themselves along by holding fast to this solidity and that as they reached them, and letting go of what was passed. She did not clutch hold of memorial services much herself, but then, her needs were different. She smoothed away at the corners of her lips the shadow of the tolerant smile she had suppressed for Renie's sake.

'Hullo, Renie! Nice of you to come and see us! Sit down there by the fire. Dad's in the parlour—he'll be in as soon as he hears your voice.'

They did not see her very often now, which made it easier to guess what had brought her on this occasion. Mrs Parrish knew all about young Chris Blakeway, and felt relieved and pleased about him, as though she were getting a difficult daughter off her hands. She was serenely sure that he knew how to play his hand; this lapse into the old devotional solemnity would not daunt him.

Tom came in from the parlour, carrying in his hand the little inlaid box that held his medals. He kissed Renie, as he had always been used to do after he once became reconciled to Jack's bringing a girl home at all; and seeing them there thus, mouth to mouth, was like seeing a piece of the past cut out and presented afresh, out of context. It was like trying to recreate a pattern of which the main piece has been lost. It made the emptiness ache again in Mrs

167

Parrish's heart.

'Hullo, girl, how've you been?' He tipped out the contents of the box upon a corner of the table, clear of the waves of sheeting, and began to tell the medals one by one through his hands, a rosary without a religion. 'It's been a long time since I thought about these things. I missed the last few parade services— thought I was getting too old for these capers. But I think I shall turn out tomorrow afternoon.'

He had thought of nothing else for ten or eleven days, his eyes fixed upon the solemn occasion with a daily increasing ardour. For years he had been getting slack about turning out on Armistice parades; old fellows begin to think the day for that sort of thing's over, in a changing world like this. Then another generation turns and looks back in going, and the eyes recall them to their duty in a world which has not changed at all, in which young men die for the same patriotisms, the same ideals of freedom and chivalry, as they did when the old men were young. He owed it to his boy to turn out among the veterans, to show his breastful of medals with the best, to remind them all that he had a personal stake in this sad but splendid ceremonial.

He told the medals through his fingers, lovingly polishing them into brightness with the ball of his thumb and the sleeve of his second-best jacket. 'That's the Mons Star. Ever seen it before? There's not so many of us left now with that, you know. And this is from First Ypres—I'm proud of that, too. I well remember that town—smashed to bits, it was. Talk of the blitz, the blitz never did no worse to any town than shells did to Ypres—'

The girl accepted each little star and disc of metal from him reverently, holding her breath at their

168

holiness, devouring their boasts and flourishes with her large eyes, worshipping at the same shrine with him. From the wall the boy stared over their heads, sceptical, silent and afraid, containing his monstrous doubt until it should be knowledge, trusting no one, believing nothing.

'I'd like to come to the service with *you*,' said Renie, looking up at Mrs Parrish over a handful of glory, 'if you wouldn't mind. My people will be coming, I expect, but if I could sit with you—because of Jack! I'd like it! I know Mr Parrish will be in the parade, but you'll be going, too, and we could go together.'

Mr Parrish said heartily. 'You know, girl she'll be glad to have you with her, a day like that. It isn't every girl who'd have thought about it.'

'Well, I'm proud of him, too; I'd like to be with his mother, I would really.'

Mrs Parrish had said nothing. Her hollow-cheeked face with its crooked, humorous mouth and fine, commanding eyes was gazing at them thoughtfully above the sewing-machine, and her hands lay still in the folds of the sheet. It amazed her, though she did not look amazed, that it should never occur to either of them to suppose that Jack Parrish's mother might prefer not to attend his canonisation. But since they took everything so peacefully for granted, she could not feel that this was the time to argue out the case. They were perfectly happy in identifying her with their fervour, and it was no part of her duty to shatter their happiness in order to establish her own honesty. That could take care of itself, one way or another. So she merely smiled reassuringly at Renie, and said affectionately that she was a good girl. She meant every word of it. Chris Blakeway was doing well for

169

himself, and good luck to him.

'I'll come for you about a quarter to two,' said Renie earnestly, 'then we can be at the church in plenty of time to watch the parade, and if we slip into church a little bit before the band stops playing we ought to get a good seat, close to the stone, because most people won't want to go in until the parade ends.' She was beginning to glow with pleasurable anticipation, though remembered sadness clouded her eyes still; for in Renie joy and sorrow were exquisitely reconciled. 'Have you seen the stone? I do want to see it, they say it's ever so fine.'

The innocent words lingered in Mrs Parrish's ears long after Renie had gone home; into the dusk and the dark she was still recalling the urgent, serious, kind little voice exclaiming that the stone was ever so fine. It ought to be, she thought, it's the sole payment for God knows how many lives, for all the years of experience they missed, and all the things they might have done for the world. And we're expected to be content with it! And the strange thing is, that people *will* be content. Nobody's going to get up and say: 'Is *that* all? It's a swindle. We've all been cheated!' No one. Not even me, she thought with finality. Why is that? Is it because we know, at the bottom of it all, what nobody ever says, that we who are cheated helped to do the cheating? All that way round in search of the truth, to come up against a mirror in the end? And after that, what? After that, one might well be silent, and leave off searching for what was already found.

When he had sorted all his medals, and brushed his bowler hat and his black suit, and left all ready for the next day, Tom went out for his usual Saturday pint, and because everyone at the local would be discussing the band music for next day, or the hymns, or the ex-officers who would be taking the parade, with much professional detail in the case of all three subjects, she knew he would not come home until closing time. Normally the drink was only the excuse for a little trip into pleasant company, a half-hour of exercise, maybe a game of darts; but tonight it was serious business.

The house felt very lonely to her without him. Towards nine o'clock she put on her hat and coat, and went out into the town. The wind was cool but not yet cold, the shop-windows were lit, and the pavements populous with the coupled young. The tower of St Michael's was floodlit, she could see its single grey turret glowing against the night sky, and the flag in calm and elegant motion in the wind above it. Beyond the tower the more frequent trees of the residential side of town arched gleaming gilded heads in the light.

It looked a gracious and dignified place, this Caldington. She walked with her head up, for the pleasure of watching it; and when she came to the lane which turned in towards the nearest gate of the churchyard, she turned with it. She wanted to see the stone which was said to be so fine, the charm which was to lay so many unquiet ghosts. In her heart she suspected already that she would not be there to see it at the unveiling.

Imagine, she thought, as she pushed open the heavy door and looked into the vast obscurity of the nave, entering a competition for a design in stone to commemorate the deaths of hundreds of young men, in a war they never properly understood—for who did? Who had even troubled to investigate it very closely?—in a battle grossly mismanaged, and

171

conducted apparently wantonly, while discussions about making peace were actually hanging fire for want of goodwill upon either side! As if anybody could ever hope to get all that into one piece of stone, about one foot by two! As if anyone with more imaginative insight than—say—the generals who had made the battle, would have the temerity to try! Yes, it would be worth seeing, the prize-winning entry in a contest like that. A pure, cold curiosity possessed her, the analyst's curiosity, willing to take things irreparably apart in order to perfect her knowledge of them. It was a stranger in her mind, yet she felt at ease with it, as if it had always been with her. Perhaps, after all, the ambitious young man who had made the stone was not quite a human creature—not a whole one. Or perhaps he was old, and had atrophied with years. Either way, he must surely be incomplete.

The church was lit by only one small hanging light in the centre of the nave, and the candles in the sanctuary. Its lofty roof soared into a sky-like darkness, and all its corners retreated into deep shadow. The candles wavered as the door closed softly behind her, and their shuddering light, flung upward along the tormented lines of the Rector's German crucifix, caused the body on the cross to writhe and start. The arched and staring ribs, the labouring muscles of the belly, the thighs, the arms, all heaved and strained momentarily in an anguish of light and shadow, and then relaxed into a stillness not of death, but of endurance. The crossed feet, half worn away, thrust downward upon the nail, so that for an instant he seemed very near, almost within touch if she stretched out her hand. Then he was only a little image, a long way off upon the altar, and the

172

church was too big and too cold for comfort.

The stone was set into the left-hand wall of the nave, perhaps two-thirds of the way along towards the chancel. There was no missing it, because a square yard of the wall there was draped in a large Union Jack and the colours of the 4th Midshires, with a knot of artificial poppies holding the folds in place at the top. Two pews had been closed off with a red silk cord to allow access to the stone for the unveiling, but there was a young man standing by the wall now with the folds of the flags raised in both hands, and his head and shoulders inclined to the left to allow the light from the single lamp to play upon what he saw. The cord had not kept him out, nor was there in his attitude anything of that furtively humble manner most people feel compelled to assume as soon as they enter a church. His face was in shadow, but the steady, critical attention he was giving to the stone was implicit in the very set of his head and the sweep of his spread arms. He did not hear Mrs Parrish come in. Her feet made no sound upon the matting of the aisle, and she closed the door very softly, unwilling to disturb his intent scrutiny.

Then, for no reason, he turned and looked at her, letting the drapings of the stone fall back into place. His head went up and his brows drew a little together, and then as abruptly unloosed their attentive knot, and he smiled. The broad, fair forehead smoothed, the eyes widened, caught the light, and flashed bluely. It was amazing how much positive colour they had, and how it manifested itself even here, where almost everything was grey.

'Good evening!' he said.

His voice sounded very clear and quiet at that distance, and rang a soft, solemn echo from the far

173

crannies of the roof. The completeness of his recognition of her was all in that greeting, and she knew that if he did not add her name it was not because he had forgotten it, but rather because they were already too close for that. The intimacy of the smile and the quick brightening of his eyes would have been marred by a name. He dropped his hands, and stood facing her, smiling, waiting for her to join him.

Mrs Parrish said: 'Good evening!' with equal gladness and gravity, and went to him directly. The red cord was linked across the pews by the bosses which decorated their ends; she lifted it aside, and closed it again after her like a gate, and crossed to the wall the faint, hollow sound of her footsteps upon wood suddenly large in the silence.

'Did you come just to look at this, too?'

'Your father's going to unveil it, isn't he?' she said gently. 'You'd have seen it then.'

'I know. I don't know why I had to come in now. I was just on my way home from the Unicorn, and I took the short cut through here—I can go out by the wicket gate in the back wall, you know, and it saves going quite a long way round. And when I was here, I suddenly thought I'd like to see exactly what he is going to unveil.'

He had been escorting Stephie back to the Unicorn; her parents had left earlier in the evening, for Crozier had local business to get through during the weekend, and his wife could not imagine him dealing adequately with agents and local officials without her moral influence to stiffen him. But Stephie had stayed, and since Ginnie had thoughtlessly run the car out of petrol he had been able to suggest that they should walk back into town.

174

They had not taken any short cuts then, but by mutual consent had selected the pleasantest and longest ways, all through the ghostly unlit alleys of the park, on the sodden layers of leaves, talking and laughing ardently all the way; arm-in-arm, hip-to-hip, he curbing his step, she lengthening hers. It was a thrilling but precarious proximity they had felt together, needing every moment the intent and exhausting care an abnormal child demands of its parents. On his way home in the darkness, alone, he had found himself only too aware of the dangers and despairs implicit in it among the exhilaration and joy. It made him happy, but it frightened him, too; it was new to him that the two could go together.

'What's it like?' asked Mrs Parrish, watching his face instead of looking at the stone. For he was a real, a live young man, not yet despoiled.

'I don't know.' He took hold of the draped flags again, and parted them firmly; then with a glance which she interpreted at once, as if she had been conversing with him in silence for years, surrendered the nearer one to her. They stood back to let in the faint light to the stone, and looked at it together. His frown had come back; it was partly perplexity and partly a positive conviction that something was wrong.

The panel showed three young men in a carefully anonymous uniform, crouching in a shallow trench. The background of geometrical hills was drawn in with a few severe lines. The man on the right was upright upon one knee, levelling a sub-machine-gun, the second kneeling lower beside him, the third lying forward upon his rifle. They had the over-simplification of all heroic monuments, the large, squared shoulders, the monolithic throats and heads

175

of antique sculpture, and faces of gods, with broad cheekbones, full, squared, final mouths, and great formalised eye-sockets under down-drawn brows. In the sockets were nothing but oval stones; the bodies were stones, and immovable.

'Do you like it?' asked Mrs Parrish.

'No,' he said, with a mildness beyond all appeal.

'Why not?'

'They're not people. They're rocks. They don't really see anything coming to them. The eyebrows are made as if the eyes should be looking right into the distance, but they're not really looking anywhere at all. They wouldn't see if they did. They're quite blank.'

It was true that nowhere in these three creatures was there any sign of awareness or intelligence. The blank, beautiful face of non-identity was in its way a truth; it was what they had made of Jack, among many others.

'I know nothing about sculpture,' said Mrs Parrish. 'I daresay this is just to fit in with a fashion.'

'No, he meant it to be like that. Rocks, not people. So that everybody should think of them like that, and feel quite good about it. To make it seem that they weren't afraid, and didn't suffer. But of course, they did.'

She was silent, because it seemed to her imperative that she should not prompt him. He turned his head, and looked at her gravely. 'This isn't what you wanted.' It was not a question; he was quite sure of her.

'No. But it's nothing to me. I only wanted to see if it was what I expected.'

'I didn't have any ideas about it. But you can see why it won. It makes it all right, for everybody.' He

176

drew together the folds of the flags again, scrupulously settling them as he had found them, and it was rather as if he had buried the heroes in the gesture, once for all. They had not made it all right for him.

'What *should* we have done for them?' he asked.

'Nothing. It's too late for that. We should have kept quiet. They may have something to be proud of. We haven't.'

He leaned his large young hands upon the back of the pew between them, and let his weight lie forward upon them until the edges of the spread fingers looked white. Without any desperation or any appeal he said slowly: 'I don't know what to do.'

She waited, and was silent; and in a moment he looked up into her face, and his opening brows shed their habitual little frown of thought, and his eyelids rolled back widely until the light found that startling blue of his eyes again. 'I've thought about asking people—different people. When you came in tonight, I thought of asking you.'

'I shouldn't be able to tell you,' she said. 'Nobody could.'

'No—I've realised that. But I thought that perhaps—without actually setting out to tell me, without knowing anything about it—somebody might give me a sort of sign.'

'They might,' she said.

She wanted to tell him not to rely on it, but she stopped herself in time, because she saw that even that necessity he would have to discover for himself.

He stirred and sighed. 'Oh, well ... I shall have to go home. It's getting pretty late, isn't it?'

They left the church together, he punctiliously steadying the heavy door for her, and letting it roll

177

back gently into place after them. To the corner of the grey, buttressed wall their paths lay together, then separated; hers leading back to the town and the modest back-streets, his to the dignified suburban roads of the residential district, and the shrubberies, and the park.

Before them, as they left the darkness of the porch, the rectory lay, one end of the house quite near, and the churchyard wall running away from it on either side in grey of stone and black of ivy. There was one lit window on the ground floor, the curtains undrawn, and the long shaft of light probing the night above the graves. Edmund walked into it, and there upon impulse halted, looking along the spear of radiance full into the window, with the inspired curiosity of a child, since he did not expect anyone to be paying any attention to him.

They were now at the corner of the church, where the ways divided, and Mrs Parrish halted, too, one step already taken upon her own path. The light did not reach the spot where she stood. She watched Edmund's brows draw down protectively, the eyes narrow to stare into brightness; she saw all the lines of his face grow sharp and clear, shining abruptly out of the shadowy air.

Into the window she did not look at all. There was a man sitting there, deep within the room, but Edmund saw him clearly. He was sitting at a table, with his hands linked before him, and staring straight into Edmund's eyes, and even at that distance the light bound them together so significantly that for a long minute neither of them could drag his gaze away. Then the Rector jumped up from his chair and took a few quick steps towards the uncurtained window, and Edmund, released by the movement,
178

and deeply mortified at being caught out in such a lapse, sprang aside out of the light and, with a hurried 'Good night!' to Mrs Parrish, fled along the path to the wicket gate.

He could only suppose that Mr Faulkner had advanced upon the window in annoyance, to rebuke his thoughtless impudence by drawing the curtains, and he did not want to see the snub delivered, even if he had incurred it fairly. His cheeks were burning already at the thought of it. Thank goodness the encounter had been too brief and distant for him to be identified! He let himself out by the gate under the knot of trees at the churchyard's end, and made for home at his fastest walk, never once looking back.

*   *   *

He sat with the sheets of his sermon neatly aligned upon the blotter before him, with his linked hands held hard down upon them, as though he were restraining the matter in those few thousand words from rising and taking possession of his mind. He was afraid of relaxing the steel grip he had upon his own intellect, for fear some other power should seize the initiative from him.

The words were good words. He had lived a long time, he knew the right words for every occasion, the right response to every challenge. They were good words. Why should not a man eulogise physical courage and personal sacrifice? There was nothing false about the words, for he knew the things the young men had done one for another, there in the stained and scorched and honeycombed hills of that afflicted country. All the world knew the incredible, the fabulous acts they had performed, the terrible

179

heroisms men achieve when the hope of life has left them, when they have already ceased to live except in a thousand lives, each one agonising instant long, flowing one after another to a thousand deaths.

Had he ever denied, was he denying now, that the courage and the self-sacrifice of which they were capable had often been abused by cynical misdirection, and cruelly spent in unworthy and mistaken causes? Had he said, had he dared to say, that this had not happened to them? Was he praising their splendour, or the misuse that had been made of it?

What is a lie? he thought. Is this a lie, that they were heroes? What else have I tried to say, that they should open their silent and unwavering eyes inside my heart, and with those eyes as silently reject me?

He knew what it would be like, he had conducted dozens of Remembrance Day services in his time and this was only the same thing with a more grievous urgency. If only the soldier with the always changing face would go away from the threshold, or close his patient and unsatisfied eyes, and die within the mind as he had died in the flesh, all those thousands of miles from home!

He had read his sermon through, beginning briskly, intent to span it and keep firm hold of reality, so that there should be nothing to fear. But he was afraid. Oh, my God, I fear Thee! Do I? As much as I fear the raised eyebrows and the polite astonishment of my fellow-men? I do not want to be a Christian martyr! In particular I do not want to be a Christian martyr in the worst of taste, disrupting with incongruous moral rage a civic occasion of such solemnity as this, hurting the feelings of the innocents who believe absolutely in what they are celebrating,

180

and clawing away the rags from the nakedness of those who are intent to persuade themselves that they believe. What is required of me, God? I am perplexed. If this is not what I ought to say, then I do not even know what I should put in its place.

How can it be right to take away people's faith from them, and leave them to starve? What else should I be doing, if I attacked their conviction that this was good, and well done? And was it not done well? Do the evils that crept into the holy war utterly damn it, with all its believers?

He was staring through the window all the time that he sat there, his hands numbed with the force of the pressure they used to hold the dead men down in their graves. Beyond his undrawn curtains the lane of light sprang across the churchyard, leaping the grey stones and the green mounds and the low white curbs, and touched the wall of the church. He had meant only to read his work through, put it back into its drawer, and go back to his wife and daughters beside the sitting-room fire; a matter of fifteen minutes, perhaps. He had been sitting here now for half an hour, and had no power to rise and go, because there was no answer, and no one to give any answer except himself. He stared before him along the lane of light, and saw nothing because his eyes were focused far beyond the stones of the church wall; and when he became conscious of the young man, he had no idea of how long he had been standing there.

He was at the curve of the path, standing perfectly still in the narrow channel of light, his face raised, a tall young man in a dark overcoat. The light which spread and diffused between them gathered again radiantly into the bright planes of the uplifted

181

forehead and the fine cheekbones, and outlined violently the full, firm length of a youthful mouth and the rounded jut of the strong chin below it. The colour of the eyes he could not hope to see, but he saw their brilliance, and received from them a sensation of ever-strengthening light, and it was at them and into them that he found himself looking when the awareness of the apparition first transfixed his heart.

The tall, slender form did not withdraw into the darkest place this time, the face did not evade him with changing, melting features of shadow and anonymity, the eyes were not veiled; they opened wide to him, wide as the night, he was lost in their immense, aloof, calm and intent regard. But he had only a man's eyes, subject to distance and illusion, he could not read the face now that it lay open to him, he still did not know whether he was damned. Only across the dark churchyard and in silence would the angel speak to him.

He jumped to his feet, and in haste and agony sprang to the window. He meant to call out, and he could not speak. But by the time his face was close to the glass and his hand at the sash, the space of light by the church wall was empty, the visitant vanished.

All the time he knew in his heart that this was a man, like other young men except that the hand of God had brought him again with purpose, and with purpose moved him to depart. Nothing absolved him from the laws of gravity and space and time. He had been there, and at the movement to arrest him he had taken flight, and whatever his haste now, haste could overtake him. The Rector threw open the door of his study, and ran down the corridor to the garden-room, and out into the moist, mild coolness of the night. There was a door which led from the garden

182

into the churchyard, and a mere thread of a path brought him stumbling between the graves to the corner of the church.

There was someone standing there still, but in the darkness now, close to the buttress of the wall. He felt rather than saw the figure, motionless, shadow among shadows. He slowed his pace to a steady walk, coming out of the night with held breath and bounding heart. He was filled with an exquisite sense of relief and joy, because God had not abandoned him, after all, and the dread which was one with his joy did not mar it. Thus in fear and ardour believers approach revelation.

He did not know what he was going to say to this angel who was nonetheless a man and a stranger, but he knew that if he could only meet him inescapably at last the words would come to him, and that they would be the right words. He trusted the hour, because he was sick with the need. To be reassured, to see at last not only the light in the eyes, but their acceptance of him, to know that he had done all that was required of him, and that no extreme sacrifice, no exile into the wilderness, was demanded of him now!

He went forward slowly, and his foot touched for the first time the gravel of the path. The figure in the shadows moved, turning its head to look at him, and there grew out of the darkness before his eyes, silent and motionless between him and the way which the young man had taken, the form of a woman. A middle-aged woman in a shabby black coat and hat, a thin woman with a worn and wonderful face, and large, neutral, confounding eyes. Even in the dark he knew her, and felt the shock of superstitious fear turn the air of the night suddenly cold about him. He could not pass her. She stood in the centre of the way, gazing at him steadily, knowing him through and through, and her eyes between him and the fugitive angel were barrier enough. He thought for an instant, with despairing anger: 'She has no right to keep me from him—*he* is not her son.' And fierce upon the heels of that thought, the answer: 'But of course—they are all her sons.'

'Good night!' said Mrs Parrish, as mildly as one says it to an innocent stranger passing in the darkness of the street.

'Good night!' he said, averting his eyes from her; and hastening his steps, slipped away from her and went into the church.

CHAPTER SEVEN

THE BLOOD-SACRIFICE

The great day began with a grey and rainy morning, but by noon the clouds had broken, the last shower faded into a faint but indubitable rainbow, and the sun came out upon the watery streets. All the puddles changed to silver, and cast back into the shining air scarlet and blue reflections of poppies and sky, as the parade of ex-soldiers gathered in the square. The air of Caldington rang with martial music. The band of the Second Midshires played for the parade, and the town band for the procession of the Mayor and Corporation. The Boy Scouts and Wolf Cubs, proceeding independently from their club hut on the edge of the recreation ground, made their own shrill, brisk noise with bugles and drums, and needed no other announcement of their approach.

Inside St Michael's almost all the pews in the front half of the church were marked 'Reserved', or corded off like the two which led to the memorial stone under its solemn drapings. First there were all the civic dignitaries to be seated, right in front, together with the two Members of Parliament and their families. Then the borough officials, the local magistrates and several other distinguished guests, the ex-servicemen from the parade, the officers of two or three Friendly Societies, and the Women's Branch of the British Legion. The Scouts and Cubs, the Girl Guides and Brownies, were banished to the back of the church, and the deafening company of the town band, which was accommodated on chairs in the porch of the west door.

After all these important people had been accounted for, the rest of the seats were open to the general public, and in spite of Renie's intelligent guessing, large numbers of people had preferred to sacrifice even the spectacle of the parade, rather than risk not getting a seat. There had not been so much competition for a place in church in the two years Charles Faulkner had been in the parish. By the time the regimental band had played the parade to its impressive dismissal outside the lich-gate, and the town band inside had begun a muted voluntary for the civic procession, the ushers were placing single chairs at the end of all the rear pews, and packing the Sunday-school children into the dusty gallery alongside the organ-loft.

The Mayor led the advance up the aisle, his unaccustomed feet stepping out of time to the music in a crisp, impervious syncopation. Dallas and Crozier followed him sedately, shoulder to shoulder in civic solidarity. Their families were apparently held to be inseparable from them, for they found themselves ushered into the same august front pew, immediately behind the seat which would presently be occupied by the lady members of the choir.

Edmund had been prepared, even rather anxious, to take a back seat, but fate had allotted him the middle place in the pew, between his mother and the Mayor. He felt conspicuous, though he was seldom troubled by any such consciousness; and the slight discomfort, and his resentment of it, had given his face an unusual severity, and his movements an exaggerated fastidiousness and arrogance, austere and precise as a cat's, as though he were trying to appear extremely sophisticated. Ginnie noticed it, as she noticed everything about him at all times, and as usual misinterpreted it happily; she thought that he was very much moved by the solemnity of the occasion, and adored his charming, childlike appropriateness. She considered that it was his father's earnest adaptability coming out in him.

Well, at any rate there was plenty of knee-room, he thought approvingly; even legs the length of his could feel at home in St Michael's Church. He settled himself with deliberation, slid to his knees, and suddenly stopped short of the perfunctory, cheerful prayer which usually followed automatically, or sometimes didn't even bother to come at all. He had been brought up to say his prayers regularly every night, like a good little boy, because life was pleasant and tidy like that, and Ginnie had been brought up in the same way before him, and enjoyed, in turn, both roles in the ritual. Through all the years in which he'd had nothing serious to pray about, and in any case had never really wondered whether there was anyone listening if he had needed something badly, he'd been

186

able to rush into words with bright, light enthusiasm; and now that he had something of a desperate need, and was for the first time consciously convinced that he had a listener, he was without words or thoughts, because he did not know what he had a right to ask, how much of a trouble which was essentially his own it was fair to shuffle off upon God.

He said silently into his shielding hands: 'Oh, God, let there be some way that I can find out what I ought to do. Let there be somebody to give me a sign.' That was all he felt he could ask. The doing, once he was sure, was obviously his responsibility.

Within his closed eyelids he saw his own answer, a sudden image of the Rector's face, and though he was almost sure that he had been thinking of this man all along as the person most likely to help him, and had produced the omen himself, with very little help from God, he accepted it politely, and let his mind rest upon it with relief and hope. Probably nothing would happen, but it was nice to lean on the thought that something might. And after all, so it might, if he waited, and didn't try to strain miracles out of the empty air. He sat back, settling himself gravely, listening to the persistent shuffling of feet in the aisle behind him.

The ex-servicemen were coming in now, the sound of their steps beat rhythmically, keeping time even when slowed almost to a standstill; they could never unlearn what they had learned. There was another sound, too, a cheerful, small, metallic sound like the distant clashing of horse-brasses. Breast after breast of medals jingled into the pews behind him. He knew the sound, even though it was still novel to him; and until the rhythm was broken he did not turn his head, but sat with thoughtful face and lowered, shadowy eyes.

Then the hollow place in the beat assailed his ear, and he had to look round before he could identify it. Of course, the even, unmatched thump of a single foot, and in the silence between, the rubber-shod step of crutches! Then another of them. Then one with two feet, but one an artificial one; he was adroit and young, but still Edmund's ear caught the unevenness of the two paces.

Then there was a new sound, a curious creak, soft and persistent, that brought his chin stealthily on to his shoulder again; and that was an invalid chair, in which a great fleshy figure lay, gross and still, deprived of exercise God knew how many years ago. They wheeled him into the wide space of the chancel, and set the chair against the wall there, so that he would not be in the way. Probably he had been spending most of his waking hours like that for years and years, parked somewhere where he wouldn't be in the way.

Edmund felt the music attacking him already, the highly-charged atmosphere tightening the nerves of his throat, stinging his eyes, constricting his breathing. He knew just how it happened to others, because he could feel it happening to him. Once he caught a glimpse of Stephie in profile, hemmed in by the imposing bulk of her mother, at the end of the pew under the dappling glow from one of the Flemish windows. Her lips were parted, her eyes wide and soft, and fixed upon the flowers and candles of the altar in a dreaming intensity. He averted his gaze from her unhappily, and filled his mind angrily with the revulsion he had felt at the passing of the invalid chair; not from its unfortunate occupant, but from this mood of emotional complacency which accepted

188

him as justified, which was willing to contemplate generations of him, past and present and to come, for the sake of an orgy like this. He bit on the thought deliberately, as on an aching tooth, to keep himself from relaxing and breathing in the hypnotic emanations of collective emotion, the incense of sentimentality.

Now everyone was in, and he heard the door of the church closed. The organ broke forth suddenly, taking over from the band in a ringing voluntary, as the vestry door opened, and the choir filed in. The tremendous, heaving, disquieting sound of a thousand people all rising together almost drowned out the organ for a moment. Edmund felt the excited crowd acquiring instant by instant a single, enfolding personality, from which it would take all the obstinacy in the world to hold himself detached.

He was waiting for the Rector to appear, and craned to catch the first clear glimpse of him, for he had never yet seen him so closely. The lean, weathered face, hollowed into dramatic shadow by the crossing lights, comforted him because it did not share the communal rapture. It seemed to him strained and sad, with a sadness which lay in the pits of the eyes like a cloudy darkness, lit at the heart with a secret, self-devouring light. Edmund fastened his own eyes thankfully upon a countenance so immune from any touch of the collective ecstasy, and opened his ears with relief to a voice so unhysterical. His first impression had not been at fault, he thought. This was a proud and sincere old man, without attitudes, standing up erect within his own personality. The day could be saved yet, there could be a flame of reality left alive in it, a genuine conscience could speak out of it, even if everybody was soon going to be too

189

drunk to listen. What he had to do was hang on to his own reason, and keep from getting drunk, so that if the sign he had asked for fell into his hands he should not let it slip through his fingers and be lost.

When the choir were all in their places, the Rector turned on the chancel steps, facing down the aisle, and from the obscurity there under the organ-loft, where they had been waiting for their cue, the standard-bearers came pacing slowly and solemnly, two by two and surrendered their burdens to the temporary care of the Church: four regimental colours, the British Legion banner, two standards of Friendly Societies, the Boy Scouts' flag, the Girl Guides' flag. When the Rector had ranged them in the sanctuary, propped against the wall on either side of the altar, the Gothic crucifix grew small and pale and worn among so much colour and pageantry, and had the beleaguered look of some little local deity in decline, watching his shrine swing irrevocably towards a rededication.

The hymns were the usual hymns, 'For all the Saints', 'Ten thousand times ten thousand', all the ones with magnificent shouting tunes, and the dual implication that these dead soldiers were all willing martyrs, and therefore what happened to them here was of comparative unimportance besides their crowns hereafter. The Lessons were very much what might have been expected, too. Crozier read them in a full, ringing voice, rolling the words of the prophet Isaiah from his tongue like notes of trumpets:

'"He giveth power to the faint; and to them that have no might he increaseth strength.

'"Even the youths shall faint and be weary, and the young men shall utterly fail.

190

'"But they that wait upon the Lord shall renew their strength; they shall mount up with wings as eagles; they shall run, and not be weary; and they shall walk, and not faint."'

He had a passion for English prose of the high period, which was why he had whole passages of the Authorised Version tucked away complete within the capacious cupboards of his mind. He could produce from those well-furnished recesses quotations upon almost any subject, sermons to almost any text. And as he went back to his place after the reading he was thinking wryly: 'I could have found him something more appropriate. Nahum the Elkohite, for instance, had plenty of words for it:

"And there is a multitude of slain, and a great number of carcases:
And there is none end of their corpses:
They stumble upon their corpses:
Because of the multitude of the whoredoms of the well-favoured harlot,
The mistress of witchcrafts, that selleth nations through her whoredoms,
And families through her witchcrafts."

'Or if that's too steep, what about Habbakuk?

'"Oh, Lord, how long shall I cry
And Thou wilt not hear!
Even cry out unto Thee of violence,
And Thou wilt not save!"'

He had, however, given a very good performance; not for love of the game, but because he had long outlived the illusion that voices crying in the wilderness really change anything. Only now and again, between the words of the prayers, did it enter his head to wonder what he was doing there, and even then he knew the answer so perfectly that the question had no weight. 'I am conforming,' he said to himself simply, 'because I no longer have any faith in the effectiveness of noncomformity.'

'And what,' he asked further, watching the clear profile of Bill Dallas bowed beside him, with closed eyes as tranquil as a dead man's, and firmly responding mouth, 'is he doing here? He is believing in what he does. That's the difference between us. That's why, on the whole, he does it with so much less conviction.'

The Second Lesson was from the Revelation. He scarcely needed the book for it.

'"And he said to me: These are they which came out of great tribulation, and have washed their robes and made them white in the blood of the Lamb.

'"Therefore are they before the throne of God, and serve him day and night in his temple; and he that sitteth on the throne shall dwell among them.

'"They shall hunger no more, neither thirst any more; neither shall the sun light on them, nor any heat.

'"For the Lamb, which is in the midst of the throne shall feed them, and shall lead them unto living fountains of waters; and God shall wipe away all tears from their eyes."'

'And ask, of course,' he reflected, resigning the centre of the stage to Dallas with no reluctance at all, 'no awkward questions of anybody, such as: "Cain, where is thy brother?"' He resumed his seat to the soft, remote chords of the organ, and watched Dallas cross the aisle and loop back the red cord to let himself into the holy place.

The Rector, standing at the chancel steps, said the dedicatory prayer. Dallas, his face taut with the solemnity of the moment, unfastened the knot of poppies with reverent hands, and lifted aside with great tenderness the folds of the flags, and the three demigods stared out at him blankly, with the same stony stare they had levelled upon darkness. The town band broke into 'O God, our help in ages past', and everybody burst into song.

Charles Faulkner turned to kneel at the altar as soon as the hymn began. He had not once looked towards the act of homage at the rival altar, nor did he now lift his head from his hands. This was another man's hour, but his was coming. Even when he rose and walked slowly out of the sanctuary, and began to climb the steps of the pulpit, he still did not look towards the stone. His eyes were fixed before him, and when he had reached his place they remained so, wide-open in their dark pits upon the refuge of greying late-afternoon air above the serried heads of his flock. He felt them though he did not yet look directly at them, a corrugation of pale faces lifted towards him, a sudden absolute silence of expectation after the Amen had ended.

'In the name of the Father, and of the Son, and of the Holy Ghost, Amen.'

The long sigh of their subsiding, the rustle of their skirts, the pulling-up of trouser legs, the throat-clearing ripple of coughs across the surface of the lake, the experimental stirrings and readjustments,

193

the composure, the hush.

He would have to look down at them now, and they would become people. He would let his eyes pass, like the hypnotic stroking passage of a hand across a tensed forehead, over the raised faces, gathering to him slowly all the avid, waiting glances. A sign of the cross made above them with his eyes, once from wall to wall across the church, once from the shadowy recesses under the organ-loft at the back, to the officials and their families sitting close beneath the pulpit.

The second arm of the cross ended, and the silence was not broken. He was staring down into the eyes of the angel.

*   *   *

The moment of recognition rounded and fell into the silence like a great golden tear. For the third time they remained gazing at each other, and both the darkness and the distance had fallen back from them now, so that there was nothing at all to impede the marriage of their eyes.

The young man's face was quite unlike any of the others, although, like them, it was all attention and expectation. What made it different was the stature of his faith, the quality of the utterance he awaited. His face was very young, younger even than it had seemed last night in the shaft of light from the study window, fresh and fair and candid, with fine, clear bones that showed through the adolescent flesh. It was not, like the others, rapt and complacent, awaiting the shock of pleasurable emotion, but deeply troubled within its stillness; and the eyes had positive colour at last, a blueness as intense as the

194

Flemish blue of the Virgin's robe in the window. Their look as they held him was like what prayer should be, furious, demanding, confident, aching with longing, incandescent with hope, resolute with certainty, all desire and all conviction.

Who would have looked for him here, among the established ones? Who would ever have thought he might appear at last as that man's son? The woman was not here between them now; her absence was something of which Faulkner was aware in the deepest places of his heart, where reason could not penetrate. She had withdrawn herself because the time for her to stand between them was past, because it was the day on which they were appointed to encounter. Their eyes clung, locked, unable to break free. 'You will know,' the boy's silence said, 'what you have to say.'

He knew what he had to say. His hands fastened hard upon the rim of the pulpit before him. The sermon he was commanded to preach flashed fully-grown into his mind, like the instantaneous vision of a world transformed as the lightning passes. 'Yes,' he thought, drowning far down beneath the engulfing blueness of the boy's believing eyes, 'I know what I have to say. We go about to cover and confuse with graceful complexities those things which a true Christian would see as blazingly simple. But now all the irrelevancies are washed clean away again, and nothing is left but what you want of me, and all you want of me is the truth. The truth, which changing its name does not change, which no costume will disguise, no rulebook make out of order, nor passage of time render old or invalid.'

He strained down upon his hands, and lifted his head, and now the blue of the eyes was the illimitable blue of air, and sustained him like a hawk upon the mere tremor of the wings of his own inspiration. He soared, feeling the compromise, the limitations fall from him like shed jesses, riding the gale on which the angel's radiant passage uplifted him.

'The twentieth chapter of the book Exodus, the thirteenth verse:

'"Thou shalt not kill!"

'Not: "Thou shall not kill except in self-defence". Not: "Thou shalt not kill except in a good cause". Not: "Thou shalt not kill except when a law of the country sanctions it". But: "Thou shalt not kill!" Not: "Thou shalt not die". The grass withereth, the flower fadeth, all flesh is grass. Thou shalt die, soon or late, well or ill. But: "Thou shalt not kill!"'

'We are here to remember the deaths of many young men who killed and were killed. In that they killed, they were guilty of murder, and in that they were killed, those are guilty of murder who sent them into the forefront of the battle. Do not be deceived into thinking that any murder among all these murders goes unrecorded, unremembered, unrepaid.

'Every man has but one life, of which he is only the custodian; but of that he *is* the custodian, and he must be answerable for what he does with it, and therefore the choice of how it shall be spent must also be his, and cannot be arrogated to any other human creatures by the name of a state, or a legal code, or a tradition, or a church, or what you please to name it.

'It is the duty of man to value and cherish the life of which he is in charge. It ought to be used to the full, it ought to be ventured with, and to bear fruit; but he is still the judge of what ventures are justifiable, of what

196

fruit is profitable to harvest. His is the privilege and the burden of choosing for what he shall spend the single coin he has in care, for he can spend it only once. And when he has found the worth-while thing for which his life seems a fair payment, let him buy it, and pay for it, and ask no man's leave.

'But beware how you lay hands on the lives of other people, and spend them; for the first is misappropriation and theft, and the second is murder. Do not let anyone or anything persuade you, by the use of prettier names than these, that the acts are less, and less culpable, than I have said. Do not think that a little sacrifice of either stones or bread can make restitution: death is death, and no restitution is possible. What crowns God may choose to give, leave to God. It may be that His choice will abandon both you and your victims. It is by *your* acts, not by the acts of any other human creature, that *you* are saved or damned.

'Remember, then, for we are here to remember them, these young men who allowed themselves, in their inexperience, to be robbed of their birthright of choice between salvation and damnation. Remember, also, the millstones waiting for the necks of those who offended and caused to offend these heroic and misguided little ones. The more promise they had, the greater the sin that they were robbed of it. The finer qualities they possessed, the higher will be the account charged against those who dispossessed them. The cleaner their hands were, the dearer the price will be to those who constrained them to shed blood. As for the comfort we take and have taken in believing that they resigned their rights, their cleanness, and their lives willingly, in the day of judgment that, too, will be answered. Then we shall hear from their own mouths how many will say: "Yes" to the indictment. For the rest, be ready to make your answer, as I must be ready to make mine. For as you were silent while these things happened, so was I silent.

'We are members one of another, all sons of the same father. All killings are fratricide, all wars are civil war. This is the law which is around, and beyond, and before, and surviving, your law. And by your law shall no man living be justified.

'Therefore do not put your trust in music and praise, however loud, or poppies, however red, or stones, however magically blessed; for the accusation will still be heard, and the blood will still stain, and the dead will still rise.

'Be not deceived! God is not mocked!'

*   *   *

The words wrote themselves like fire through his mind and heart, he opened his lips, struggling for a speech which should be audible to others, since this only the angel heard. Out of the forgotten spaces of the nave the massed faces swam back into his sight, fixed, puzzled, tremulous with a slight stirring of unrest because of the moments of delay. The accumulation of eyes, returning terribly, weighed upon him, leaden and mindless, bearing him down out of the strong and intoxicating air of prophecy, down to the company of the Mayor, and the Members of Parliament, and the Corporation, and the ordered hierarchies of law within law. He had duties, he had a fixed place; they too expected, they too needed.

A terrible weariness and sadness came on him. He
198

looked despairingly into the young man's eyes, and they were again eyes, and not the deeps of the sea any longer, nor the airy spaces of heaven. He was too old, he had made too many concessions to the world, he could not face the wilderness! He let his gaze pass once again from wall to wall, and instead of being alone he knew himself compassed about with a great cloud of witnesses, absolved from ever being solitary and unblessed. The relief was all he needed to give him strength.

He drew breath, and gave out his text in a firm, resonant voice:

'The first book of the Maccabees, the third chapter, portions of the second and ninth verses:

'"He received unto him such as were ready to perish—and they fought with cheerfulness the battle of Israel."'

Once the first irretrievable sentence was launched, there was a wonderful and awful sense of ease in speaking the well-prepared words. He was committed. The imprisoned voice within, threshing against the bars of his mind, might lament in its frenzy: 'What have you done?' But there was always the unanswerable answer: 'It's done!'

This going downhill was easy, the very sense of descent absolved him of effort. All the assuaged and flattered eyes, bright and drunken with emotion, sustained him, like a firm paving under his feet, upon the road he had chosen. Nevertheless, in choosing he had lost the power of choice. He was committed, and he must go forward.

The afternoon was advancing, but was that why it seemed to him so dark within the church? The centre

199

of light had shifted from the deep brilliance of the windows to the discreetly shaded lamps, the emeralds and rubies and sapphires of the Flemish glass had dulled to pebbles of queer and ugly shapes between the strips of lead. Over everything within his sight a greyness had spread like dust, from the moment that the ardour of belief and desire had faded out of the young man's face.

The unwavering regard of the eyes did not once leave him, though the light had left them. All the lines of the face had composed themselves into a new, cold clarity, the quivering, confident look of extreme youth and brightness was gone. The lids relaxed upon eyes of a steel-blue calm, distant and sharp as spears. There was a very slight curl at the lips; it might have been a smile, or a grimace of fastidious distaste, it might have been only the shadow lying in the firm, deep shaping of the mouth, but it had a terrible, pure scorn about it.

'We live in a world of social and moral upheaval, in which values are being overturned about us, in the name of that very humanism which we had considered, within the framework of Christianity, to be the basis of our own code of ethics. But even in this world, whenever the moment of crisis poses the most immediate of all questions, whether we are willing to die for our beliefs, the answer is an unchanged: Yes. There have always been some who have fallen short, but still, when the demand is made, the lives are offered. Even in the confusion of this present time the supreme sacrifice is made freely, without doubts or regrets, when the need arises.

'Do not despair of man, while there are young men like these. Do not speak of the degeneration of modern youth, while this stone remains here to refute

200

the charge. Remember rather the words of our Lord: "For he that will save his life shall lose it, but he that loseth his life for my sake, the same shall save it."

'"Blessed are the dead which die in the Lord."'

For My sake! The letters of the young man who was dead confronted him again out of the air, and though he put them by with the compelling flow of his own oratory, they rode upon the tide and shone, and would not be submerged. Were these things done for My sake? Have I to praise men, thank them, ask My Father to give them crowns of glory, for burning to death with jellied petrol their fellow-men, also My children? Be not deceived, God is not mocked!

But there was no turning back, the words continued to flow of themselves, because of the pleased compulsion of the eyes, all the eyes of the world, drawing him to them, embracing him, taking comfort in the absolution afforded them by his damnation.

The young man in the front pew quietly leaned forward, laid his hymn-book and prayer-book meticulously together upon the ledge, gathered up his gloves and hat, and rose to his feet.

The movements were so slow and so gently deliberate that at first no one seemed capable of feeling, much less showing, any surprise. The boy looked up for an instant, and raised his eyes once, with a perfect and final simplicity of rejection, to the Rector's face. He looked at it thoughtfully, as though he were wondering what he had found in it five minutes ago to interest him, or make him hope for better than this; and there was in the momentary glance a renewed flash of the ardent light in his eyes,

201

so that the Rector should never be able to forget the beauty and gallantry of the opportunity he had abandoned, or fail to recognise the person he had betrayed.

Then the young man turned towards the aisle and looked down at the astonished Mayor, with a polite little inclination of the head and a tentative gesture of his hand requesting pardon and passage. The Mayor, too startled to make any resistance to a will so positive, drew in his feet and stood up to let the boy pass.

A faint, long sigh passed quivering through the church, and though there was scarcely any jarring sound from below to disturb him, the flow of the Rector's speech shook and halted, resuming with an effort and in a higher key. The alignment of all the glances had changed, the eyes were following the young man's implacable departure. His mother put out an anxious hand, too late to arrest him. His father looked up into his face with a forbidding and reproachful frown; but the polite, demanding head bowed its way past him, the slender, haughty body waited for his releasing movement, and there was nothing he could do but draw back and let him go.

The boy walked away down the aisle without undue haste, and with no deliberate noise nor any attempt to silence his steps. The firm, fatal sound of every footfall echoed hollowly through a sudden terrible silence, for the thread of the Rector's discourse had snapped in his brain, the end of his sentence had recoiled out of his grasp, and he stood clutching the rim of the pulpit and staring, with stunned and tragic eyes, after the receding flight of the angel.

He heard the door open and close, heard the first

faint, withdrawing steps upon the gravel outside, then silence. So deep, so absolute a silence that it brought to his ears, across the glebe from the small-holding and through the solid stone walls, the sound of a cock crowing.

*   *   *

Edmund walked down the path and out at the lich-gate, and the slowness had already passed from his step, and the over-emphasis from his movements. He felt inordinately light in mind and body, rather as though he had been sick, he thought honestly, trying to find a simile for the sensation. He had certainly shed something which had been up to now essential luggage to him; he had a bewildered idea that he ought to feel it as a loss, but instead it felt like a liberation.

So after all he owed nothing to any of them, and after all he had discovered that he could get along without borrowing. That was what happened, then, when you looked for a sign from Heaven. He had fixed all the energy and enthusiasm he had upon drawing down the lightning, and he had got probably the only answer he deserved, a plain intimation that if he needed help from a third party in making up his mind, he might just as well realise his limitations right away, and fall meekly into line like the rest.

The odd part about it was that he felt better now, not at all deserted, not at all snubbed, only rather as if God had rounded on him in justifiable exasperation, and said: 'Look here, young man, if you can't think of a better way to deal with a problem than running to me with silly questions about it, all you'll get will be short answers. Now go and use the wits I gave you,

203

as you very well know you were meant to, and make the best job you can of it without trying to shuffle it off on other people. And if you *do* need me, I'll be around.'

Very well, then, since that was the answer, since there was no help to be looked for from any creature outside himself, he could and he would think the thing out for himself, take his own decisions, accept the risks involved, make his own mistakes and pay for them himself. Commit his own crimes, if that should turn out to be the way other people looked at them, and take the rap for them himself. Whatever happened! And no whining afterwards, either!

Surely so abrupt an acceptance of so large and daunting a responsibility should have come upon him as a weight. Instead, it came upon him as a lightness, even a happiness. It would not have taken much to make him break into laughter as he went out into the street, or to shake his demure, authoritative walk into a dance step.

He'd begun his career of independence on the spot. He hoped it hadn't looked too insufferably rude, but he'd meant it to be unmistakable. He didn't want to hurt anyone's feelings just for the sake of hurting them, but to stay and listen in silence to humbug in which the speaker himself did not believe would have been to condone it, even to identify himself with it.

'There'll be a row,' warned the schoolboy in him, with candour. 'They'll ask you who the devil you think you are to judge, and call you a self-opinionated little prig.'

'I shall be called worse things than that before the finish,' he replied, unshaken. 'I'll survive it.'

'Well, it might not be so far off the beam, at that,' stated the irrepressible critic, faithfully frank, and

204

uncomplimentary as a young brother.

'I'll survive that, too. If I am a prig, I am, and that's that, and I can't help it. I'd rather be a prig than a humbug, any day.'

He knew that it was not really as easy and as gay as this, but the intoxication of the first unsupported steps was new, and legitimate. He had a right to feel it at least as wholeheartedly as he would feel the knocks and the depressions later. It was of no use whatever to try to prepare himself for those until they came. The thing was to meet everything as it arrived, and deal honestly with it, and then stand by what he'd done.

It was past four o'clock and already dusk, a watery, silvery twilight, full of gleams of lambent light from the puddles in the lane, from the wet windows, the sills and the washed doorsteps. The lamps in the quiet Sunday streets were lit, and a few solitary figures moved gently homeward towards firelight and tea. The sky was silken-grey above the glimmering slate-black roofs, and the air was mild and moist.

On the edge of the pavement by the Post Office he halted, and stood for a few minutes, considering where he should go, and what he should do. There was no point in going home, since no one would be there. They were all dining at the Unicorn this evening, and had intended driving there after the service, with the Croziers. He hesitated, wondering if his parents would be sufficiently upset about his behaviour to want to go home first, and see if they found him there; but he did not think it likely. In his father's position one had to preserve the public equanimity of one's life, meet all obligations, keep all engagements. Family scenes were deferred until duty was done. He might as well consider himself free until

205

seven o'clock at the Unicorn. He would probably need all that time for the amount of thinking he had to do.

He took the first alleyway on the right, heading for the edge of town, and the low hills that rose in meadow and woodland towards Harbury Ring. The fields would be wet, but the woods had open pathways among the firs, deep in needles, and good walking even after rain. There would be no people, unless someone else had problems like his to work out; and if he had, there was room for him.

The way towards the hills brought him through the rim of the poorer side of Caldington, along the streets of Victorian and Edwardian shop-fronts, solid and ugly, with lace-curtained windows and fanlighted doors. In the squat, square windows on the first floors there were geraniums in ceramic pots, or aspidistras in brass tubs, sustained on bamboo stands, as though the rooms could never escape from the date of their origin. From the front doors here and there a solitary figure emerged with a letter for the corner pillar-box, and, having disposed of it, slipped back as quietly into the tiny enclosed world of lamplight within.

He came to a terrace of six red-brick houses, shabby and pretentious and sad, with tired little bushes of box in their narrow front-gardens. At Number 4 a woman was just taking her key from inside a shell on the end of the step, and fitting it into the lock.

He had not been thinking of her, but he knew her at once, by the very way she stood, by the twice-altered coat which still showed signs of its old shape, and yet hung with grace and style upon her gaunt shoulders. He hesitated at the gate, his hand lingering upon a post from which the paint was flaking in long strips.

206

'Mrs Parrish—'

He did not know why he had called to her. He did not need her, he needed no one, and he had no real reason in the world for troubling her. It was just that he could not pass by without speaking to her; in some way which he did not trouble to examine it would have been a dereliction of a dear duty. When she turned at the call, she already knew who was there; the smoke-grey eyes looked for him with a smile.

'I thought you were in church. They're not finished yet, surely?'

Surprise was now something as unlikely between them as was embarrassment, but a kind of shyness revisited him when he was with her, and left him more monosyllabic than usual. He shook his head, and stood there for a minute in silence, holding his hat in his hand. His thick, light hair gathered to itself what was left of the amorphous light. She came down towards the gate with the key in her hand.

'Do you want to come in? There's nobody here but me.'

'No, thank you, I'm going on in a minute. I just saw you there, and I wanted—' No, there was nothing he had wanted from her, more than just to speak, and hear her speak. The less you need people, sometimes it seems, the more you value and understand them. 'You didn't go to the church?'

'I went as far as the door,' she said, with her crooked smile. 'My son's girl wanted me to go with her. I don't suppose I ever really intended to go in, but I didn't *know* until I got there. So I came over faint, and thought perhaps I'd better come home. She wanted to come back with me—No, she didn't want, but she thought she ought to offer, poor kid! I told her I'd be all right if I came back and lay down for a bit. She'll be all right, too, in there among the rest of 'em, she won't need me.'

'But you didn't come straight home,' he said, returning the smile.

'What was there to come home for?' The simplicity of her loneliness, about which she made so few and such uncalculated remarks, went into his heart as greenly, freshly and fiercely as on the first day he had ever seen her. He averted his eyes from the unbearable tranquillity of her face. 'How did it all go?' she asked. 'Was everybody happy?'

'Yes—I think they were.'

'All but you,' she said. 'They're never through all that business yet. What happened?'

'I walked out.' He looked fixedly at his hand, which was marching its fingers slowly along the top of the gate, one beyond another, and his long brows gathered into a slow, considering frown. 'Nothing happened, really. I just didn't like it, none of it seemed true to me. Most of the people there believed in it. But *he* didn't! So I came out.' He looked up at her suddenly, his eyes flaring wide and dark. 'Mrs Parrish, did you go to anybody else, about your son? After my father, I mean?'

'No,' she said, her voice very quiet. 'I stopped looking for anybody to take the blame, very soon after that.'

'Why?' he asked, almost inaudibly.

'Because it came round in a circle, home to me. I let it happen, as much as anybody else. It was something I hadn't bargained for, finding myself looking into a mirror at the end of it. So I didn't go any further. Why should I? I'd arrived.'

'Oh, no!' he said in a soft cry of protest. 'What could you have done?'

208

'Not much. But I didn't do it—whatever it was.'

'But then it must have been everybody's fault—everybody who didn't—didn't—'

Mrs Parrish smiled, and for once she let herself smile at him as at a child, instead of a contemporary. 'Everybody who didn't at least get up and walk out. You did.'

'Yes, now, but now is too late.'

'No,' she said, 'now's perfect. You've only come to it now, and, even at that, you've come very early. You let Jack alone, he's never going to come knocking at your door asking for anything.'

She would have liked to do something for him, but there was nothing he needed, from her or from anyone, except the given and reflected warmth one human being can shed upon another and receive again undiminished; and that he felt already, he was relaxed and half-smiling and at ease in the glow of it. 'You've found out,' she said, 'what you want to do?'

'I shall.' He sounded wonderfully secure, and his eyes had a resplendent confidence. 'I found out that there was only one place to look for the answer, at any rate.'

Yes, she thought, here goes another of the younger generation looking for the answers to everything inside himself—what the churchmen, poor souls, call trying to live without God, as if they didn't know what *he* knows perfectly well, that that's exactly where God is, supposing one believes in him at all. The one place a man can't fail to find him, supposing he is what one hopes and trusts and feels he is, as constant as churches and governments are capricious, and as honest as they are devious.

'Wish me luck!' said Edmund, his smile broadening into a boyish grin; and he held out a large

209

young hand suddenly over the top of the gate. She took it, and her fingers felt worn and rough and strong in his.

'I do, all the luck you need.' She did not say that he would need plenty, even with his courage and obstinacy, but she knew that he was aware of her thoughts, and that the quality of the smile was partly for her reassurance. He wanted her to feel sure of him, and to think of him afterwards with the calm of certainty, even if she never saw him again after this third encounter. He need not have been anxious upon that head; she would have staked her life upon him without an unquiet moment.

'Good-bye, Mrs Parrish!'

'Good-bye, Edmund!'

He made her the slightest of formal bows, and put on his hat, and went on along the darkening street, leaving the memory of his withdrawing smile warm and luminous in her mind, and the big, vigorous, impulsive grip of his hand still tingling through her fingers. She watched him until he flashed through the last pool of lamplight at the corner, striding blithely, and vanished into the darkness beyond. Then she went into the house, taking his warmth with her, and knew that never again could she be altogether separated from him, or left utterly without a son.

CHAPTER EIGHT

THE INNOCENT

When Edmund entered the Unicorn it was past seven o'clock, and Stephie Crozier was just emerging from the lounge and looking towards the street with an angrily anxious face. When she saw him she pretended that she had come out in search of a Sunday paper, snatching up the *Observer* from one of the worn easy chairs with a determined gesture of satisfaction, which was spoiled next moment by the face of intense displeasure she turned on him.

'So you decided to come, after all. I thought you were scared to show yourself, after that performance.'

Edmund hung up his hat and coat, and looked at her over his shoulder with an almost teasing smile.

'Not scared—just busy. But I didn't mean to be so late. Where are they all? My people didn't start worrying about whether I was ill, or anything, did they? I never thought about that until afterwards, but you never know with Mummy.'

She stood clutching the *Observer* and scowling at him over it, her lower lip caught between her fierce little teeth, and then released it to say, with freezing dignity: 'We haven't discussed you at all, and nobody seems to be worrying in the least about your health. They're all in the lounge. You'd better come and show yourself.'

Edmund paused in front of an ill-lit mirror to settle his tie, and pass a perfunctory hand over his hair. Fresh air and rapid walking had whipped more colour than usual into his cheeks, and he looked rosily healthy, and, he was afraid, inconsiderately unrepentant. Even rather frivolous, because of that enchanted smile which was purely the result of seeing Stephie again. He made an experimental grimace or two at himself, trying to achieve a decently severe gravity; but when he raised his eyes a little, and met hers suddenly in the glass, the sight of so much rage, and doubt, and bewilderment, and unwilling curiosity, was fatal to the attempt at a properly sober expression. The smile rushed back, with an irresistible eruption of laughter on its heels.

Stephie's eyes flamed. 'It isn't funny! You make a scene like that, you insult everybody, the Rector, the town, the ex-service men, those dead boys—'

'I didn't insult them. I thought they were already being insulted, that's why I walked out.' He turned to face her, calmer by far than she thought he ought to be. 'There's no time now, we'll have to go in, but later I'll tell you all about it.'

'I don't want to hear it! If you felt like that, why did you come to the service at all? Nobody forced you to. Why did you have to make a public scene like that, walking out in the middle of the sermon—such rotten taste!' she said furiously, selecting with accuracy the stone she thought would hurt most.

But somewhere behind her rage, he thought as he looked at her, there was a secret fountain of grudging sympathy for him as a contemporary with the odds against him. Hesitating outside the door of the lounge, he consented to sound for it. 'Are they fearfully upset?'

The heat of her resentment mellowed bewilderingly into the warmth of her comradeship. 'Nobody's said anything, of course. I think your father *is*, though. After all, you did rather put him in a nasty spot, you know, knocking the Rector right off his stroke like that. Honestly, for a minute I thought he was going to collapse. We all felt *awful*! But he came round all right, and started off again, and went the rest of the way pretty well. Still, it was a nasty moment; you can't wonder if your father's mad as a hatter about it. I mean, in *his* position—' Her limpid

212

silvery eyes were almost friendly now, her tone confidential, though still severe. Probably that was how it would always be, even when he had known her for years and years upon this plane of intimacy. They would still fight about everything, and like each other through all the warfare, but still be unable to stop fighting; and between blows they would comfort each other. But never would either of them accept an idea from the other, or surrender a point of principle, or learn anything, or teach anything; and never, never would they understand each other, or discover how to make peace between them.

Edmund reached for the handle of the door, and their faces were close together, so that the clarity of her features swam out of focus for that instant into a starry, dreamlike beauty. Their arms touched, and they both flushed, drawing apart again with a confused smile. All the potential sweetness and bitterness of the future visited them in the contact, but there was nothing to be said about it yet, it was too new, too disquieting, too fragile to be explored. The next moment Edmund was saying, with his provoking smile:

'Don't worry, your evening won't be spoiled by scenes of carnage. We Dallases always take our rows home with us.'

All the same, it was with some trepidation that he entered the lounge on Stephie's heels.

They were all sitting over drinks at a corner table, and when they looked up at his entrance he had a queer feeling that the whole tableau, the casually interrupted conversation, the elaborate carelessness of their attitudes, even the bright, social friendliness of their faces, had been arranged with infinite pains for this moment. Everyone looked at him, except his father, who continued his interrupted sentence to its close without allowing his attention to be deflected. Mrs Crozier said brightly: 'Ah, here he is!' and Ginnie came bounding out of her chair to meet him. Maybe they hadn't actually talked about him, but he had never for an instant been off Ginnie's mind, that was clear in the relief, and the reproach, and the pure pleasure of her face at the sight of him.

'Eddie—so there you are! We wondered where on earth you'd got to, you're awfully late!' She stood squarely in his path to halt him well out of earshot of the others, and straightened again the tie on which he had already spent his attention, so that she could whisper up to him: 'Darling, how cruel! Why *did* you? Were you ill? Such a *bad* impression! Darling, it *was* naughty!'

'I know!' he said as softly, tempering the special smile he kept for her with an appearance as near contrition as he could manage. 'But I'm behaving now, and everything's going to be all right, really. Don't worry, darling Mummy! Come on and back me up till the party's over.'

She gave him a despairing look of helpless affection and foreboding reproach, and then crossed the room sunnily smiling, her arm in his. Stephie had already joined the rest of the party, and only a few solitary people besides were scattered about the room. There was space enough even for the overtones; and besides, everyone was expert in pretending that nothing had happened. The social mechanism had already gone smoothly into action. Mrs Crozier had moved up on her alcove seat to make room for him, and Crozier was on his feet, asking if he would like a sherry.

'I'll keep you company. Don't worry, a Unicorn

214

dinner won't be spoiled by ten extra minutes.'

'Thanks, then I will, please. I'm sorry to be so late, I went off walking, and miscalculated a bit on the time it would take me to get back.'

'Walking, an evening like this, and in the dark?' said Mrs Crozier, breaking off in the middle of a sentence addressed to his father, and settling him beside her with an imperious pressure of one hand upon his arm. 'And it's raining again, too, I can hear it! Ginnie, your child is crazy.'

'I often think all children are,' said Ginnie helplessly, but with a certain resigned serenity. 'But one gets so used to it that one hardly notices. It isn't so bad unless one tries to make sense out of the things they do. As long as one goes right ahead, being surprised at nothing, like Alice in Wonderland, things work out quite well, on the whole. But of course it's fatal to try to find a *logic* about it.'

Dallas was sitting in a deep chair, his face in shadow. The sudden lift of his deliberately lowered lids at this speech, the look he gave Ginnie, half-acknowledging, half-rejecting her ingenuous plea for amnesty, drew Edmund's eyes as infallibly as if it had been aimed at him. And indeed he had expected the first upward glance to be for him, and an unmistakable index to his father's feelings towards him. He had looked for a direct, brief and menacing stare of displeasure, launched at him with hearty intent to discomfort, and then, perhaps, to be let severely alone until afterwards, to chew the cud of anxiety until they had leisure and privacy for the row proper. His father was not one of those cool, sanctimonious parents who must conduct these affairs in the manner of an assize judge; he had a fine, positive but fair temper, the kind children respect,

215

and their occasional head-on clashes had been hot while they lasted, though soon and serenely forgotten.

Now the admired face in repose looked heavy and still; if there was honest anger in it, Edmund could not find it, and he needed it, because he needed everything to be as he had expected it, as he was prepared for it. He would have been only too glad to be met with the perfectly straightforward rage to which parents are entitled when their sons transgress their particular code of behaviour, or even the more painful resentment of a public figure badly let down by his own child on an important occasion. But this closed quietness, stony-lidded eyes evading him and composed brows drawn down into a knot of unfathomable anxiety, confounded and depressed him.

He fixed his eyes urgently upon his father, and stared at him above the glass all the time he was drinking his sherry, in a manner which should have drawn the answering regard of any but a man in a deep sleep. Not a look answered him. Yet his father could become animated enough for the others, could smile and crack wry jokes with Crozier over the previous week's business in the House, and skate expertly over the rare issues on which they might have been too seriously divided. But he would not so much as look at his son.

Under this sentence of banishment, which dismayed him more than he had believed possible, Edmund sighed and submitted, for there was no hope of appeal while all these people were present to complicate matters. There was nothing to be done but wait for the interminable evening to drag out its length to a departure at last; then they could get rid of
216

everybody, and argue their hearts out at one another in blessed peace, and come to an understanding.

Stephie, watching his persistent efforts to catch his father's eye, and much too cocksure to explore the subtleties of the pursuit with any accuracy, leaned and whispered in his ear: 'I wonder you aren't ashamed to look him in the face!' But still no revelation invaded Edmund's senses. It was taken for granted, by Edmund most of all, that he was the only one who had cause to shirk the encounter; nothing could ever have moved him to consider the absurd possibility that his father, his immaculate, admired father, might be ashamed to meet his eyes, or mortally afraid of the homeward journey when there would be no Croziers to deploy between them, and the moment of truth could no longer be delayed.

*   *   *

The first words Dallas addressed directly to his son were a rather curt refusal when the boy offered to drive on the way home; and even the offer, to tell the truth, had been made to elicit a response of any kind, rather than have the constraint last a moment longer.

Exiled to the back seat of the car, and with even Ginnie too upset to talk to him in his father's presence, Edmund sat and thought of Stephie. There was no need in the world to think of what he would have to say to his father when the time came, because that would be simplicity itself. He had done all the thinking he needed in the wet, dark woods, with the resinous warmth wrapping him round mysteriously, and the thick silent inches of needles muffling his feet and gushing forth earthy scents at every step. He had no more need of thought now than a traveller who

217

has arrived has of trains. He felt pleasantly tired, physically and mentally, and at the same time alert and excited, as if after a journey and before the event for which the journey was made.

So in the meantime he thought of Stephie, who had maintained her inimical face to the last glimpse, and yet had suppressed her strictures to the considerate whisper of a neutral, if not of an ally. At their last private moment he had asked her point-blank: 'Do you really think I did something so awful!' A man ought not to need approval, but he does need respect, from those people who are close to him; and at this crisis it seemed to have happened to them both unawares that they had drawn disconcertingly close.

Without knowing what she did she had given him the perfect answer, still jutting her angry chin at him and drawing down her displeased brows: '*I* didn't like it. But I suppose you think you had a proper reason for it, because at least you *are straight.*'

The words, and the emphasis she had distributed so generously among them, had started a small, positive glow of happiness in him. In the back seat of the car, driving homeward through the moist, mild night, he let the little fire burn up steadily, while he tried to balance the future upon this one severe and honourable gesture of hers, and knew all the time that the odds against him were so great that he might as well give up. But so they were over other issues, and he already knew that, too, and felt no inclination at all to give up his convictions, his recusant intentions, or Stephie. He was acquiring wisdom at a speed which made him feel slightly intoxicated; he could tell himself honestly that Stephie would prove an exceedingly difficult and perilous achievement, and still continue determined to attempt her; just as

218

he could foresee all the probable results of the course he had selected for himself, and still embark on it with undiminished resolution and unclouded cheerfulness. The great thing, he thought with all the astonished pleasure of certainty, is to choose.

As soon as the car stopped before the front door he slid out and reached a hand to Ginnie, who was distractedly gathering up her scattered belongings. His father was slow to speak, and allowed him to run up the steps and open the door in silence; but Edmund was so sure he would be called back that even when Ginnie had entered the house he stood waiting upon the top step, looking back rather sadly over his shoulder.

From within the car Dallas called: 'Eddie!'

'Yes?' He came back with relief and alacrity, taking the steps in one flying leap, and leaning in at the window.

Now there was no escaping him; the sound of his name had blown down the protective wall of silence, and let him in joyously to the sack of the city. The trumpet-blasts that flattened the defences of Jericho were not more fatally effective. He stood there within touch, bending his long young back and bowing his fair head eagerly into the car, his face not a yard from his father's face, and his ready smile palpable even in the dark, a quickening warmth on the air. Dallas, with senses erected and quivering, felt after any tremor of uncertainty in the boy's response, but there was nothing there but an absolute acceptance, open as a flower in the sun. He was ready to be criticised, but it would not matter to him; he did not feel that he, for his part, had criticised anybody, and the only ground they had for resenting him, that he knew of, was that in their view what he had done was wrong. A

219

view he did not share, but he had no stones in his hands to throw back. Only saints, fanatics and idiots are as single-minded as all that; yet Eddie was none of the three.

Dallas felt again the superstitious dread which had touched him in the church, not as the boy had forced his imperious passage to freedom, but as the door had closed after his going. Suddenly the taste of the sonorous words had grown acrid and bitter in his mouth, the light had soured into a greyness, the knocking of his heart, angry in his breast, had changed in an instant to the beat of a bell tolling, and he had recognised within his own being, like a gushing of dark blood, the abrupt effusion of an overwhelming grief. There had been one instant in which he would have given his position, his reputation, even his life, to have been there with the boy, closing the door pointedly behind him upon the celebrations held to the glory of negation and death.

It had lasted no more than a moment; a man in his position could not see things as sharply as that for a longer time and go on living. What he could remember of it now was not the remorse and the revulsion, but only the surge of anger with which he had fought it off and re-established his equilibrium. If he never felt it again, yet a recollection of sickening insecurity would always be with him, as long as he lived, simply because it had happened once, and was for ever thereafter a horrible possibility. He owed that to Eddie. He had been very near to hating him for it, and he felt the same jealous resentment rising in him now, because the boy stood there so immaculately innocent of all superiority, so unoffending, and all ordinary, compromising mortals fell off from his bright completeness into

220

outer darkness.

'Yes?' sighed Edmund, patient under the long scrutiny.

'I want to have a talk with you, young man.'

'Good!' said Edmund, gratified rather than resigned. 'I was beginning to be scared you didn't. I want to talk to you, too.' He waited for his orders with a dutifully inclined ear. He was much happier now; everything was going to be straightforward, even the row, if that was still the right word for it. They had never yet failed to understand each other, and he was no longer afraid that communication would fail tonight.

'Go and wait for me in the snuggery. I'll come to you when I've put the car away. Oh, and try to side-track your mother—we want to keep her out of this, she'd only worry.'

Edmund turned obediently and loped up the steps and into the house, and went to look for Ginnie. She was kneeling before the sitting-room fire, hunting vaguely through the medium wave-band for light music, and looking, for Ginnie, a little sad; but as soon as he came and dropped to the rug beside her she abandoned the wireless, and took him by the shoulders, holding him facing her while she searched his countenance, and frowned disapproval at his smiling placidity.

'Eddie Dallas, I ought to be very angry with you!'

'Do, then, darling, if it helps. But you don't have to make the effort unless you really want to, because Dad's about to do it for you both.' He put his long arms round her and hugged her warmly, and laughed at the grave face she was making.

'No—seriously, it was very naughty of you, and I'm not going to let you laugh about it. Darling, you

221

know how much these things can compromise a man in Daddy's position. What on earth will people think?'

'Of me, Mummy, not of him! People aren't so beastly unfair as to blame *him* for what *I* do, surely!'

'What do you know about people? You're just a baby, with everything to learn about the world. You'll find it,' she said with sage severity, 'a very unfair sort of place before you're done with it. And in any case, you know very well that the families of men who go into politics, like Daddy, must always take care to avoid the sort of behaviour that might damage their fathers' careers. It was very inconsiderate and very unkind of you, and I'm very cross with you, do you hear?'

She shook him; it was the worst she had ever managed to do, however cross he had made her. And all he did was tighten his arms again, and squeeze her breathless, and hide his irresistible laughter under her right ear, in the cyclamen georgette scarf that smelled of French fern. It was because of Ginnie's helplessness to deal with bad behaviour that he had had to become such a good child at so early an age, and save all his worst animal spirits for school, where his reputation had been by no means so angelic.

'Eddie—you're crushing me to death, you great bear!' She pushed him off, and he let her smooth her ruffled plumage. 'No, but really, *why* did you? Darling, you hurt him so much, and me, too. It wasn't like you, and it's made us very unhappy.'

Ginnie warning him sternly of the blows the world had in store for him, and chiding his heedless youth, melted his heart in fond, loving laughter, but Ginnie in her uncomprehending affection, torn between her two darlings and wanting to comfort both, moved

222

him to self-reproach in spite of all his resolution.

'I'm sorry, I didn't mean to do that, but the way it turned out, I really couldn't help it. Look, I'm going to talk to Dad now, and when we've had it out he'll understand perfectly, and I promise you it will be *over*—see?'

'Oh, Eddie, you're not going to have it out *now*? Not *tonight*!' Ginnie believed in sleeping again and again and again upon anything unpleasant, until it faded out from sheer weariness and absolved everyone from worrying about it any longer.

'Of course tonight! You don't want it hanging about, do you, making everyone miserable?'

'But it's too new, and he's angry, and if he's too hard on you...'

'Oh, Mummy darling, don't be silly! Don't you know you can trust him to be absolutely fair any time, angry or not? What *do* you think the poor lamb's going to do to me?'

'Oh, you, who's worrying about you, little wretch!' She patted his cheek, reducing what she had at first intended to be an admonishing slap into an impulsive caress. 'I don't want *him* to upset himself, that's all.'

'I'll be as meek as milk. Don't you worry about anything, because there's no need. Now I'm going, and you've got to give us half an hour or so to ourselves. Promise!'

'You neither of you pay the slightest attention to me,' she said, more truly than she knew, and with the scowl of an angry little girl.

'Mummy, how can you! You know we both adore you.' He stood up and, taking her hands, drew her up after him. 'Make us something nice, while we argue, there's an angel! We're both going to be hungry.'

Along this comforting side-alley her mind
223

consented to wander thoughtfully. She said: 'There are some mushrooms Nora brought—could you eat an omelette at this hour, and still sleep easily?'

'Could I? You go and make it, and I'll guarantee the rest.'

He led her to the kitchen in his arm, and shut her in there gently but firmly. Sometimes she complained that she stood in too much awe of Mrs Windsor to venture to amuse herself in her own kitchen, so she could have fun now, with the domestic tyrant already in bed. And as for all the fibs he had told her, his father would help him to make them good once they had straightened out their differences.

The room Dallas used as office and study was in a retired corner at the shrubbery side of the house, withdrawn alike from front-door bells and the domestic noises of the kitchen. Edmund went in and turned on the electric fire, and waited; and in a few minutes he heard the light, deliberate footsteps of his father approaching the door.

*　　　*　　　*

On his slow and reluctant way round from the garage he had almost managed to persuade himself that the mountain was really no more than a molehill. The kid was subject to mental growing pains, like any other intelligent boy coming to maturity in this terrible and wonderful century, and the twinges would probably continue to pinch them all from now on; but this particular manifestation would have blown over within a week.

But as soon as he entered the room, and saw the fair head spring round to greet him, and the eager mouth already quick with words, he knew that he had

224

not misread the signs. The affair might well be bigger than he had supposed; it would not prove to be less. If there had been any way of turning aside from the interview now, he would have taken it, but there was none; for Edmund wanted it with all his determined heart, and there could be no authority strong enough to deflect him from it.

'Well, sit down,' said Dallas, closing the door behind him. 'Pull the big chair up to the fire.' He brought its mate round upon creaking casters to face it across the hearth, and then turned away again to fetch cigarettes and lighter from the desk. 'Will you smoke?'

Edmund grinned, and said: 'Not till we've got this off our chests, thanks!' and was instantly ashamed of the note of levity left over from playing with Ginnie. Recoiling into a severe gravity, he pulled up his trouser-legs meticulously, and seated himself well back in the deep chair, settling himself squarely and flattening his hands upon the worn leather arms. No, thought Dallas, of course, Eddie wasn't the one who needed something to do with his hands; a cigarette would be only an irritating distraction to him. To Dallas, on the other hand, it represented a way of retaining his self-respect, a delicate microcosmic hold upon sanity and dignity.

He was horribly afraid that Edmund would see he was afraid, but there might still be salvation in Edmund's own nature; the eyes with which he looked at his parents, though acute and critical enough, had grown used to accepting certain qualities and relationships as inviolable, and might fail to re-examine them even in new circumstances. My past performances, he thought, may yet save me.

'You realise, of course,' he began abruptly, 'that
225

you put me in a very unpleasant position this afternoon. It was an important public occasion, and I had an official part in it, and you chose to stage an unmistakable demonstration against it. You couldn't have timed your gesture better if you'd set out to do me the greatest possible damage. I'm giving you credit for believing you had rather better reasons than that for what you did, but, whatever your motives, it was done very rudely, and in the worst possible taste. Well, I suppose you have quite a lot to say for yourself? I'm listening.'

Edmund braced his shoulders firmly against the back of the chair, and said simply: 'I don't think anyone will blame you for it, you know. You're more likely to get a good deal of sympathy, because, after all, other people can connect, too, and they're hardly likely to think you had any hand in putting yourself in a spot like that. Maybe I should have realised that you'd feel involved, but I just thought if anyone collected the kicks it would be me, and that was all right, because I asked for them. I'm glad,' he added thoughtfully, 'that it came over as an unmistakable demonstration; I suppose that's what I meant it to be. But it wasn't just that I wanted to be as offensive as possible. If I'd known how it was going to be, and how I was going to feel about it, I needn't have made any scene—I shouldn't have been there. For your sake, I'm sorry I couldn't stick it out, but if I'd stayed there and kept quiet it would have been as good as associating myself with everything that was being done and said. And I found I couldn't put my name to it. That's all!'

Dallas sat down opposite him, and remained leaning forward, with his forearms pressed along his thighs, and his fine, muscular hands tightly linked.

226

'So in order to dissent, it was necessary for you to interrupt the sermon by getting up and striding out as obtrusively as possible—shaking off the dust of your feet for a witness against us, I suppose!'

'I had to make it clear where I stood. I can't bear not to do everything I do in the daylight. If that's selfish,' he said firmly, 'it's one of the things I'm selfish about, and I can't help it.'

He was answering without heat, because his confidence in his critic's will to understand and be just to him was absolute; only a man secure in his own actions and satisfied of his own integrity could so serenely take these things for granted in others.

'But what *was* it that offended you so much? What was unexpected about the service?'

'Nothing was unexpected, that was just it! I'd hoped there would be something different, and there wasn't. It wasn't enough to push them off round the world to be killed, we had to get together and get drunk on a lot of sickening lies about how they loved it, and how nice it was of them to suggest it, when we know very well they hated it, and wouldn't have been there at all if they'd had any say in the matter. Well, I didn't want to associate myself with that kind of vote of thanks. I can't stand humbug!' he said, with the first vehemence he had displayed, and with a fierce flush of disgust mantling his cheeks.

'You think all that was humbug? You never made any such charge before. If you felt like that, you should have talked to me about it beforehand, and you needn't have come with us. But what you did was inexcusable.' He was growing careless, the helpless rage of personal despair making him want to hit out and hurt as he was being hurt; and he must not allow himself to be separated from Edmund, it was a

227

deprivation he could not contemplate. He looked down into his tightly knotted hands, and forced his voice to a gentler level. 'Look, Eddie! If this is all that important to you, you must help me to understand. Make yourself clearer! Do you think I'm a humbug?'

'No, of course not!' Edmund's voice leaped up indignantly. '*I* don't think you belonged there, but of course you believed in it, or I know you wouldn't touch it.'

'And all the others? The ex-servicemen? The bandsmen? The relatives of the soldiers who were killed? Were they humbugs?'

'Not consciously—at least, not many of them. But I think they come to affairs like that for the same reasons miserable people take to drink. What with the music, and the medals, and the marching, they all get beautifully lit up together, and they see all the neighbours getting lit up, too—and you know, if enough people are doing the same things all round you, you feel awfully safe and approved. But they wouldn't *need* to get so high unless they really knew, deep down inside, that there was something wrong with it. But *I* should have been a humbug if I'd stayed, that's what I meant. So I got out. What else could I have done?'

It really seemed to him as simple as that. He either trusted everyone to understand and respect his motives, or he simply didn't care about the ones who wouldn't have the insight and the generosity to interpret him correctly. He had no notion of the devious ways people's minds worked, the pleasure they could get out of misrepresenting motives and misreporting actions, the rage, in particular, with which they would turn on and tear anyone who insisted on dragging himself clear of their collective

228

hypocrisies. Or was it incredibly true that he had a very clear notion of what the world could do to him, and yet was so single-minded that he could actually afford not to care? He'd had a sheltered life, to all appearances, but it was only just becoming apparent how much of it he had somehow contrived to live outside the shelter, and how much, in his unworldliness, he knew about the world.

'I can see that you felt strongly about it, and that you did what seemed right to you, but I can't acquit you of rudeness.' He made the extreme effort necessary to raise his eyes from the smoke of his cigarette to Edmund's face, and the buoyant tranquillity he could not match filled him with a jealous fury. 'You insisted on the last ounce of your own honesty, like a man resigning from a political party over a tiny little point of policy, and no doubt felt very comfortable and virtuous as you went off and left the rest of us wrestling with realities. It didn't matter to you that you'd made everyone else feel very uncomfortable, and wounded the feelings of a lot of decent people by insulting their sacred beliefs. You'd better look out, Eddie, you're going to end up as one of those moral people who think about nothing but saving their own souls, and damn all the rest!'

'It wasn't so much my soul as my self-respect,' said Edmund, with a sudden, unabashed grin. 'And it wasn't so much a case of feeling virtuous as of feeling real again. Nothing in that place was real today. Don't you worry, none of the devotees is going to suffer any permanent damage from my little lapse in manners. Rage won't hurt them—be another jolly good cathartic.'

'At least you owe an apology to the Rector, and you'll go to him and make it in person!'

The grin faded rapidly, but not so rapidly as to indicate any loss of composure on Edmund's part. He sat silent for a moment, staring steadily at his father with a face of meditative affection, and eyes brilliantly wide and deep in their blueness. There was no way of saying some things without shocking, and no way round the issue without saying them.

'No,' he said gently. 'I won't.'

'Edmund!' The flash of anger, violent though it was, sounded curiously weak and precarious in his own ears. He stiffened in his chair, reaching out a hand trembling with rage to grind out his mangled cigarette in the ashtray.

'I know, and I don't blame you, but I'm not sorry about it, and I won't say I am. *He* wouldn't want it, either. Let him alone!' said Edmund. 'He was the one person there who agreed with me.'

'*Agreed* with you? How on earth can you make that out? You heard him—you stayed long enough to get his drift.'

'Yes, I heard him. He didn't believe a word of what he was saying.' Edmund's voice remained calm; he had got over the shock of betrayal by this time, he was pre-occupied with his own decisions, not with those of Charles Faulkner. 'I heard him, all right. I was paying particular attention, because I thought he was quite a person, and I had an idea that he was going to say something I was waiting for, something that would solve things for me. You know, when you have to make up your mind about something, how it's easier to count paving-stones or look out for crows than think? Well—I'd sort of elected him, and I was waiting to find something specially for me in what he said. I couldn't believe a man like that would come out with all the same old claptrap. Well, that's

230

what the Church is *for*, isn't it?—to illuminate things? But all I got was my knuckles rapped, and it couldn't have stayed darker. So I've done without an oracle.'

Dallas had come out at the other side of anger, and now there was very little left but fear. He sat looking at his son, and in spite of the fire he felt very cold.

'What do you mean by that?'

'There's something I've had on my mind for a long time now, and I didn't know what I ought to do, or even quite how I felt about it. It's such a complicated business. One can't claim privileges other people don't have. But on the other hand one can't accept something one's reason and conscience absolutely reject—not even accept it under protest, because even that's shuffling off the responsibility on somebody else. I've been thinking about it ever since that day of the Miners' Rally—the evening Mrs Parrish came to see you. Do you remember?'

The name was spoken, the inescapable name, and she was there in the room with them; and beside her was the boy, her son, in his implacable humility. They were waiting for the processes of justice to move; and they were moving now, slowly, obliquely, in the manner of all the machinery of law, not replacing what was lost, but balancing it with a second loss, not turning back death, but repaying it with a ruin the double of death.

'Yes. I remember.' He rose from his chair, because he could no longer sustain the beloved burden of Edmund's eyes. The only thing he could do to cover his distress was to go to the wall-cupboard and get himself a drink, and he needed it badly; but when he had it he was appalled to see how the glass shook in his hand, and he had to keep his shoulder turned upon Edmund while he tried to steady himself, and waited for the whisky to take effect.

'That was when I started thinking about it, because this business of military service was something that applied to me, too, and if it had been as wrong as all that for him, it was high time I began to consider what I was going to do about it. You don't mind my going into all this now, do you, Dad? You see, I'm supposed to register early in December, so we've got to talk about it pretty soon.'

'Yes—we'd have to have it out pretty soon.' He was tracing with fixed eyes the outlines of a charcoal drawing which hung above his desk; but the voice sounded all right, he hoped: level, friendly, ready to see reason. 'Why not now? Of course, go ahead.'

'Well, after what happened this afternoon I saw it was up to me, and when I walked out of church I went off to think it out properly. And of course, I saw that I couldn't claim deferment, or let anyone else claim it for me. I can't take what the others can't have as well. You must see that.'

It was what he had seen behind the blue eyes on the very night when all this coil had begun, and then he had dreaded it and backed away from it as though his world must end with it; yet now it was relief that came flooding into Dallas's mind like sudden sunlight. He stood aghast at his own abject gratitude, for if this was all, he had been wasting all his agonies of apprehension. Edmund was bowing to the necessity of conscription just as tamely as his father, it seemed, without a critical glance. All that had been worrying him was the thought of accepting privileges; it was not principle that set him apart. There was no longer any need to feel ashamed in his presence, or brace oneself against an implied criticism which had all along been no more than imaginary. A flush of hopeful warmth flamed through his physical coldness, and he turned with a smiling face to meet the confident eyes of his son.

'I wish there could be some way,' burst out Edmund, his own responsive smile blazing forth under this first gleam of encouragement, 'of accepting the risks and hardships without accepting the rest of it. I know it's only vanity, but I do hate backing out from the dangerous part of it. But that's impossible, I suppose—you can't have everything the way you want it. And anyhow, the kind of nastiness I shall be courting may make up for the lack of flying bullets.'

There was a silence of incomprehension; it seemed very long, and so rarefied that it was difficult to breathe. Then Dallas asked, in a very low voice: 'What do you mean? I don't understand!'

'Well, obviously I can't agree to be conscripted, can I?' Edmund was very patient, because they were at the perilous heart of the matter now. His voice had become carefully gentle, as if to a child who should not be hustled or startled. 'I can't put myself in the false position of promising what I've no intention of performing, and I can't acknowledge anyone's right to tell me to kill people. If you go into the army, you give them a blank cheque—they can use you as a killing machine wherever they like, and you've already agreed to it in advance. Well, I can't do that. I can't see how any responsible person can do it. So I can't take the oath, or whatever it is, in good faith, can I? And I can't take it any other way, obviously. So I won't serve.'

It could not have been simpler. He said it with the absolute, inflexible wholeness of Stephen Daedalus, and he was about as likely to be moved from if for

233

father, or mother, or friends, or country.

'Are you trying to say,' asked Dallas in a tone of extreme and brittle carefulness, 'that you're a conscientious objector? Do you intend to go to a tribunal and ask for exemption?'

'I don't intend to ask for anything.' A sparkle of disdainful amusement came into his eyes; he leaned forward in his chair, and allowed himself one scornful gesture of his hand, brushing the inexpressibly mean safeguards of law out of his way. 'I've *got* what's important to me, all I have to do is prevent anybody from taking it from me or persuading me to give it up. But anyhow, you see, I don't think I am a conscientious objector, so it doesn't arise. I don't go as far as they do—or maybe it's rather that I go a slightly different way. I daresay it would be nice to be one, as a matter of fact, because it's a beautifully definite sort of position. But it isn't the same with me.'

He cast a sudden glance at his watch, and began to hurry a little, because he had asked Ginnie for only half an hour, and he did not want to have to finish this difficult exposition in her presence. It was not so bad now that the ice was broken, and his father was really taking it very well; Edmund took comfort in his quietness and attentiveness.

'At first it did seem to me that I wanted to be an out-and-out pacifist, and I still think I'm very near that position. But when I thought back to the last war, and the things that happened then, I knew that if I'd been old enough I'd have been in it, with all my might. So there *could* arise circumstances in which I'd be willing to fight, and to kill, too. I don't know that it's a thing I *like* realising about myself, but I know it's the truth. I don't even mind the thought of military training very much, if it was only the training—I might be jolly good at it, I might even like it. So you see, evidently I can't claim to be a conscientious objector, can I? I hope I never shall want to kill anybody, but I've got to have the right to make my own decisions, commit my own crimes if I must, make my own mistakes. Even guaranteeing in advance that you'll *never* fight, in *any* circumstances, is just another way of cutting off your own head. How can you be sure what you may feel you have to do, some day? No, I'm not going to renounce, even in that way, the right to decide for myself when I'll fight and when I won't, and whether I'll kill or whether I won't—yes, and who I'll kill if I ever come to that! I'll answer for my own actions, and I'll keep them mine. It's the *choice* that's got to be my own, and then the crimes will be my own, too. I'm *not going to abdicate*.'

To Dallas, a little warmed by the whisky and the speed with which he had drunk it, this conversation had become almost too fantastic to be taken seriously. He heard the round, firm young voice uttering with a kind of fiery deliberation these outrageous sentiments, these lawless intentions, and they had a placid, dreamlike inappropriateness from his son's lips, so that he could not believe in them. From the very extreme of his discomfiture he rebounded into as treacherous an optimism. Young boys struck these attitudes, the universities were full of little islands of martyrdom and enthusiasm, and the only fatal mistake in dealing with them was to take them seriously. That woman had had a profound effect on Eddie, without doubt, but with patience and good sense he could be coaxed out of his eccentric fervour, and in time forget the whole affair.

Don't lose your temper, he warned himself, having

235

reached a level of self-confidence at which he almost believed he could feel returning anger. Whatever you do, keep him assured of your sympathy; but short of infringing that, let him know that he's seventeen, and hardly dry behind the ears yet, and that you won't stand any nonsense.

He turned, with the calculated calm these rapid and sanguine reflections had helped him to re-establish, and met the lively blue of Edmund's eyes, studying him from a face dauntingly reposeful and adult.

'Now listen to me! These heroics are all very understandable, Eddie, and I've a good deal of sympathy with them. But you'd better realise right away that you simply can't do that kind of thing, so it's no use indulging high-falutin dreams about suffering in the cause. When it comes to the point, you'll do your two years like everybody else, and like it, and you'll go where you're sent and do what you're told, and probably do it very well, too. You'll go through with it, in spite of all your fine sentiments about a man's right to his own conscience, because there's a law to enforce it, and you'll find that in practice you have no alternative.'

Edmund's eyes opened still wider, and deepened into a more intense blue with the flashing arrogance of his smile. The faint but definite *hauteur* in the lift of his head was something he had inherited from his father, but unconscious imitation had increased the likeness, too.

'Don't be silly!' he said indulgently. 'There's always an alternative.'

It was an echo of something he had never heard, but Dallas remembered it only too well, and it crossed the troubled sky of his memory like a comet of ill-omen. The frail little candle-flame of hope began to fail. More harshly he said:

'There is, for those who're modest enough to submit to a perfectly legitimate test of conscience, but it seems you're not. Do you imagine you can take a case like the one you've been making to any tribunal, and expect to be listened to? Don't be a silly little fool, Eddie! You'd better drop this ridiculous pose at once, it isn't going to get you anywhere.'

'I told you,' said Edmund, with a quick little frown of impatience, and a note of distinct asperity in his voice, 'that I never supposed a tribunal would listen to me. I wouldn't go near one in any case. I don't acknowledge the right of any bench to poke into my morals, unless I commit a crime. But if I refuse to submit myself for medical examination, then they'll *have* a crime to deal with, and we shall all know where we are, and they can behave like decent human beings, and say flat out that the law says they're to do this and that to me, and we can all keep our dignity. I wouldn't mind stating as much of my case as they'd listen to, in a perfectly sensible police-court. And, of course, I'd simply go on refusing service.'

'Are you out of your mind?' It was almost a shout of exasperation this time, and Dallas had come back to the hearth, and was standing over him furiously. 'Do you know what would happen to you on a charge like that? You'd go to prison for anything up to six months!'

Edmund stared back at him with irate calm, and said sharply: 'Yes, that's what I supposed. Do you think you're telling me something I haven't taken into account?'

'Good God, how do I keep my hands off you! And if they were long-suffering enough to offer you the option of a fine, I suppose you'd expect me to pay it, and get you out of your mess? Well, let me tell you, you'd better not count on it!'

The roused young face softened again, the hint of a mischievously affectionate smile trembled in the corners of his lips. 'You're a bit of an old humbug, after all,' said Edmund. 'But, actually, Dad, you *won't* pay any fines for me, and I won't pay any for myself, either. It isn't that I want to go to gaol as much as all that, but, you see, it wouldn't be the thing to flourish my defiance in front of the world, like that, and then crawl out of it just because we happen to have enough money for a twenty-pound fine, or whatever it is, when plenty of other boys might have to go to prison in the same circumstances. But don't worry, I'd make it all quite clear. I'd refuse to pay myself, and ask the court not to accept it from you, because I'd tell them I don't consider it fair to involve you in any way, when you don't agree with my feelings about conscription. I think they'd listen to me. But even if they took the money from you, and threw me out, they'd only have the whole job to do again the next time I was called for a medical. And the next, and the next, and finally they'd have to take me at my word. So you might as well save your money, mightn't you? I'm not sure,' he said, with a speculative and awed smile dawning in his eyes, 'how we go on from there. I think I did hear of a case where a fellow went back to gaol three times, but I don't know how long they keep it up. But if I stick to my guns and go on saying no, we shall find out, shan't we?'

He meant exactly what he said, there was no longer any possibility of doubting it. A certain almost pleasurable curiosity, even, mingled with his natural

238

apprehension on the subject. As for any sense of grief or shame, it was useless trying to evoke either in him; he had been brought up on the heroic stuff of the social war, in which half the legendary heroes had gone to prison for their beliefs. Why shouldn't he do the same? And why should he be ashamed of it? Edmund had been well taught, he knew all about the sway of principle; what he did not know was the frustration of being confronted suddenly, at forty-five, with the inflexible ghost of your own declared beliefs, a monster in whom you have never, in your heart, really believed.

Dallas made an attempt to reach him, though he knew already that he was far out of reach.

'And what do you suppose your life will be like afterwards? Do you think you're going to find it easy to become a doctor, and make a decent life for yourself, with two or three prison terms behind you?'

'I don't see why not,' said Edmund, friendly but unrelenting. 'There's nothing so new about it. If you stand by me, I'll get through and qualify some time, somehow. But, in any case, there are other things a fellow can do. I've got hands, and I'm honest.'

He meant that, too; he would let his ambitions go, if need be, to keep his integrity, and he would not even feel any very deep regret for them from the moment that their sacrifice became inevitable. The words he was using tonight he was using without flourishes, not flying them like hawks, as once he might have done in his exuberance.

'And what about your mother's feelings? Haven't you thought of her at all?' That was the most unworthy, the meanest weapon of all, for what he really meant was: 'What about your father's political career?' though he was ashamed to say it. The dream

239

of office, that almost ripe fruit leaning to his hand, that golden apple he had made a feint of risking with his half-qualms and his restrained protests, had fallen through his fingers now, and nothing like it would ever drop in his direction again. Parties can afford to respect members with sons in prison, but not to honour them. Respect costs nothing in weight and effectiveness, but votes are votes, and the great British public still doesn't like recusants who won't fight and kill to order. The dream of advancement was over, and slowly, slowly, everything else was crumbling after it.

'Don't be silly!' said Edmund for the second time, with a faintly reproachful smile. 'You know as well as I do that Mummy doesn't have to understand what's going on at all. We can make it quite easy for her. She believes every word you tell her. You've only got to tell her that it's perfectly all right, and a matter of principle, and that I'm doing the only honest thing I can do, and she'll be perfectly satisfied. I mean, she'll miss me, of course, and she'll be miserable while I'm away, but she won't be *ashamed*.'

Dallas thought in the heart of his despair: 'No—not of you!' Aloud he said, in an almost pleading voice: 'There's time to think it over, you know, before December. I can go fully into the legal side of it, too. I think we ought to talk about this again, Eddie, when you've considered it quietly for a week or two.' But all the time he knew it would be useless.

'Of course!' said Edmund cheerfully. 'As often as you like. But I don't think I'm likely to change.'

He turned his head suddenly, hearing faintly from the hall his mother's voice calling. 'That's Mummy ready for us. She promised us half an hour—that's pretty good timing.' He rose from his chair,

240

stretching upward to his tallest, and turned towards the door, expecting his father to follow.

In a sudden harsh cry, Dallas flung after him: 'You're treating this whole thing like a game! You don't realise what you're taking on! Do you know the sort of things they'll say about you?'

Edmund halted at the door, turning over his shoulder a face altogether open, and grave, and mature. 'I know some of them, the rest I shall find out when the time comes. No, I'm not making light of it, and if I don't know everything it will mean, I've thought enough about it to know I'll take it, kicks included. But what do you want me to do? Sit down and howl about it? I'm only doing what a lot of other people have done before me, probably with worse chances than mine. Don't think I'm going to just survive the months in prison, and live for the day I come out, as if I'd got something to forget and live down. I'm going to be interested in everything, and odd bits I'm even going to like. They're people inside, too. It's all experience; I'm not ducking any of it. It makes it simple for me, you see, because it really is the only honourable thing I can do.'

'And have you considered the effect your action may have on other boys? You claim the right to administer your own affairs, but have you the right to put this high-flown idea into the heads of other boys, and get them into the same kind of trouble you're taking on?' He thanked God, as he clutched at the tenuous argument, that Edmund could not guess how little he cared for all the other eighteen-year-olds in the world.

'Certainly I've the right,' said Edmund vigorously. 'At least as much right to recruit by example as the Government has to recruit by compulsion—I should have said a good deal more. At least there's only one person whose actions I can *command*, and I'll see that nobody uses *him* to do their dirty work for them.'

'But, my God, child, what do you suppose would happen if everybody made the same claims you're making?'

'I wish they would!' said Edmund, his eyes shining. 'Governments would have to think twice, then, before they started the shooting, or let other people get so desperate that they'd start it. They'd have to convince enough of us, first, that there was really something worth fighting about, and no way of tackling it but fighting. They wouldn't often manage that, so they'd have to find other ways of carrying on the world. But if ever they *did* manage it, they'd find they had the most single-minded, the most effective, the most reliable, the least corrupt army in history.' He reached for the handle of the door, and stood in the doorway, still looking back. 'Are you coming? We'd better not keep her waiting, or she'll think we're beating each other up, or something.'

Dallas stood unmoving, an extraordinary bitterness of hate and love flowing like gall into his mouth. He knew that it was all over, that nothing he could say or do would ever turn the wheel back again. In a voice whose dullness a boy might easily mistake for calm he said: 'You've delivered your soul now, haven't you? You feel good about it—holier than the rest of us!'

Edmund made that mistake. He thought that he was being stung deliberately, every considered thrust a test of his sincerity; and he remained placidity itself because he had every reason to know that he would stand the strain. He left behind him, as postscript to an interview which had turned out, on the whole, better than he had feared, his most filial and disarming smile.

'I just feel free,' he said amiably, and started away purposefully towards his supper.

Dallas stood on the hearth with the empty glass in his hand, and stared at the door which had closed so firmly upon the boy's going. He had no company now but his own conscience and the ruin of his hopes, which were raining slowly and lightly as leaves about him in the silent and secret disintegration of his life. The woman who had filled the boy's mouth with echoes was gone, too, gone with him, satisfied because he had done his part of her work for her more perfectly and finally than any other creature could have done it. And the other young man, the thin, distrustful young thing who hovered about the thresholds of his temporal and spiritual masters, waiting for justice, he might well put on his cap now, and leave this bankrupt presence. There was nothing here for anyone.

With the myth of a career the older illusions of service, of chivalry, of love for humanity, were crumbling and blowing away in the desolate wind. Dallas was alone in a room filled with the desiccated wreckage of the hypocrisies Edmund had touched unaware with his practical, valiant innocence, and shattered: the unchristianity of Christendom, the insincerity of political ideals, the corrupted and compromised virtue of adaptable man. There was nothing else in the room now but the shadow of the next election, and the calumnies the boy would have to bear.

Even the last illusion, the illusion that at this pass he cared most about the boy, was slipping away like gossamer from his nakedness. He saw himself in the

243

mirror of his own mind for the first time without disguises, and he shut his eyes within lids which hid nothing, upon tears which were all for himself.

*   *   *

Edmund lay awake until after midnight, gazing open-eyed into the contented deeps of his mind, and watching his boats burn. In spite of the chilling dews of the night, which sometimes caused him to shiver a little, they made a lovely blaze.

'That was tough while it lasted,' he thought, 'and I'm glad it's over. When he's had time to get used to the idea, I know he'll understand. It came as a shock, and then, he was trying me out a little, to make sure I wasn't just dramatising myself. But he'll understand that I mean it, when the time gets closer.

'I'll see that it shan't reflect on him. I'll make it clear that he disapproves of what I'm doing, but simply believes that everybody has to fight out an issue like that for himself, and do what seems right to him. Then I hope it won't lose him any votes. It might even bring in a few, because there are plenty of generous people who'll appreciate his standing by me in the circumstances.

'Besides, they know *he* was a soldier, so they can't chuck any stones on that account. I might even be a soldier myself some day, and if ever I am, I'll be a damned good one, too, only if it ever does happen it will be as a volunteer, and it will be because I've got a cause I really believe in. I know it could happen, because of last time. But, somehow, I don't see it happening again very easily. If it ever does, I shall know, all right. Until then, it won't be any good anyone telling me, This is it!

'It won't be long, now—less than a month. So I've got a lot of thinking and planning to do. Because I've got to do it properly. It isn't merely a matter of going through with it, but of getting it *right*. I won't make any more trouble than I can help, for anyone—that isn't the idea. I know there's a law, and policemen and magistrates have to administer it, and they'll only be doing their job, and I'll be as decent to them as I can. I'll even write and let the medical board know I don't intend to submit myself and why, so that they can take action as soon as they like. I'll let them know I'm expecting it. I'll plead guilty, of course, and be as helpful as I can in court, not to waste their time—and then, too, if the magistrates aren't too fed up with me they're more likely to ask me to explain my attitude, and that's what I want. Yes, I do want that, it's important. Because of the others! I don't suppose there'll be any rush into gaol, but just supposing there are a few others in this county who feel as I do, but all of them thinking they're alone—it might help them over the jump to know that somebody else took it first, and in just this way. So that's another reason why I've got to get everything right, not only to show them it *can* be done, but even *how* it should be done.

'All the same,' he owned, stretching out luxuriously into the first languorous, shadowy ease of sleepiness, 'I'm scared! I'm horribly scared, but I'm excited, too, and interested, and in a way I wouldn't have missed it. And in a queer way, even, it seems almost a pity to miss the army, only I don't seriously think there's time for it in one life.

'Stephie isn't going to like it.' He smiled at the very thought of her, a little tremulously, and his cheeks burned invisibly in the darkness. 'I don't suppose she'll speak to me for a long time. But she won't like it when people say the things they're going to say, either—even if she's said them all herself, first. Stephie'll turn round and fight the other way if the odds begin to look too grim. She's younger than I am,' he thought, steadying his mind upon the few months between them as upon a rock. 'She has plenty of time to get over hating me. I can wait.'

He turned his head upon the pillow, and saw through the open window a space of clear, dark sky, from which the ragged rain-clouds were recoiling distractedly in all directions, and a few stars flung into the breach like a handful of soldiers, forlorn but undismayed, ready to hold off the assaults of an ordered army.

'I'm scared! Of course I am! Much more scared than I should be of going into battle! If only I *could* have the dangers without taking on the rest of it! It hurts like the devil to think you're putting yourself in a position where you can even *seem* to be ducking out and leaving the risks to the others, and that's the way I feel when I think of *them*. That's the worst thing of all. But I can make up for it later. Doctors, of all people, can get into some dangerous places, and take some terrifying risks, and for something worth doing, too! And in the meantime, there's prison. I'll be a model prisoner, if I've got to be one at all. I'll put into it everything it'll take, and whatever there is to be got out of it, I'll get. Let's have some style about it!

'Dad doesn't know it yet, but it isn't only on principle that I wouldn't pay a fine to get out of it. I even want it, if I can't have the flying bullets. I'm not brave enough to do without some sort of honourable wounds to show.'

The fire of commital was burning down gradually

246

into a comfortable, steady glow, and with its dwindling into the dark his eyes were closing. 'I wonder if Mrs Parrish will read about the case in the paper?' he thought, very near to sleep. 'I think she'll think I did right—I hope she will. You have to begin somewhere, and until you're sure of yourself you can't do anything for the others. Well, soon I shall be sure. Then we'll see how to go on—then we'll see...'

He fell asleep. The few little outpost stars, holding their places stubbornly between the whirling, stormy onslaughts of cloud, shone with an impervious cheerfulness. They were so sparse that they could look in reason for nothing but obliteration; yet they had the jaunty look of expecting victory.

*   *   *

In a grove of the Kenya highlands, at a late hour of the same night, between the curving, rustling tops of the trees, spaces of the same sky showed, velvet-black and brittle with stars. The Devonshire private, nineteen years old and sick for home, clenched his cold hands on his rifle, in the thick darkness beneath the leaves, where the patrol held their places every one in a walled-up isolation, embraced, shrouded, marooned in darkness.

Not far from where they crouched in cover, a foot moved softly, a tremor of leaves stirred. A torch flashed along the track. Transfixed in the beam shone for an instant an intolerably anguished and terrified face, dark brown, with a doe's moist, distended and tragic eyes, on the forehead and cheekbones iris-grey highlights, under the throat and in the hollows of the cheeks purple shadows. The everted lips opened and cried out lingeringly in a thin keen of despair, and a

247

hand of pathetic length and elegance brushed open across the eyes. Then a Stengun rattled its short outcry, and like a violent wind swept the face and the hand backward in a burst of blood, and left the circle of feeble light vacant.

Back along the track light feet were running madly. The patrol broke crashing out of the bamboo and pounded after.

The second-lieutenant went forward, and shone his torch dispassionately upon the half-dead body. This one was a woman, young, with the heart-rending slenderness and grace of tall African peoples. Her shoulder and jaw were shattered, but her eyes were open and wildly intelligent, and she was threshing and moaning, one hand burrowing its long fingers into the earth with the last reflex contortions, the other, the good one, half-hidden under her body.

'Poor devil, she's had it!' said the second-lieutenant, flinching. 'Much better finish her!' he said, and thudded after his patrol along the dark track.

The Devonshire private came out of his shielding darkness, dropping the rifle with which he had never killed anything, and fell on his knees in the grass beside the Kikuyu girl. His small torch brought down the whole night into her eyes, which dreaded and implored him. He touched her, and she shrank from him, writhing back some inches along the bloodstained grass. Her hand came up from under her body with a knife clutched in it, and slashed upward at him with all that remained of her life fervent behind the blow.

He did not see the movement clearly, because his eyes were full of tears. The knife sheared into his neck, and his blood leaped out from the severed artery and filled the darkness with scalding heat. He remained for a moment still kneeling upright over her, and then sank forward slowly, and toppled into the fallen bow of her arm.

Her breast was soft under his breast. He felt death fusing them. Her arm in the agony of going folded round him, clinging. Her beautiful, long, murderous, dispossessed fingers spread gently in the hollow of his back, pressing him to her heart. Their blood ran down and mingled in the grass.